Perfect Family

A. G. Hawkins

Copyright © 2024 by A.G. Hawkins

www.aghawkins.org

All rights reserved.

Cover Art by K. B. Barrett Designs

Editing by On the Same Page

No portion of this book may be reproduced in any form without written permission from the publisher or author, except as permitted by U.S. copyright law.

This is a work of fiction. Names, characters, places, and incidents either are the product of the author's imagination or are used fictitiously. Any resemblance to actual persons, living or dead, events, or locales is entirely coincidental.

To those who have been made to feel small.

If you or someone you know
is a victim of domestic violence and needs assistance,
please visit: https://www.thehotline.org/,
call (800) 799-7233,
or text "START" to 88788

Author's Note

Dear Readers,

When you read my stories, I hope to write relatable characters. My characters go through situations, sometimes dark. For a longer list of what tropes or types of situations you may see within this story or any of my others, you can visit my website: aghawkins.org.

Thank you,

A. G. Hawkins

Chapter 1

Margot

Ask anyone in the Waverly Park subdivision, and they would all agree that the Lewis family was perfect.

Margot Lewis slipped her manicured feet into her expensive name-brand heels before changing her mind and choosing some flats instead. Her last piece of clothing to throw on was her light zip-up jacket. She secured each sleeve down before heading down the stairs and toward the kitchen.

"Ah, there she is," her husband, Jeffery, greeted with a bright smile. He came toward her, handing her a large cup of freshly brewed coffee. She took it as he leaned forward, giving her a kiss.

"*Oooooo.*" They broke apart and laughed as they turned to face their daughter, Ari, who was eating her breakfast. She wore her green soccer jersey, and her blonde curls were drawn up into two matching pigtails with white ribbon. The white skin of her cheeks was tinged pink. Margot bent down to roll up Ari's one knee-high sock that had fallen down to her cleats. As she stood, she pressed a kiss to the top of Ari's head.

"Did Daddy do your hair?" Margot asked, bouncing one of Ari's curls in the palm of her hand.

Ari giggled. "No, Mommy! Nanny Fay did!"

"Ah, of course, Nanny Fay did." Margot grinned.

"I did make her breakfast," Jeffery spoke up. He was stunning. It didn't matter they had been married for ten years, every time she looked at him, she was blown away. He kept himself tan with fake tanner, and Margot was pretty sure she'd never seen him without his tan. His raven hair now had a few streaks of gray in it. She liked it, made him look even more handsome. She touched his perfect jaw, giving him a wink.

"And is that mine?" she asked, pointing to the plate of protein pancakes, eggs, and turkey bacon behind him.

"It is."

"Good, I'm starved."

As she took the seat next to her daughter, Jeffery sat across from her. They ate breakfast together every morning, and most of those mornings Jeffery made that breakfast for them. With Jeffery's hectic schedule, this was the main time he could spend with them. He never missed it.

"Are you coming to my first game, Daddy?" Ari asked. The seven-year-old dunked her pancake into the syrup before taking a bite. Syrup dripped down her chin. With a baby wipe, Margot wiped it away.

"I can't, baby doll. Daddy has to work today."

Margot didn't quite understand what her husband's job was. She just knew he dealt with investing and helping others invest. He often traveled around town for his job, going to people's businesses and sometimes to people's houses. Though it kept him busy, he did it all to provide her and Ari with the best life possible. They were so lucky to have him. He would do anything for them.

Ari sighed loudly, dropping her head.

"I'm going to be there," Margot told her. "And Nanny Fay is going to record it so you can watch it with Daddy tomorrow."

"No work tomorrow?" Ari asked Jeffery, lifting her head and eyeing him through her thick bangs.

"No work. Daddy doesn't work on Sundays." He gave Ari a wink, which made her lips curl into a smile.

"Good. So you'll watch the game and play checkers with me?"

"Yes, of course, whatever you want."

Seemingly content, Ari went back to eating her breakfast. Margot glanced across the table at her husband, reaching out toward him. Their fingers touched before Margot placed her hand in Jeffery's. They met eyes. Jeffery's thumb rubbed her wrist.

"It's about time to go," Nanny Fay called out from the doorway. Margot's hand slipped out of her husband's as she checked the time on her watch.

"Oh, yes. Hurry up and eat, Ari. Your game starts in half an hour."

She stood, picking up her plate as well as some of the other dishes on the table. Jeffery also stood.

"I'll handle this." His hand brushed against her wrist once more before he took the items from her hands. She smiled. Though she knew he'd only be setting them down next to the sink. Their housekeeper, Janet, would do the dishes when she arrived in a little bit.

She helped Ari clean off her face and then get out of her chair. Ari scampered off toward Nanny Fay, leaving Jeffery and Margot alone. Jeffery put the dishes by the sink and then came over to Margot, lovingly taking her cheek into his hands.

"I love you, darling," he murmured before capturing her lips in his own. Margot melted against him, digging her hands into his back until Ari's voice interrupted them again.

"I should go," Margot said. "I love you too. Will tonight be a late night?"

"Likely," Jeffery answered. "But stay up."

"I will," Margot promised. Regretfully, she pulled away. "See you tonight."

Last year, Ari danced. But this year, she'd insisted on doing soccer with her friends from school. Margot knew very little about the sport, but she'd signed Ari up for the eight and under team where her friends also played. They'd had two practices and this was their first game. Margot searched for her friend Victoria, who sat over in her folding chair with a large cooler sitting next to her.

Victoria became her first friend when she moved to Georgia. They met because Victoria's husband, John, worked with Jeffery. It had been nice to have someone she could call and meet up with in a new place where she didn't know anyone other than her husband. Their relationship grew when they both got pregnant around the same time. During that time, Victoria introduced her to her other friends, and then their friend group was formed. Victoria and the rest of the group was ten or more years younger than Margot. They had just celebrated Victoria's thirty-second birthday a few months ago, while Margot was forty-six. It usually wasn't an issue. They all got along just fine.

"Oh, you made it!" Victoria said, waving her over. Margot took in everything around her. She hadn't thought about needing somewhere to sit. "Here, I brought an extra seat." Victoria pointed to the red chair beside her.

"Nanny Fay, you sit," Margot offered. Nanny Fay had been working for her since the day Ari was born. Before Ari, she'd been Jeffery's nanny. So she was more than just the nanny, she was family.

"You can't stand the whole game!" Victoria argued. Margot waved her off and again pointed to the chair for Nanny Fay to sit. Nanny Fay did so while pulling out her camera to film the event for Jeffery.

"Where's Jordyn?"

"Over there." Victoria waved to her daughter, who paused what she was doing to wave back. As she smiled, she could see her missing front teeth. "She's so glad Ari's on her team."

"How many children are on the team?"

"Twelve."

"Ah. And how long does a game typically take?" She swatted the air. The mosquitos were already out for the day.

"About forty-five minutes, but today is a double hitter. So we'll be here about two hours."

Margot gave her a tight smile and was grateful she'd chosen to wear her flats today. She dug inside her purse for her sunglasses. When she found them, she used them like a headband to keep her hair off her face, glad it wasn't sunny out making it too hot like it could get on these fall mornings.

"Well, tell me about the other parents and kids. Are these the same children who were on Jordyn's team last year?"

"Yes," Victoria said. "Over there are the sporty parents." She pointed to a group of parents who were all in matching chairs and matching shirts. Upon closer inspection, Margot saw their shirts had the team's name as well as their children's names on the shirts. "They get a little intense, forgetting these are just a bunch of kids playing. Last time that one"—she pointed to a woman with a green hat—"got kicked out."

"Wow, that is intense. And I thought dance moms were bad."

"Oh they are, just a different breed." Victoria laughed. "And that's Cassie and Mark. They're cool. They live about a neighborhood over from us. You'll like them. They have two kids on the team—the twins, Holly and Lucy."

"And who is she?" Margot pointed to a woman who stood over in the corner. She had rich brown skin, with tight curly brown hair that was pulled up halfway. She wore a pink sports coat and had on large sunglasses, making it appear as though she didn't want to be there. The woman was well put together, dressed as nicely as Margot was. The two of them stood out like sore thumbs on the soccer field next to everyone else in their T-shirts and shorts.

"Oh, that's Claire."

"And who is her child?"

"Um, Zachary. He's not her kid, though, she's his guardian." Victoria pointed out one of the two boys on the team. He was the smallest one with the pale pink skin, messy light brown hair, and bright green socks. "Claire's cool. She's not as into the sports, kind of like you," Victoria teased.

"I'm learning it. I have figured out that they kick the ball into the net."

A whistle blew, signaling the start of the game. This was all new to Margot. Nanny Fay had taken Ari to her practices. They both had landed during her Zumba classes, which Jeffery insisted she not miss. Thankfully, the class was over now because the instructor was moving. She wouldn't have to miss any more practices.

"Go, Ari!" Margot yelled. She jumped up and clapped her hands. "Wow, she's really good at this!"

"You'll be a soccer mom before you know it."

"Nanny Fay, did you catch that on camera?"

"Yes." Nanny Fay was grinning. She loved Ari just as much as she and Jeffery did.

By the time the second game ended, Margot needed a shower. Even though it was fall, the humidity had soaked through her clothes. Ari rushed past her and toward the spot where snacks were being passed out. A parent, one of the intense soccer moms, was handing each child a bag of chips and juice. Margot stepped behind Ari to make sure she used her manners.

"Thank you!" Ari said when she got her snack.

"You did so well!" Margot gushed.

"Where's Nanny Fay?"

"She went to cool down the car. She was getting hot. Here, let me open the chips for you." She took the chips from her daughter and pinched the top so they'd open smoothly. Behind her, a parent complained about the unhealthiness of the snack and how she would be bringing carrots and water on her day. She thought about how Jeffery might say the same, as he was ever the advocate for all their healthy eating habits, but Margot supposed one bag of chips wouldn't hurt.

After handing the chips back to Ari, a shiver ran down her spine. She glanced over, realizing someone had their eyes on her. It was Claire. But she wasn't looking at Margot's face—her eyes were drawn to her wrist. Margot looked down, spotting the circular bruise around her wrist on display before she quickly pulled her jacket sleeve back down. Her eyes shot back up toward Claire, who held a knowing expression on her face. Claire started walking toward her, but before she could say anything the little boy from earlier came up to her and tugged on her sleeve.

"Come on, Aunt Claire! James promised me ice cream after the game." Claire's eyes shot back over to her before they dashed off in the opposite direction.

"What do you know about that Claire person?" Margot turned toward Victoria, who was helping her daughter open her juice.

"Not much. Why?"

"No reason." Margot looked back over her shoulder, but no one was there anymore.

As Margot and Ari headed toward their car, she felt a sensation bubble up in the pit of her stomach. She touched her wrist and glanced around, sure someone was watching her. But she shook it off. She was imagining things. That woman probably wasn't even looking at her earlier.

She got into her car, smiled back at her daughter, and thought about how happy she was. They were the perfect family.

Chapter 2

Margot

Margot dropped her book into her lap as her husband slid into bed for the evening. His lips immediately went to her neck, and he pushed her back onto the bed, bringing his kisses to her collarbone.

"Well, hello," she said, grinning. Jeffery glanced up at her before his hand reached for her wrist and brought it to him. He kissed along the purpled bruise, and a tear slipped down his cheek. Margot touched his chin, forcing him to look up at her. "It was an accident."

"I never, ever want to hurt you, Margot. I love you."

"I know you do." She pulled him toward her, and he rested his head on her chest. Her fingers ran up and down his back. "It just happened. No need to speak of it again."

They lapsed into silence. She tugged her sleeve back over the bruise, not wanting to look at it. She kept that moment when it happened right at the edge of her memory, unable to get it to disappear.

"How was Ari's game?" Jeffery asked a minute later.

"Oh, great." Margot brightened. Jeffery sat up, staring at her as if he was ready to take in every word she said. "She's a pro."

"Well, of course she is. We should hire her a personal coach."

Margot laughed. "She's seven." Though Margot shouldn't be surprised. Jeffery had also insisted Ari take private lessons in dance the year before. Margot had a theory that was why she hated it. Yet, when Jeffery had his mind on something, it was hard to change it.

"But if she's really talented, we should tap into the talent now." Jeffery stood from the bed. He pulled his phone from his pocket and typed over the keyboard. Margot's brows furrowed.

"It's nearly midnight. Don't you think it's a little late to call anyone?"

Jeffery ignored her, placing the phone to his ear. "Manny!" he said. "Hey, who is that soccer coach you have for David?" A pause. "Uh-huh. Price?" Another pause. "Great. Send me over his info, thanks."

Jeffery dropped the phone onto the bedside table and then sat next to Margot, taking her hands in his own.

"I'll see about him coming after school a couple days a week."

Margot nodded. "Of course."

"Here, drink some water," Margot said, offering a glass to her husband as he swung their daughter on the playset out back. She wiped her forehead with her sleeve. "It's been such a warm October."

"That's the south for you. Ten years here, and you still haven't adjusted."

"I don't think I ever will." She pulled her thick, blonde locks up into a ponytail. Before she could tie it in its place, Jeffery's hand covered hers.

"Leave it down," he said with a smile. "Your hair looks so pretty today."

Margot hesitated before allowing her hair to fall back over her shoulders.

"Of course," Jeffery began before moving closer to kiss her cheek, "you're always pretty to me."

"Mommy, can we play a game?" Ari jumped off the swing, allowing the dirt to gather up around her feet.

"Sure sweetie, what game?"

"Actually..." Jeffery broke in as he looked at his watch. "Mommy has to go upstairs and get changed."

Margot narrowed her eyes, confused.

"What? I don't have anywhere to go."

"Yes, you do," Jeffery said slyly. His lips curled up, and he gave her a small wink. "Your outfit is sitting out on the bed."

"What have you done?" Margot asked, giggling. Jeffery took her hand and brought her closer to him so their noses touched.

"*Oooooooo*," Ari called from behind. "Daddy's surprising Mommy!"

"Did you know about this?" Margot turned toward Ari, who shook her head. "What is it?" she asked Jeffery.

"It's a surprise. Now, go on upstairs and see what's sitting out for you to wear."

"Okay." Margot kept her hand entangled with Jeffery's before slowly pulling away and going inside to see what surprise Jeffery had planned for her.

This wasn't that surprising, actually. About once a month, he sprung on her a special date night out somewhere. It was always fun trying to figure out what the next event might be. Just the month before, he surprised her with a couples massage at the Four Seasons downtown. He was always doing things like that, making her feel special.

When she reached the bedroom, she spotted a green long-sleeve dress lying on the bed with a shoe box and small present beside it. Now this was a surprise. She was used to getting a new dress and shoes, but not usually a present. Opening it, she found beautiful gold jewelry inside. The necklace had a square emerald pendant that matched the earrings and bracelet. She opened the shoe box. New gold Gucci heels sat inside.

"So, what do you think?"

Jeffery leaned against their bedroom doorframe. He had rolled up his sleeves, showing off his toned arms. He grinned at her, stepping inside the bedroom and shutting the door behind him.

"I love it," Margot gushed. "You spoil me too much."

"Never," Jeffery said. His fingers brushed along her cheekbone. "You and Ari are my everything. I would be nothing without you." He took her hand and brought it up to his lips, kissing her knuckles.

"Where are we headed tonight?"

"No, no. No clues."

"Hm." Margot rested her head against Jeffery's cheek as his fingers played with the hem of her top. She stopped him, straightening. "What about Ari?"

"She's with Nanny Fay. Don't worry. We have time."

She and Jeffery went to the nicest steak house right inside the city that had rooftop seating. It was their favorite place to go, but Margot still found herself fretting over the prices on the menu. Even after being married for as long as they had been, she still hadn't gotten used to spending freely. She had grown up well off, but not rich. Her family had nice things, but they still were careful with their spending. Her parents taught her to save, not spend.

As they sat on the rooftop sipping on cocktails, the lights around the city were a sight to behold. Margot took it all in. She never got tired of its beauty.

"Our anniversary is in a few months. Ten years," Jeffery said, drawing Margot's attention back to him.

Margot nodded and smiled. "Ten years has felt like one. It's all going by so quickly."

"I've booked us a flight to Paris."

"Oh?" Margot placed her glass down on the table. Her fingers traced over the rim. "Paris? Will we all be going as a family?"

Jeffery laughed. "As a family? It's our anniversary, Margot. Ari will stay here with Nanny Fay. *We're* going to Paris."

"It's just..." There was an uneasy feeling in the pit of her stomach. "I've never been away from Ari overnight, except for when—"

"That was seven years ago," Jeffery cut her off, waving his hand in the air. "You can be away from her. Stop feeling so guilty about it."

Margot's hands squirmed anxiously in her lap, and she pressed her thumb into her palm up and down to soothe the heaviness on her chest.

"But I'm just not sure about being away from her, and so far away. What if there's an emergency?"

A flash of frustration passed over Jeffery's eyes before he offered her a gentle smile.

"She'll be with Nanny Fay. Nanny loves our girl as much as we do. She'll take great care of her. You and I haven't been on a proper holiday with one another since before Ari was born. Now is the time."

Beads of sweat formed on the back of her neck as panic consumed her. She blinked and lifted her drink to take a few sips. Jeffery moved his seat next to hers. His hand cupped her chin.

"This is what we need, Margot. Time away from here. It'll be good for not only us, but you, as well."

"But—"

"It's happening. We're going. End of discussion."

Jeffery moved his chair back over to his side of the table. He motioned for their waiter to bring him another drink. Margot wanted to go home; the lights no longer looked as pretty and it had suddenly gotten colder. She tightened her hand around the glass, trying to suppress those thoughts.

"You know that I love you," Jeffery said once the waiter walked away. "Right?"

He stared at her, waiting for her to speak. His eyes softened as he smiled back at her. His hand slipped across the table, taking hers in his own. She swallowed down the lump that had formed in her throat. She did love Jeffery, very much. She reminded herself that her anxiety was the one in the way. Traveling with her husband had always been a dream of hers, but since Ari had been born she'd been too afraid to leave her for long stretches of time. Every time they'd traveled it had been with her and the nanny. But Jeffery was right—it was time for them to travel as a couple. She was grateful for him, pushing her to experience things out of her comfort zone. He only did it because he cared.

"Always."

The next day, Margot researched restaurants and museums they could visit in Paris in an attempt to make herself more at ease about the trip without Ari. As she added another museum to her list of places she wanted to visit, her phone rang.

"Hey," she answered, excited to hear from Jeffery during the day. "I was just researching places for us to visit while we're in Paris."

"Oh darling, don't you know I've already got all of that planned?"

Margot's chest deflated. "Right, of course you have. Silly me."

"Anyway, I completely forgot that you need to get a dress."

"I have several dresses."

"Yes, but a new one. We have a black tie event—color scheme is black and white—on Friday night. The stylist is heading over now with a few dresses. Try them on and pick your favorite."

"Oh, okay, what event are we going to?" Margot closed her laptop and crumpled the paper with the list she'd made up in her hand, throwing it into the small bin by the desk.

"Um, a fundraiser for the Taylor Foundation. I don't know much about it. Our company bought a few tables and we're expected to attend. Oh, I have to go. Martin will be there at one with the dresses. Goodbye. Love you."

"Good—" The line cut off. She sighed, checking the time on the wall's clock. It was noon. She had an hour to shower and change before the stylist came over. But before she did that, she opened her laptop back up to search the foundation.

The website opened to a disturbing painting of a fist against a wall. Her stomach lurched. As she scrolled down the page, she found the summary of the foundation.

The Taylor Foundation is here to help victims of domestic violence. The Taylor Foundation was founded by Claire Donahue in honor of her friend, Taylor, who was a victim of domestic abuse.

Claire Donahue. Margot paused. Why did that name sound familiar? She scanned the page, finding a link that took her to more information about the founder. When she clicked on it, she immediately knew. She was the woman from the soccer game. The one who'd looked at her strangely, and made her feel uncomfortable. Margot swallowed before closing her laptop again. Once more, she was getting into her head.

Chapter 3

Margot

Instrumental pop music played throughout the ballroom as guests chattered and walked around. Margot held tightly to Jeffery's arm, never being fond of crowded events.

"There's an auction table. Would you like to go and look?" Jeffery offered. He pointed to the long black table. A line of people gathered there, looking over the items and making offers. Margot shook her head.

"I would really like to find our seats." She dug at the side of her dress, which pinched into her hips. This hadn't been her first choice. She'd preferred the looser black dress, which felt silky beneath her fingertips. But Martin insisted she wear this one, and after some questions, she realized this was what Jeffery had chosen for her to wear. After she heard that, she laughed. He always knew what she looked best in.

Jeffery grabbed her hand and pulled it away from her hip before darting a glare at her. She straightened.

"We have to go around and talk with people. Look, there's Victoria and John. Let's go and say hello."

Margot felt relief at seeing someone she recognized. She quickened her pace until she reached her friends.

"I didn't know you would be here tonight," Margot said, being drawn aside by Victoria. The guys both walked away toward the bar. John and Jeffery worked for the same company, but in different branches. Jeffery, as the head of his branch, had been trying to recruit John to his branch for the past couple of years.

"Oh yes, we come every year."

"Oh, I didn't know that."

"Well, John's branch manager uses, um, the founder...you know, the woman from soccer the other day."

"Claire?"

"Yes! Her parents are the company's lawyers, so they send us invites every year. I think this is the fourth year of this fundraiser. I'm not sure. But it's always a great event. There's live music that'll start, and the food is to die for."

"It seems nice," Margot said. She grabbed an appetizer from a passing tray. The shrimp cocktail was delicious, she had to agree.

"Ah, there's John's boss. I should go and say hi. I'll find you in a little bit?"

Margot tightly grinned before giving Victoria a quick peck on the cheek. She did the same in return. Then Margot searched around for Jeffery, but she couldn't find him anywhere. Her heart pounded in her chest. She reminded herself that she was fine and she was safe.

"Margot, right?" a friendly voice asked. Margot glanced up to see a stunning woman in front of her wearing a floor-length white dress. It took her a moment to place that she was Claire. The moment she realized who it was, she scanned the area to see if there was a way to make a quick escape. Something about Claire made her nervous. But she shook it away, and forced herself to smile.

"Yes, and you're Claire?" she asked, her voice a pitch too high.

"Yes, hi." Claire reached out to take Margot's hand and give it a shake. "Sorry I didn't introduce myself at the soccer game last weekend. You're new to the team this year?"

"Yes. Ari decided she wanted to play with her friend instead of taking dance. Though I thought she loved dancing last year, turns out she did not. She's super athletic. I think she might want to play more sports this year." Margot finally shut herself up, cursing herself internally for saying so much at once.

"Zachary just likes being with his friends," Claire said. "He's not really athletic. He's more artsy, like his mom was." There was a wistful look on her face that disappeared just as quickly as it had come. "And I'll be honest, I don't really love the outdoorsy stuff." She chuckled.

"Me neither," Margot replied, feeling more at ease. "This is impressive, what you've done here."

"Oh, it's all thanks to donors and the local shelters and domestic helplines around here. I just do what I can."

"Well, I think it's amazing. Do you provide help directly, or...?"

"No, I work with the local shelters in the area. They do all the heavy lifting. I can't take any of the credit. I just help fund money for them to use."

Claire dug into her small, black and white striped clutch and pulled out a black business card. She took Margot's hand in her own, wedging the card into her hand.

"This is for my business. I'm a party planner. You look like you could use some help," Claire said, meeting her eyes intently as if her words had a different meaning. "Just call that number on the card or send a text message, and I'll have someone contact you right away." Claire held onto her hand for a beat too long before finally letting go.

She gave Margot a curt nod and then dashed off in the direction of someone else.

"That was odd," Margot said to herself. She brought the business card up for a better look. There was little on it besides a small round design, as well as a phone number and a different number to text. No name or anything else. Finding it strange, Margot tucked the card into her purse, deciding she'd try to figure out what it meant later.

"Ah, there you are," Jeffery's voice rang. Margot smiled up at him. "Sorry about that, John and the boys convinced me to sign up for several auctions."

"Oh boy, what did you sign up for?"

"Horse lessons, a wine of the month club…"

"You already know how to ride a horse. You own three."

"I know, but Ari could take them." He brought his arm around her shoulders, and the two of them started walking down to where their seats were. "I don't remember what else I signed up for."

"I guess it'll be a surprise to see if we win any," Margot said as he pulled out the chair for her to take a seat. She grabbed her phone out of her clutch to see that Nanny Fay had sent a picture of Ari. She smiled, touching the picture, wishing she was home with her.

"Oh, I remember! I did one for you! For belly dancing lessons!"

Margot jerked her head up from her phone. "What?"

"Yes, you'll love it."

"If we get it," Margot squeaked.

"Oh, we will. I made sure we'd get them all."

And they did get most of them. By the end of the night, they were now proud owners of a new grill, several different types of lessons, and a few bottles of wine. None of these were things that they needed. However, they didn't get the belly dancing lessons, and for that she was relieved.

"See, I told you I'd win them. I'd say we gave a lot to this foundation." He smiled, raising his wine glass with their table. Margot grinned along with him. The table clapped. His smile widened. Jeffery loved nothing more than to be the center of attention. It's where he glowed.

"What do you like best about the foundation?" Margot asked him as the noise settled down.

"Hm?"

"What do you like best about the foundation?" she repeated.

"That it helps people, of course," Jeffery told her. He sipped on his wine. Margot frowned. It seemed he knew nothing about this foundation at all.

Chapter 4

Claire

Claire had never given one of her cards out at one of these events. In fact, she'd only given them out a few times. Generally, she stayed out of that part of it, not wanting to get involved again. Yet, something about Margot and the bruise she'd seen the other day had her alarm bells going off. So the moment she saw her at the event this evening, she knew she needed to at least try to help.

Her heart was still tender from losing her best friend to domestic violence. It was easier to help by fundraising and letting others handle the harder stuff. It's why she dropped the card off so quickly. Easier that way to keep her distance, but she could still offer help where she was sure it was needed.

"Another successful night," someone said in her ear. Claire jumped before turning around to face Max. He grinned at her, his blue eyes sparkling. His tanned white skin looked shiny under the lights and his dirty blond hair was slicked back. He wore a tux with a bow tie.

"You made it. I thought you had to work tonight," Claire said, trying not to sound as excited as she actually was to see him. Max was her best friend and her closest confidant since they had met four years prior when she hired him as the PI to help find her missing friend. She went to him about everything, and he was always there no matter the reason.

"I did, but the case ended early. Lilianna figured it out."

"Really?" Claire asked, impressed. "Your little sister will be taking over the business before you know it."

Max chuckled and shook his head. "I don't think so. She got lucky this time."

"Well, I'm glad you were able to come tonight," Claire told him sincerely.

"I always try to come. It's important to me too, to be here."

"I know," Claire said. She blinked a few times. All evening she'd been able to stay strong, but something about Max being here brought the tears to her eyes. She touched the side of her eye with her finger and forced the tears to stay back.

"No one thinks you're any less strong if you cry, Claire."

"I'm not crying," she bit, making Max laugh.

"Oh, sure, sure."

"It's nice to see you," Claire said, changing the subject. She met his eyes, flutters in her chest. She went to reach out toward him, but stopped herself.

"Are your parents here? Any of your siblings here? James? Simone?" He made a face as though he was trying to recall her other two siblings' names.

"My parents are. But no, Simone couldn't make it. And James...well..." She waved her hand as if to explain it all. Max nodded in understanding.

"Ah."

Claire reached forward and wiped a stray piece of flint off Max's shirt.

Max grabbed a glass of wine off one of the trays from one of the servers walking past and then took a sip.

"What food do you have? Anything good?"

"It's always good. My parties are amazing," Claire said.

"Of course they are."

Again, their eyes met. The butterflies flapped rapidly in her stomach. She checked her watch. "It's about time for my goodnight speech. But thanks for coming. Really, it means a lot." Quickly, she dashed away, not looking back at where he stood. Though she was certain he looked just as confused as she felt.

After her speech, Claire spotted the woman again. She sat next to her husband at one of the tables. She looked uncomfortable with everyone else at the table. Her body sat inward, toward her husband. While she laughed when the others laughed, it was only to hide her discomfort. At least, that's how it looked to Claire.

"Tonight was wonderful," Claire's mom, Kim, said as she came up beside her.

"Are you leaving?" Claire asked. Her father, Jack, joined them. He held one of the gift bags they gave to the guests in his hands.

"Yes, it's past our bedtime."

"Or your wine and reality TV time," Claire said teasingly. Her father gave a knowing nod. Kim rolled her eyes.

"You did great," Kim told her, again. She kissed Claire's cheek.

"So far we've earned about thirty thousand dollars and that's just from the tables. I'll be curious to see what the final total is with the auctions. I tried to calculate it, but..."

"I calculated around ten grand," her dad said.

"Wow," Kim exclaimed.

"Yes, wow," Claire agreed. "Did Max come by and say hello to you?"

"Oh yes," Kim said. "I like him. He would be perfect for you."

"Me?" Claire shook her head. "Mom, I'm not dating anyone, especially not Max."

"And why not?"

"It's complicated. He found Taylor. He's just my friend." She sighed, not wanting to rehash this again. It was difficult when she didn't even understand her own feelings surrounding Max. "Aren't you going to be late for your favorite show?"

"It'll record." Her mom glanced around. "Is Max still here?"

"I don't know," Claire said. She hadn't seen him since their brief talk earlier.

"All right, we really should go home," Jack interrupted. Claire gave her father a grateful smile, knowing he understood how uncomfortable the conversation made her. He kissed the top of her head. "Goodbye, sweetie. Will you and Zachary be over for dinner tomorrow?"

"Yes, of course."

After she ushered her parents outside, she remained by the front door. She wasn't ready for the end of the evening. For the past several years of doing this fundraiser, the end of the night was the hardest. The months leading up to it kept her busy, kept her focused on making sure the night was perfect and a testament to her friend, Taylor. But once it was over, that hardness hit her like a ton of bricks.

She took a deep breath, enjoying the fresh air before checking her phone to see if she had any messages from the sitter. There was just one.

Zachary is asleep. He was perfectly behaved. No need to rush back. All is good here.

Claire texted back, *Good to hear. I'll be back by midnight.*

She put her phone back into her clutch before stepping back inside. Max was across the room. He still hadn't left. Her lips curled upward, but she forced them back into their neutral state.

"Ms. Donahue?"

She turned to face the young server who held a tray full of desserts which were about to be passed out for the end of the event.

"Yes?"

"We're low on the champagne."

"Of course we are..." Claire shook herself, and got back to work.

Chapter 5

Margot

They rode in near silence on the way home from the fundraiser. As the driver drove down the dark road toward their neighborhood, Margot stared at her nails. The nail polish on her left ring finger had chipped. She ran her finger over it, wondering when over the night it could have happened.

"I'll make an appointment for you to have that fixed tomorrow," Jeffery said. He brought his hand over hers, interlocking their fingers. Margot rested her head on Jeffery's shoulder. Her eyes were growing heavy. Riding in the car at night had a way of lulling her to sleep.

Jeffery kissed the top of her head. She cuddled up closer to him. These moments were the ones she loved the most with him, when it was just the two of them with no one to impress. Even with the driver up front, it still was just about her and him in this moment. He rubbed her shoulder. She felt safe with him. She loved him. She wished there could be more of this right here.

"I love you," she said. Against her head, Jeffery let out a happy chuckle.

"Oh, I love you too."

"What if, next weekend, we just drove somewhere and looked at the stars?" Margot suggested.

"Where could we even do that?" Jeffery asked.

"I don't know. I'm sure we could find somewhere out of the city. We could just put on something comfortable and go out somewhere. Maybe take some food and a blanket." She tried to recall the last time they'd done something so simple. Almost every weekend, they had something major they had to do, whether it be a fancy dinner, an event to go to, or something he'd planned to do as a family.

"We can't next weekend," he told her. "We're taking Ari to the play Saturday night."

"The weekend after?" She sat up so she could look him in the eye.

"Plans that weekend too, but we'll find a date," he promised. He kissed her, his thumb brushing against her cheek as he pulled her closer. And for a moment, she really believed it to be true.

Jeffery kissed her again when they entered the house. He pressed her up against the door, trailing sloppy kisses from her lips to her shoulder. She giggled nervously, worried Nanny Fay would catch them acting like teenagers out in the open.

"Jeffery," she said between kisses. "Jeffery, we should continue this upstairs."

Jeffery stepped back. "Margot, Nanny Fay is asleep. Ari is asleep. This is our house. We can do whatever we want."

"I know, but still…" Margot took the opportunity to walk around him and farther into the house. She slipped off her shoes before picking them up to carry to her closet.

The house was still. Even with bare feet, she could hear every step she took. Jeffery held his shoes as well. Shoes in the house were a big no-no. After marrying Jeffery, she had to make a lot of small changes about how she did things. Jeffery liked a meticulous home. He had gently guided her on putting her cups into the dishwasher when she was finished with them and making sure nothing was kept around the house. By now, ten years later, she'd gotten more used to it.

When she reached her bathroom, Margot tore the dress off her and dropped it onto the bathroom floor. She rubbed the spot on her hip where the dress had pinched at her all night before pulling the pins out of her hair. Each blonde lock fell down in a nearly perfect curl. Once all her hair was down, she ran her fingers through it and rubbed at the back of her neck where tension had gathered throughout the night.

"Why is this dress on the floor?" Jeffery boomed. Margot jumped and turned.

"I-I was just so glad to get it off. It didn't fit me very well," she said.

"That's a very expensive dress, Margot. And you just throw it on the floor." He lifted it up, shaking it out and folding it over his upper arm. Margot couldn't believe she'd done that. Nice dresses did not go on the floor—ever.

"I'm sorry. I wasn't thinking," Margot said. She looked at him through the mirror, unsure which way this conversation was going to go. It was late and he'd been drinking, so that made it even harder to tell.

"No, you weren't," he agreed. But then he chuckled, moving forward and kissing the back of her head. "You're always a bit of a klutz, aren't you? I'll have this dry cleaned and put back in your closet. Why don't you take a shower? You look tense."

Margot nodded. He kissed her bare shoulder and then left her alone in the bathroom. She turned the shower on and waited for the water to warm. Her mind went to the card Claire handed her tonight. She still was not sure what that was about.

As she stepped into the hot water, she allowed it to wash over her. She couldn't get that stupid card out of her head. She needed to figure it out. Scrubbing her hair, she tried to push it out of her mind. It was late. But it wouldn't leave her alone.

Once she got out of the shower and dressed in her pajamas, Margot searched for the card in her clutch. Checking in the bedroom to make sure Jeffery had fallen asleep, she gave the number on the card a call. Something about the way Claire had spoken to her and the way the card looked made her think it wasn't actually a card for party planning, but maybe she had imagined it. Her curiosity wouldn't let her rest until she called to know for sure.

"Are you in immediate danger?" a voice on the other end asked.

"Um, no. Who is this?"

"This is the Women's Resource Center to End Domestic Violence located in Georgia, who is this?"

"I-I got the wrong number." Margot hung up her phone. She clutched the business card in her hand, anger coursing through her. Why on earth would Claire give her this? Why would she lie about what it was? She was not an abused woman. She was a loved woman in a great relationship. Her hand curved around the business card, ready to throw it into the bin.

However, something in her told her to keep it. She didn't know why.

Quietly, she tiptoed across their vast room to the closet where her purse hung, deciding it would be the safest place to keep it. The door creaked. She paused, looking over at her husband, who was still blissfully asleep. She lifted the purse, keeping her eyes on her husband as she hid the card in the back zip pocket. As she placed her purse back on the door, it creaked again. Jeffery turned in the bed.

"Come to bed," he grumbled, his eyes still closed.

"Coming!"

Chapter 6

Claire

Claire sat on the bench by the window, drinking her coffee and watching the sun come up. It was still early, so she had about half an hour before Zachary would be awake and asking for breakfast.

"We've got to stop doing this."

Claire turned her head. Max sat up in her bed, bringing his hands up as he yawned. As per usual, she called him after she got home and he came right over. All she ever had to do was call. He never told her no.

"I don't know," Claire said with a grin. "Last night was fun."

"It was," Max agreed. He slid from the bed, grabbing his boxers from the ground and putting them on. He then made his way over toward her and gave her a kiss. "But I think it's time for you to let me take you out on a proper date. These random one-night stands we keep having aren't enough."

"I think they are. I quite like them. I didn't hear you complaining last night." Claire rose a brow. Max sighed, sitting across from her.

"But I would like to take you out to dinner, do something more than what this is."

"I've told you I'm not ready. I'm still figuring out this life, being a mother to a child who lost his mom."

Max's eyes softened. He touched her knee, giving it a loving squeeze.

"Claire, it's been four years. You can't use that excuse anymore for why we can't be a couple."

Claire huffed, standing and removing her knee from his grasp.

"If you want more—"

"Aunt Claire?" Zachary's voice came on the other side of her bedroom door.

"Shit!" Claire cursed under her breath. "Shit!" She walked over to the door and spoke through it. "Um, I'll be out in a minute. Why don't you grab your tablet and play for a bit?"

"Okay!"

She turned, pressing her body against the door.

"You have to go."

"Go?" Max asked.

"Yes, go out the window!"

"We're on the second floor," Max said. "We have this discussion every time. I am not going out of a second-floor window."

"Ugh, don't be so dramatic. Okay, regular then? Um, hide in the bathroom until I can get him distracted. I should have woken you up earlier, but I thought we had another half hour. He's up early today."

"Or, we can stop this charade, and I come down and have breakfast with you."

"What? No, absolutely not. Zachary is not ready for that."

Max paused from grabbing his shirt and looked at her.

"He's not, or you're not?"

Claire couldn't respond.

"Just hide, all right? I'll text you when it's safe to come downstairs."

Claire stepped out of her room, pausing at the door. Her hand rested on the knob, debating going back inside to Max. But she pushed that thought away. She moved forward, finding Zachary on his bed with his soccer uniform on. Right, soccer was today.

"Hey, bud," Claire said, standing in Zachary's doorway. He glanced up from his tablet in his lap.

"Hey."

She turned to look down the hallway. If Max exited her room Zachary would easily be able to see him.

"Why don't we go downstairs and get breakfast?"

"Sure." Zachary plopped his tablet down on the bed next to him before jumping off and running ahead. Claire shook her head. No matter how much product Claire put on his hair, his dark hair stuck up in the back.

Claire was lucky. Zachary was a pretty easy child. He hardly ever gave her any trouble and was an angel at school. He was so much like his mother. Smart, too. Taylor would have been so proud.

"Can we have your cinnamon rolls for breakfast?" Zachary asked, looking up at her hopefully.

"Not today. Your game is in an hour. Tomorrow?"

"Okay." Zachary jumped from the third to bottom step down to the final one. Claire cringed. The one thing she still hadn't adjusted to was just how much energy he had.

"I'll make pancakes. How about that?"

"Yes!" Zachary ran into the kitchen. Claire rubbed her eyes. She still had to get dressed and face the morning.

Her phone dinged.

Can I come out yet?

No, not yet. Just stay.

I'm not a dog.

"I wish you were. You would listen better," Claire murmured under her breath.

"What, Aunt Claire?" Zachary called from the kitchen.

"Nothing!"

Claire checked the view from the kitchen to the stairs. Max could make it without being noticed. They'd probably only done this about a hundred times at this point over the past four years. Of course, it had started with her needing someone to stay with her overnight. Her grief had been palpable, and she'd hated being alone. At some point, it had turned into whatever this was. She hadn't lied to her mom that this was complicated.

"You're being weird," Zachary said when Claire entered the kitchen.

"Me? No, no, I'm not." She grabbed the frozen pancakes from the freezer and placed them in the microwave. A couple of years ago, she'd given up on trying to make most things from scratch. "Go sit at the table, and here, you can watch a show." There was a small TV in the kitchen she'd put up years ago for when she wanted to bake and watch her morning shows. She turned on some cartoons before blocking off the way between the kitchen and the living room.

Now, and be quiet!

Creaks echoed through the house with every step Max made. Claire tensed, keeping her eyes on Zachary, but he didn't seem bothered. She waved Max away when he gave her a wave. All was well until the moment Max turned the front doorknob.

BEEP. BEEP. BEEP.

"Shit!" Claire curled her hands together. She'd forgotten the house alarm. The late night and early morning had gotten to her.

"Aunt Claire?!"

"Everything's all right. Just eat your breakfast." She ran toward Max, motioning for him to exit the house quickly. She shot toward the panel and turned off the alarm. The sound quieted. For a split second, Claire relaxed. Well, until she realized Max was still standing in the doorway and his eyes were on Zachary.

"Max? Were you trying to break into our house?" Zachary eyed him carefully. Zachary knew Max as her friend. Every so often, they would swing by Max's PI office to take him baked goods. They also always went to his office whenever Zachary had a fundraiser for school. Max was a sucker for those things. They could always sell two hundred dollars of goods easily then. Zachary liked Max, but Claire still tried to keep the relationship casual. She didn't want Zachary to get too attached to anyone who might not stay around.

Panicked, Claire looked between Max and Zachary. Four years and they'd never been caught. She should have known their time was up.

"No, no, of course not," Claire answered. "He came by to, um…"

"I had to bring your aunt Claire some paperwork is all."

"Yeah, and I forgot to turn off the alarm."

"Oh." Zachary remained in his spot, not looking convinced.

"Go on, eat your breakfast. We have to leave in a little bit." Claire attempted to shoo him away.

"Max, want to come to my game?" Zachary had the sweetest smile on his face.

"Sure. I would love to come to your—"

"No!" Claire interrupted. "Um, no, he can't today, bud. He's got an important meeting, remember, Max?" Max shot her a look before giving Zachary a sympathetic smile.

"She's right. I forgot. Maybe next time."

"Now go and eat," Claire said again. This time, Zachary did as he was asked. She spun on her heel to face Max. "You can't come to his games. You can't be in his life. Not like that."

"And why not? You bring him by the office sometimes when you come and visit."

"That's different."

"How?"

Claire didn't have a good answer for him.

"Please, just go," she said.

Max pressed his lips into a thin line. "Fine," he said in a monotone voice. "I'll leave."

He passed her, making his way to the front door. She hated herself for not being able to be the person he needed her to be, a person who was ready to settle down, a person without trauma. As she turned to try to say something to fix this, the words caught in her throat. He glanced back at her, opened the door, and left.

Chapter 7

Margot

Margot had never been one to enjoy waking up early, but since becoming a mother she'd adapted. However, early morning soccer Saturdays might be one she could never get used to. Selfishly, she hoped Ari would decide she no longer wanted to pursue soccer after this season.

She pulled Ari's thick, blonde curls into a high ponytail and tied a ribbon with soccer balls on it for the final touch. Ari grinned before turning and wrapping her arms around Margot's neck.

"Thank you, Mommy! I love it!"

"Of course." She hugged her back. "Anything for my sweet girl."

"Do you think we'll win?" Ari asked.

"Maybe," Margot answered. "But what's important is that you have fun."

"Daddy thinks it's important to win."

Margot's heart broke a little.

"Daddy just wants you to be happy," Margot said. Ari shrugged. She jumped off the chair.

"I know that! He loves me! But he also likes to win." Ari reached her arms out to her sides, and she turned and turned several times.

Margot laughed. "You're going to get dizzy."

"I like it!" She stopped, took a step forward, and fell onto her bottom with a loud chuckle.

"You're silly."

"We're going to be late!" Nanny Fay yelled from the bottom of the stairs.

Margot groaned to herself, not wanting Ari to see. Nanny Fay was always rushing them, it seemed. Or always felt like she was on top of everything they should be doing, making Margot feel inferior. She annoyed Margot, which made her feel guilty. Nanny Fay was like family; she adored Ari. Margot should be more grateful for what she added to their lives than annoyed by it.

"We're coming!"

This time, Margot came prepared. She bought brand-new chairs just for soccer games. She carried them to the field and searched for Victoria. The kids were already on the field doing some warm-ups before the game was supposed to start. Margot kissed Ari's cheek and sent her off to join the team.

Not too far away from Victoria stood Claire. Margot inhaled sharply. She put her seat down as far away as she could get from Claire but still sit next to Victoria. Then she placed the other chair for Nanny Fay.

"Hey!" Victoria said. "How are you feeling this morning? I have the worst hangover." She grabbed the cup from her cup holder and held it up. "Bloody Mary. I need something to survive through this game."

"I'm all right. I didn't drink too much," Margot told her. She glanced back over at Claire, who seemed oblivious to Margot's gaze.

"Wasn't it fun? Jeffery is so awesome to you! He won you so many auctions. John never would do that for me," Victoria said. "The only auction he signed up for was the golf day."

"John loves you." Margot grabbed the snack bag from the ground. It was her week to pass out snacks after the game. Jeffery had picked out and packed the snacks before leaving for work that morning. There were bottles of water, oranges, and some organic grain crackers. She hoped the kids weren't too disappointed in the selection.

"I know he loves me, but he doesn't spoil me like Jeffery does you."

"Yes he does." Margot grabbed one of the oranges from the snack bag before placing it back down on the ground. She peeled it, then offered a piece to Victoria.

"No thank you. Okay, what is the plan for next weekend?"

"Hm?"

"Jeffery is always planning fun events for Fridays or Saturdays or Sundays for you guys. What is it next weekend?"

"We're going to the Fox Theatre to see a play. It's a child friendly one. I forget which, but we're going as a family."

"See? Always something. John would never."

"But isn't it nice to sometimes not do anything over the weekend?" Margot questioned.

"Ah, yes, so nice to have to cook and clean all weekend," Victoria teased. "Oh yeah, you don't have to do those things. Jeffery hires all the people. I'd love to be a stay-at-home mom if it was like how you get to."

Victoria and John were also well off, but John wasn't a fan of having help in the house all the time. However, despite what Victoria said, she did get her house cleaned once a week and got plenty of time to herself.

It just wasn't to the extent that Margot had it. And while Victoria was jealous of her, sometimes she was jealous of Victoria. She thought about how nice it would be for it just to be her, Jeffery, and Ari living in the house with occasional help.

The game started. Margot turned her attention to the game.

"Go, Zachary!" Claire yelled from the sidelines. Margot clenched her hands in her lap. She wasn't sure how she was going to manage coming to these games weekly with her here. Claire had assumed things about her and her husband that was none of her business.

"Are you all right?" Victoria asked her.

"What?" Margot realized the orange was squished in her hand. "Oh, yeah, the game just got intense."

"Intense? They just started. It's a bunch of seven- and eight-year-olds. Don't get too invested. Jordyn will likely end up running away from the ball."

Margot grabbed a tissue from her purse and wiped her hands. Then she threw the rest of the orange, orange peel, and wipe into a bag she had in her purse so she could throw it in the trash later.

Her eyes moved back over to Claire. It was going to be hard to focus on the game with her here.

As she suspected, the snacks were not a hit. While all of the kids said thank you, they all had a disappointed look on their faces. Well, all of them except Ari. She was used to these types of snacks and just took them with a sweet thank you.

"You did great today," Margot told her.

"The best one out there," Nanny Fay added. "I recorded so we can show your dad."

"Do you have to show him?" Ari asked. Margot placed her hand protectively around Ari's shoulder, remembering just how glad Ari had been to show her dad the first recording. But it hadn't gone how she'd expected. Margot recalled how he'd immediately started showing Ari how to do things differently.

"Yes. He hates he can't be at the game," Nanny Fay said.

"But then he'll just tell me what I could do better next time," Ari said with a sigh.

"It's how you get better," Nanny Fay replied.

Margot hated the way her daughter's little lips curled downward. She would have to talk to Jeffery about how nervous she was about him watching her tapes. She knew he wouldn't want to cause her to be upset.

She spotted Claire again in the parking lot. Part of her told her to let it go, but the other part of her said she needed to confront her. What did that woman know about her and Jeffery? How could she make such an assumption about their relationship?

"Nanny Fay, could you take Ari to the car? I have to go and say hi to a friend," Margot said. She handed Ari's hand to the nanny and waited until they walked away to confront Claire.

Claire stood alone at her car—perfect time for Margot to go and say something to her. The little boy went off with an older couple, probably Claire's parents. Claire placed her bag in her car and closed the door. Margot stood right behind her. She almost chickened out, but when Claire turned she realized it was too late. Claire jumped and then chuckled.

"Oh, um, Margot, right? You scared me. Is everything all right?" She tugged her sunglasses from her eyes and placed them on top of her head.

Margot's voice caught in her throat. She'd never actually been great with confrontation. She blinked. Claire's lips tightened, and she gently touched Margot's shoulder.

"Is everything all right?" she asked again, but in a whisper. "Do you need help?"

Margot stepped back and shook her head.

"No," she nearly growled. "I do *not* need your help. I am *very* happy, thank you very much."

"Oh," Claire replied. "Well, I was only—"

"You were only...what? Assuming things about my life? I don't appreciate it."

"Fine," Claire said, crossing her arms in front of her. "You're happy, good for you."

"I am. Not everyone is a damsel in distress. Just because your friend died doesn't mean everyone needs saving." Margot regretted the words the moment they came out of her mouth. "I—I'm sorry. I shouldn't have—"

"I'll leave you alone. Won't say another word to you. I'll make sure to keep my kid away from yours as well." Claire got into her car and slammed the door before driving away.

Chapter 8

Max

Max closed his laptop, finding that his sister had already finished the assessment needed for their case the day before. Sometimes it was really nice having someone else doing half the work. While he'd begrudged his sister wanting to join him as another PI, it ended up being one of the best things for his firm.

He checked his watch. The client wouldn't be in for a meeting for another hour and a half, so he had time to run out to grab something for lunch.

Loud footsteps had him checking down his hallway. Liliana wasn't working today, and he wasn't expecting anyone until his next meeting. Max sighed when he saw it was Claire. Her cheeks were pinched and her hands clenched tight at her sides—something had upset her. He wasn't doing this again. She was always pushing him away and then coming back to him whenever she was upset. He allowed it to happen on and off for the past four years. But after their last encounter and how terribly it went, he was done.

The longest they'd stayed off had been a six-month stretch a couple years ago when she'd decided he was trying to get too serious. During those six months, she never stopped by nor answered any of his calls.

But then one day, she showed up out of nowhere crying because she felt like she was screwing up being a mother to Zachary. And just like that, he'd been unable to tell her no. He always took her back.

No, this couldn't continue. Not this time. He couldn't let her pull him back in.

Claire didn't even say hi when she entered his office.

"I just tried to help her, and she acted like I was this horrible person. Me, a horrible person!" She pressed her hand against her chest to emphasize her point.

"What is this?" Max asked, confused. Claire paced in front of him.

"Like, the look. She had the look, you know?" Claire paused, staring at him like he should understand exactly what she was saying. He didn't, but he also wasn't shocked by this turn of events. Claire did this every time she came back, going on some tangent, usually before bursting into tears.

"The look?"

"The 'oh shit, someone's noticed the bruise on me' look that says, 'I'm abused by my husband.' So I slipped her one of the cards, right? That way, she could reach out if needed. And what do I get? Yelled at." She huffed.

"But why are you here?" Max asked, his brow rising. "I thought you said this morning that we should stop whatever it was we are."

Claire nodded with her stalwart face before it crumpled. Hot tears slid down her cheeks, and Max's heart fell. Immediately, his anger left him and he took her into his arms. Like always, he gave in. He couldn't help it. He loved her.

As she sobbed against his chest, he rubbed her back. He hated to see her sad. Nothing broke his heart more than that. It was why he'd put up with the last four years. He knew she was dealing with so much grief and that in time, she'd be ready to be with him. He'd just have to wait it out.

A moment later, Claire stood herself up. She wiped beneath her eyes and sunk down in the chair across from Max's desk.

"You're right," she murmured. "I did say that." Max handed her a tissue from his desk. She blew her nose. "And I was going to stick to it, but Margot, she just…I'll leave her alone. If she's content in her abusive marriage then so be it."

"You don't mean that," Max said, sitting on the edge of his desk. "You'll still help her when the time comes."

Claire shrugged. "Maybe I read the situation wrong. But if I didn't, yes, I will." She rubbed her nose with the back of her fingers.

"You will," Max agreed. "You are good at that, helping others."

Claire made a face. "I guess. Anyway, I'm fine. I'm sorry I bothered you. She just said something that hit me the wrong way. I'm fine now. I shouldn't have come. I'll leave you alone."

She stood, grabbing her purse beside her chair. Max reached for her, taking her hand within his.

"Or…you could stay? We could go out to lunch? Or maybe a date next weekend?"

Claire's eyes looked him up and down. She pulled her hand away from his.

"What would I do with Zachary?" Claire asked him. It was a weak question; they both knew it. Claire had tons of help between her parents and siblings when it came to raising that little boy.

"Have someone watch him?" Max countered.

"No, I mean, what do I tell him?"

"That you and I are going out to dinner, or tell him nothing. Not yet."

Claire stared at him. She always had this intense glare when her gaze was set on his face.

"Okay," she said.

Max tilted his head. He'd only asked her this same question multiple times over the past several years. Before now, the answer was always an astounding no.

"Wait, did you just say okay?"

Claire's lips curled upward. "Yes."

"What made you change your mind?" he asked, almost certain this was some trick she was playing on him.

Her shoulders rose and fell. "I don't know. I guess you wore me down," she teased. "No, I just...I do want us to work out. I missed you in the few hours we were apart today. Maybe it's time to try."

"You missed me?" he teased. She rolled her eyes before smiling.

Despite her tough demeanor, she really was a sweetheart when she wanted to be. Max's heart nearly leaped out of his chest. He had to play it cool as to not spook her where she'd change her mind.

"Yes, okay. I'll go on a date with you. I'll have Zachary stay over at my parents' house for the night so that you don't have to sneak out in the morning." She gave him a sly grin and wiggled her eyebrows.

"About that," Max started. "I don't think I should stay over after the date. I don't think I should stay over anymore, at least for a while, or you at my place."

"What? Wait, what do you mean?"

"I'm saying we should just date and not end each time falling into bed. Let's take it slow."

"Slow? I think we passed slow about four years ago when you slept over at my house for over a week."

"Me being over for the week?" Max remembered it being quite nice. It was when it had all started. Claire's parents were trying to be helpful. She was drowning in becoming a mom, still deep in her grief from losing her friend, and balancing everything. So they'd planned a week-long, camp-like thing at their house for Zachary and their other grandchildren to give her some sort of break. "That was fun."

"I don't think slow is our thing, Max. And slow is boring." She shrugged. Max had to force himself not to roll his eyes; he'd say the past four years would disagree.

"But now we're trying out the real thing, right? A real date, you and me."

Claire brought her hands together in front of her before rocking on her heels.

"Real? Is what we have now not real?"

"Not in the way I'd like it to be," Max said. "I want to date, to really date. Not to just fall into bed together whenever life becomes a little inconvenient or just because we happened to see each other in the same room."

"I mean, I've enjoyed it."

"I have too, but..."

"Are we allowed to kiss?" Claire interrupted.

Max narrowed his eyes. Then he laughed.

"After our date?" he asked.

"Yes."

"First date type kiss, sure. Maybe."

"Where will you take me?" she asked. "And it better be good."

"I haven't decided yet. But you'll like wherever I decide."

Claire rolled her eyes again. He hated how adorable he always found it.

"Okay. Sure. But, like, how long do we have to wait?"

"For...?"

"Max!" Claire said in frustration. "You know what I'm talking about."

"A while. It's best we wait. I want to focus on us outside of the bedroom."

"It doesn't just have to happen in the bedroom. We've done it other places. We've done it on your desk!"

Max cringed at the memory. It was not his proudest moment. They'd been arguing about something and then one thing led to another. He shook it away. That was when he realized Claire's hand was back in his. He brushed his thumb over her knuckles. She shivered.

"So our first date on Friday?"

His heart raced in his chest. It would be so simple to go back on what he said, but if he wanted this to be something he needed to take it slow. He wanted Claire and him to be more than people who just slept together from time to time.

"Friday."

Chapter 9

Margot

Every Monday, Margot met with Victoria and her other friends, Jenna and Abby, at a local coffee shop downtown. She'd gotten stuck in traffic on the way and was running late. By the time she found a place to park her car and get into the shop, her friends were already sitting at their regular table with half their food eaten.

"Margot! There you are! I tried calling you. I was worried," Victoria said. She jumped up and gave Margot a side hug.

"Traffic." She sat, glad to see that her friends had gotten her drink and muffin she always ordered. She quickly gulped down some of the lukewarm coffee, in need of the caffeine. She'd hardly slept since her confrontation with Claire. She still couldn't believe how horrible she'd been to her.

"Well, we're glad you made it," Jenna said. "We were just talking about the fundraiser on Friday night. It was so well put together."

"Yeah, it was," Margot agreed. "Did they say how much money was raised?"

"Um, I think John got an email from the foundation with that information. I'll have to ask him."

"No, it's fine," Margot said. She pinched a bit off her muffin and lifted it to her mouth. But she wasn't hungry. "What else is new?" Margot didn't want to talk about anything involving Claire Donahue. She was glad the soccer season was short and that there weren't many more weeks to go. Then the two of them could go off in different paths and never speak to one another again.

"Not much. It's tragic, though, isn't it?" Abby said. "What happened to her friend?" Abby tightened her hands around her coffee cup as she frowned.

"So tragic," Jenna agreed.

"I remember it on the news. I heard they found her body in a river. And her little boy..." Abby took a sip of her drink. "I just couldn't imagine."

"That's awful," Victoria said.

Margot's stomach turned. She thought of the little boy at the games and how young and innocent he was. Had she been too hard on Claire?

Her phone rang, and she happily got up and answered it, wanting to get away from this conversation and the guilt that was eating her up.

"Hello?" she said, walking away over toward the window.

"Come home," Jeffery's voice came through the phone.

Margot scratched the back of her head. She couldn't discern if he was happy or angry.

"Is everything all right?" she asked. "I just got to coffee with the girls."

"Come home," was all he replied. The line cut off. Her body grew cold. She tucked her phone into her pocket and went back over to her friends.

"Sorry about that," she said. "Something's come up and I have to go."

"No! You just got here!" Victoria exclaimed. "Please don't go."

Margot forced herself to grin. "Have to, it's an emergency."

All of the girls' faces grew grim. "What happened?" Jenna asked. "Did someone get hurt?"

"Nothing serious, I don't think. Just something important for Jeffery."

"Oh," Victoria said. All their faces relaxed. "He's probably surprising you."

"Maybe! See you later!"

When she exited the café, she tried to call Jeffery back. There was no response. What could he be calling about? Had he found that card? *No*, she told herself. She was getting in her head. It was probably nothing.

Parked in the garage, Margot brought down the visor to check her appearance. She combed through her blonde locks, wishing she'd carried her brush with her. She added a quick swipe of light red lipstick to her lips, hoping that would be enough.

As she exited the car, her hands began to shake at her sides. She clasped them together, unsure of why she was so anxious.

Right as she made it to the door, it opened. Jeffery stood on the other side, his face unreadable. Margot remained locked in her place.

"You're here," he said with no emotion.

"Yes, um, you said to come home, so I did." She attempted to sound lighthearted, but it came out squeaky.

Jeffery held something behind his back. Margot tried to glance around to see what it was, but every time, he'd move with her so it was impossible.

"Is...um, is everything all right?"

Slowly, Jeffery's lips curled up into a smile. He brought his hand from behind his back to reveal a small jewelry box.

"Surprise! We're going to lunch!"

"*Oh*!" Margot exclaimed. "Jeffery! You frightened me! You're never home during the day!"

Jeffery opened up the box to reveal a new charm bracelet. Margot stared at it for a long moment. This wasn't Jeffery's style. He usually went for extravagant and showy jewelry, not something someone would wear just out and about.

"Okay, so I went into the shop to find you something new and the assistant talked me into this. You hate it," Jeffery said.

"No, no, not at all," Margot said. She took the box from him.

"All the charms represent Ari."

Margot's heart warmed. She touched the small charm that held Ari's birthstone.

"I love it," she said. She slipped it on her wrist, where the bruise had faded into a memory. Jeffery made a face.

"Maybe we save it just for when we're at home." Margot touched the bracelet, not understanding why he would buy her it if he didn't want her to wear it. "Now, why don't you go and get changed for lunch? I made reservations for one."

"One? But Ari is out of school at two." Since Ari had begun school, Margot had never missed a day of picking her up.

"That's why we have Nanny Fay, Margot. She is capable of picking her up. Are you not excited that I took time off work in the middle of the day to spend time with you?"

"No, of course I am. I just…" Jeffery shot her a look. "I'm very excited. Um, what should I wear to lunch?"

No one was as excited about Jeffery being home early than Ari. After lunch, they picked her up from the house and went out for surprise ice cream at her favorite ice cream shop, a place they only got to visit once in a while because treats were just that—treats. Outside were several games set up for families to play. Ari's favorite was the large game of Connect 4. She jumped up and placed her red piece in, claiming four in a row. Jeffery gave her a high five. He always hyped her up when she won, but never let her win. He said it made the wins that much more satisfying.

Margot shook her iced coffee and smiled at her little family. She didn't know why she'd been so worried earlier when Jeffery called her. It was her anxiety; she just knew it. She allowed it to control her too much. Jeffery spoiled her and their daughter rotten. He took care of them; he made her safe.

She went up beside them and brought her arm around Jeffery's middle, bringing him closer and kissing his cheek. Jeffery grinned.

"What was that?"

"What?" Margot asked.

"You never kiss me in public," Jeffery said.

"Sure I do," Margot replied, though she knew it wasn't true. She'd never been much for public displays of affection, since they usually made her feel embarrassed. But she pushed herself out of her comfort zone so she could show him just how happy she was that he was home early.

"No you don't," Jeffery teased. He took her face lovingly into his hands and planted his lips on hers. She tensed, but his hands didn't move from her cheeks. Instead, he deepened the kiss. As she wiggled out of his touch, he laughed. "See?"

Her cheeks reddened, and she glanced around at the people outside. Not one of them was paying them any attention.

"Yeah, I guess."

That night after everyone was asleep, Margot searched for Claire's friend, Taylor, on the internet. Several articles popped up right away. She clicked on the first link.

Dylan appeared as a loving husband and father. However, behind the scenes, he was abusive. His wife had many hidden bruises. When she finally found the courage to leave him, she disappeared just a little while later. He convinced the world that he loved her. Everyone was shocked when Taylor's body was found in a lake.

Margot felt a shiver run down her spine. She shook it off, looking back at the article. There was a picture of Taylor with her little boy. Tears stung her eyes. Her friend had been right—tragic. Margot knew then she needed to apologize to Claire. She had been horrible to her.

Margot curled her hand into a fist and stared at the door in front of her. She found out where Claire Donahue worked on her internet searching the night before. She knew if she didn't come by today she would chicken out.

She knocked, and then took a big step back. She had to hold back the urge to chew on the edge of her fingernails. Jeffery hated when she did that.

The door swung open. Claire's eyes widened and then narrowed.

"What do you want?" Her voice was impatient.

"I...I wanted to apologize," Margot said. "I was horrible to you."

Claire eyed her up and down, said nothing else, and went back into her office and sat down at her desk. Margot remained in her spot for a moment, wondering if she should leave now.

"Um..."

"Well, are you going to take a seat or not?" Claire asked.

"Oh, um, yes!" Margot sat across from her. She bounced her knees. "I...I don't know what got into me the other day. You help people and thought I might need help. How could I get upset with anyone who helps people? And what I said about your friend was below the belt."

Claire sighed. "It was. But it's okay. Trust me, I've had plenty of people say worse."

"But I don't want to be that person. I don't want you to see me as that person. And I promise you that I am in a very healthy and happy relationship. My husband, Jeffery, is such a good provider for me and Ari, and he just adores us both. He does everything for us and asks nothing in return. Just yesterday he surprised me with a special lunch outing."

Claire's brows rose, unamused, and then she nodded.

"So, anyway, while I appreciate the concern, I promise you he's not one of those people."

"Fine, sure." Claire tapped her fingers on her desk. "Is that all?"

"Um, well, I thought maybe you could bring Zachary over for a playdate one day after soccer practice."

"Oh," Claire said. She furrowed her brows. "I'm not sure we need to do all of that."

"Oh, please! I'd like to get to know you more, let the kids get to know one another better. Just once?"

Claire rubbed her forehead as though all of this was giving her a headache, but she nodded.

"All right, Saturday after the game?"

"Sure!" Margot stood. "I also brought this." Margot handed Claire an envelope.

"What's this?"

"It's a donation for your foundation." Margot gave her a nervous smile.

Claire opened the envelope before closing it back up and handing it to Margot. "Why don't you keep it?" she suggested.

"But I don't need it," Margot replied. "Use it to help someone."

"May I ask you something?" Claire asked.

"Yes."

"Do you have a secret fund? Like, an emergency fund?"

"That's a personal question," Margot said.

"Well, if you do, add it to that. Or, I don't know, make one. You never know what tomorrow might bring."

"Jeffery is a good husband," Margot said strongly.

"You said that," Claire replied. "I'm not disagreeing with you. But it never hurts to have money hidden away just in case."

"I don't need it," Margot repeated. "We're very wealthy."

Claire eyed the handbag Margot held in her hands. "Yes, I can see that."

"I didn't mean it like that. I wasn't trying to—"

"Keep it," Claire said again. "Emergencies pop up all the time."

Margot tucked the envelope into the back pocket of her purse. She realized she was getting nowhere with Claire.

"So, you'll come over on Saturday after the game?"

"Yes." Though Claire didn't sound thrilled about it.

Margot grabbed a small pad and a pen off Claire's desk, quickly writing down her information on it. Then she slipped it back onto her desk.

"There, so you have my information."

"Thanks," Claire quipped, seeming less than excited to be spending any more time with her.

Margot stood there awkwardly for a moment before giving a small wave.

"Well, great, looking forward to it." Claire only looked up and gave a curt nod. "All right, well, bye."

"Uh-huh," Claire muttered. She turned her chair and started typing on her computer, leaving Margot standing there. She exited the office, deciding that had gone better than she'd expected it to.

Chapter 10

Max

"You don't want me to pick you up?" Max asked into the phone that he held between his ear and his shoulder. He unlocked the door to his apartment, kicking it open with his foot as he balanced paperwork in his hands. Once he got inside, he dropped the paperwork onto the kitchen table.

"No. You said we're starting fresh. You can't come over; you might end up in bed with me."

"Do you honestly think I can't handle that?" Max chuckled. "We're both adults."

"I know, but still..."

"Still what?"

"Just not my place for now. If you want to make up silly rules, then I get to as well."

Max scoffed. "It's not a silly rule."

"It absolutely is."

He heard water turn on through the phone. "Fine, we'll meet there. The reservation at Folley's is at seven."

"Folley's, impressive. I'm surprised you were able to snag a reservation. So, I guess I should dress up then?"

"Were you not planning on it?"

"I just didn't know what to expect."

"Now you do."

He hung up the phone, heading to start his own shower. He'd spent most of the day in his car following a suspected cheating spouse. He had to sit outside a motel for five hours waiting for the money shot of the husband kissing the mistress.

As he waited for the water to warm, he sent Claire a quick text.

I'm excited about tonight. He sent it before he could talk himself out of it, sure she would find it cheesy. But just seconds later, she responded back.

Me too.

Max checked the time on his watch for the fourth time in five minutes. It was 7:08. Eight minutes after their meeting time. Not concerning, but Claire was rarely late. He sat at the table and then stood, checking over the partition to make sure Claire hadn't arrived and didn't see him.

Again, he texted her a message to let her know he was already at their table and to let him know when she arrived. He retook his seat. His foot tapped against the floor before he chuckled at himself for being so nervous. He'd known Claire for over four years now, but it was their first official date.

He rearranged the bouquet of flowers he'd picked up for Claire on the way over from a local flower shop. He hoped she liked them. Max knew very little about flowers, so he'd asked the shop owner which ones would be best for a first date. At first, he'd handed Max a dozen red roses, but Max said no. Red roses seemed too cliché for Claire. In the end, he'd decided on a bouquet of flowers with beautiful fall colors.

"I should have gotten chocolates too," he murmured to himself.

Finally, his phone dinged with a new text message. Claire's name flashed across the screen. He grabbed it a bit too eagerly and swiped his thumb over the screen to see her message, while standing to see if he could spot her. She wasn't there. He glanced down at his phone.

Hey, so sorry, there's been an emergency. I'll call you later to explain.

What happened? he asked. There was no reply.

Max sunk back into his chair. He doubted there was a real emergency. He'd just pushed too hard for this to be something Claire wasn't ready for.

But it had been four years. Four years of on and off, of sneaking out of her bedroom in the morning. Four years of her coming to him crying whenever she was upset. Four years of him trying to be more than friends with benefits.

Maybe it was time for him to move on.

The next morning, Max found himself outside of Claire's house. He decided he was going to end it all here and now. It was what was best for the both of them.

It had been a minute since he knocked, so he knocked again. It was already ten, so he was surprised she hadn't answered yet. Then he remembered it was soccer day.

"Crap," he said under his breath. He began to walk away. By the time he reached the bottom step, he heard the door open.

"Max?" Claire asked sleepily. Max turned on his heel. Claire had her bright pink silky robe on and brown slippers on her feet. Just seeing Claire made him realize he couldn't end it. He wanted her. "What are you doing here?"

Max opened his mouth to speak when Claire gasped.

"Oh! I forgot to call you last night!" She pressed her palm against her forehead. "Shit! Sorry. Come on in."

Right inside the house sat Zachary's soccer shoes and uniform.

"Um, what's going on?" Max asked, now concerned.

"Zachary broke his arm last night," Claire explained.

"Oh no!" Max exclaimed. He felt like such a jerk for being so impatient with her for not showing up.

"Yeah, he was at my parents, and he tried jumping from the porch to the ground. He fell onto his elbow. We were at the ER until about two in the morning. He's still asleep."

Claire yawned.

"Is he okay?"

"Yes. He's going to be fine, though no soccer this week. We'll re-assess next week. I'd be okay if we're done for the season, but he's pretty bummed. Want some coffee?"

"Sure."

They entered the kitchen.

"Here, let me do it. Sit," he lightly commanded. Claire didn't argue. She sat at her kitchen table and rested her head on her hand.

"Why did you come over?" Claire asked. "Not that I'm not happy to see you."

"Just to see you," Max lied. Claire perked up.

"You're a bad liar. Why did you really come over?"

"To see why you canceled," Max sheepishly said. He grabbed the container of coffee and dumped the correct amount into the cup before taking the pot over to the sink to fill it.

"You thought I just didn't show," Claire said.

Max swallowed hard.

"I mean, I can't blame you if you thought that," Claire added. "I did think about it."

"Oh." Max's shoulders dropped. He poured the water into the coffee maker and slid the pot back into its space.

"But I was planning on going, Max. I had already dropped Zachary off with my parents and had gotten ready to go. I got the call when I was on my way to meet you. And, I just...Zachary came first."

"As he should," Max said. He sat down next to Claire. "You know, if you had let me pick you up, I would have known about Zachary and been there to help you last night."

"Yeah, I guess." She rubbed her eyes. Another yawn escaped. "Well, next time, you can pick me up."

"Really?"

Claire met his eyes. She grinned. "Yes. I'll let you pick me up next time. But you have to drop me off outside. No coming in."

"It's a deal."

Max glanced over at the coffee pot to see how close it was to finishing. His stomach growled.

"There's cereal in the pantry."

"Would you like me to fix you some?" Max slid out of his chair to see what types of cereal she had. He couldn't believe how simple this all was, that the two of them were just hanging out in her house. He didn't want to jinx it.

"Oh!" she yelled, standing out of her chair.

"Um, is everything all right?"

Claire pushed past him and into the living room. He followed her in concern to find her digging in her purse. As she did, she threw random receipts and other pieces of paper out onto the couch beside her.

"There," she said, breathing heavily and holding on to one of the pieces of paper.

"Claire?"

"Some parent from soccer. You know her—well, *of* her. The one I gave a card to and she yelled at me?" Max nodded, remembering Claire coming and crying to him. "Well, she came and apologized and insisted the kids do a playdate today after soccer. I need to text her and let her know we can't come today." She fell back onto the couch. "See, Max? You don't want this life. It's hectic. There's no time for me. And you know, I'm okay with that. I chose this for Taylor. But you didn't."

Max frowned. The nice moment was gone.

Claire pulled out her phone and typed on her screen. He could see she was texting the mom about their playdate.

The coffee pot beeped to say it was full. Max took the opportunity to go and fill up their coffee mugs. This was the time to tell her he didn't mind any of it—the soccer games, the crazy life—if it meant they got to be Max and Claire.

But by the time he came back with the coffee mugs, Zachary was awake and at the bottom of the stairs with a bright red cast on his arm.

"Good morning, bud," Claire greeted. "Are you hungry?"

Zachary narrowed his eyes, cocking his head to the side. "Why is Max here?"

"I heard you broke your arm and came to check on you," Max said easily.

Zachary shrugged as if that answer seemed good enough. "I'm good. I got this cool cast." He lifted it up in the air.

"Very cool."

"Can I have your cinnamon rolls?" Zachary asked.

Claire grinned. "Yes, I think I can make those for you." She winked.

Max followed her back into the kitchen and placed their coffee mugs on the kitchen counter. That's when he spotted a tear sliding down her cheek that she quickly swiped away.

"It's hard," she whispered. "I love him so much, but it's hard."

Max went to her side.

"Let me help you, Claire. Let me be here for you, with you," he pleaded. Claire gave him a meek smile.

"Why don't you go on back home, Max? Zachary is awake now, and I need to get these cinnamon rolls made."

"Or I could stay and help," Max suggested.

"Let's talk later," Claire replied. "Go on home."

Max sighed. "Claire, stop pushing me away."

"I'm not." Her voice rose at the end.

"Claire," he repeated.

"I'm not," she said, lower. "At least, I'm trying not to. I promise. Things are just complicated."

"They don't have to be."

"But they are. I have a child. Please, respect me on this."

Max relented, giving a nod. "All right. I'll leave."

"Thank you."

Chapter 11

Claire

The next day, Claire and Zachary arrived at Margot and Ari's house for their rescheduled playdate. The house was large, but not quite as large as the house she'd grown up in.

"Are you sure you're up to this, Zachary?" Claire asked, staring at him through the rearview mirror. This was only the fifth time she'd asked him this morning. "It's okay if you need to rest more."

"I'm good," he said. He opened his door and exited the car. Claire braced herself. She kept hoping he'd change his mind. Then she exited.

Despite his broken arm, Zachary still had all his energy. He zoomed past her and up the pathway to the front door. He knocked before Claire even made it to the front porch. The door was opened soon after. Margot and Ari stood right in the doorway. They were both dressed nicer than Claire had been expecting for a playdate. They matched in pink floral dresses and pink shoes. Claire always liked to dress up, but Zachary was a T-shirt and shorts kind of kid. She glanced down at his Spider-Man T-shirt and hoped Margot wasn't secretly judging her. Though the moment she thought that, she shrugged it away. Since when did she care?

"You're here! Oh, good! Jeffery is out back and he's so excited to meet you."

Oh goodie, Claire thought. She got to meet the husband. Even though Margot tried to convince her otherwise, she didn't trust him one bit.

Margot and Ari both went back inside for them to follow. However, before they stepped inside, Claire bent down to Zachary's level.

"We can leave whenever you want, bud," she whispered. "If your arm starts to hurt, just let me know."

"Okay!" Zachary rushed forward. Claire grabbed his hand to keep him from running inside. She had a feeling that was not allowed in this house. She was even more sure when she saw how decorated everything was inside. It reminded her of her mother's style with the light, sterile colors. Except her mother's living area was all kid friendly. She saw zero indicators that a child lived in this house.

They went through the house to the backyard. Outside was a huge playset and sandbox. At least there was a kid friendly area out here.

"Wanna play?" Ari asked. She was adorable with the way she gave Zachary a shy little smile.

"*Would* you like to play," a voice corrected. A man walked up to them with a large smile on his face. "Ari, say it correctly please."

"Would you like to play?" she tried again.

"Good girl." The man—Jeffery, Claire reminded herself—patted Ari's head.

"Yeah!" Claire didn't miss how Jeffery cringed at Zachary's use of yeah, but thankfully he didn't say anything, or else they would have had words.

The two kids ran off in the direction of the sandbox.

"Hello, Claire, it's nice to meet you," Jeffery said, reaching his hand out to take hers in his own.

"Hi," she answered. Jeffery let go of her hand and brought his arm around Margot, holding her close. Claire did the quick look over of the two as a couple. They looked happy, but Claire knew a thing or two about body language, and Margot was not comfortable. Jeffery's hand rested on her shoulder. While Margot had a bright smile on her face, her body was slightly turned away from Jeffery with her foot facing outward, as if she was ready to step away.

"I will let you both enjoy your playdate," Jeffery said.

The mood shifted the moment he was inside the house. Claire could tell Margot felt more at ease. Her shoulders had relaxed, and she no longer had the look of concern in her eyes. She pointed to some chairs outside. There, Claire saw an array of snacks and drinks.

"Oh, would you like something else? I could have the chef make us some mimosas." *Chef*, Claire thought to herself. *Fancy*. She had to keep herself from giving an eye roll.

"No, this is great." Claire grabbed a glass and poured herself some lemonade. "I'd rather not drink since I'll be driving."

"Oh, right! Poor Zachary, breaking his arm like that! Was he upset missing the game yesterday?"

"Yes," Claire said. "He likes being with the other kids. Doesn't care as much about the sport."

"Ari's the opposite. She's all about the game."

The kids ran over toward them. Neither said a word as they perused the snacks on the table. Ari grabbed one, but Zachary stared at them for a long moment. Claire wasn't surprised. She'd never seen snack choices like these before, with selections like roasted edamame seeds or seasoned chickpeas. Maybe she should have healthier options for Zachary, but that had never been her style.

"Zachary," Claire said, making the little boy look up at her. "You ask first and say thank you."

"Oh, this is just for them to grab whenever they're hungry. Kids, there are also waters and fruit in the fridge over there."

"Thanks!" Zachary said, not choosing a snack. He rushed back after Ari.

"Seems that his arm isn't holding him back," Margot said.

"Unfortunately," Claire replied. Then she shook her head. "I just mean he's a bundle of energy. Nothing slows him down until his head hits his pillow at night."

"How long have you been raising him?"

Claire inhaled. She didn't like talking about this with people she hardly knew. The only time she felt comfortable talking about Taylor was her speech once a year at the Taylor Foundation fundraiser.

"For four years," Claire said.

"What a blessing you are," Margot told her. "I mean, who else would drop their entire life to raise their friend's baby? She didn't have any other family?"

"No, and I would. I love Zachary," Claire said bitingly. Margot flinched.

"I'm sorry. I didn't mean it like that."

"It's fine," Claire bristled. Then she offered Margot a smile. "So, what do you do?"

"I'm just Mom," Margot said.

"Cool. Is that always what you wanted to be? A stay-at-home mom?"

"No," Margot answered. "Before I met Jeffery, I was a pharmacist up in Colorado."

"Colorado? Pharmacist? What brought you here?"

"I met Jeffery. He was in Colorado for a ski trip, and I was at the resort too. We hit it off. I moved here with him a month later."

Claire's eyes widened. "A month?"

"Yes." Margot laughed. "I know. It sounds wild, right? But we just hit it off. I didn't move in with him. I actually got a job at a local pharmacy, so I didn't just give up everything. But a year later we got married. After that, I quit my job and we started trying for Ari. It took us a few years; it's why I'm such an old mom."

"You're old?" Claire asked. While she had a pretty good skill at reading people, she'd never been great at guessing ages.

"Yes, I had Ari at thirty-nine. I'm forty-six now."

"Forty-six isn't old," Claire said. "I'm thirty." Claire didn't know why she told her that. She was never really good at this small conversation thing. Since she'd started caring for Zachary, she'd lost the friendship side of herself. Every so often she'd meet up with old friends for drinks and some dinner, but it happened less and less as they all got married and had kids of their own.

The sliding door opened. Immediately, Claire noticed a shift in Margot. She sat up straighter and crossed her legs.

"I am making chicken melts. How many should I make?"

"None for me or Zachary," Claire answered, almost too quickly. "We'll leave when it's time for lunch."

"Margot?"

"Yes, please. Do you need any help?"

"No, I got it," he said. "That's sweet though, you offering to help." He gave a little chuckle that made Claire think his words had a double meaning. The door slid back closed.

"I can't cook to save my life," Margot explained. "Thank goodness for the chef and Jeffery, or Ari and I would live off takeout."

Claire shrugged. She and Zachary had takeout probably three times a week. She decided her sanity was more important than home-cooked meals every night.

"Well, if you're about to eat, Zachary and I should go."

"Oh, but you've only just gotten here. The kids are having so much fun!"

Claire rested back in her seat. "Okay, we'll stay a bit longer."

"Good. I'll go and tell Jeffery to wait on lunch. Ari's snacked recently anyway."

Margot disappeared inside, and Claire watched the kids play. They really did get along well. And Margot wasn't too bad either. Perhaps it wouldn't be the worst idea to have a "mom" friend. Even four years later, that word still bothered Claire. She wasn't Mom, and she never would be, because Taylor was supposed to be.

A grasshopper hopped onto Claire's foot and she jumped up, nearly screaming. Claire was not one for bugs. She placed her hand over her heart to find it racing. That's when she spotted something through the window. Out of curiosity, she narrowed her eyes to get a better look. Jeffery was near Margot, and she looked uncomfortable. Claire stepped closer. Jeffery reached up toward Margot's hair. Claire's mind flashed back to seeing Taylor and Dylan in a similar situation. Her heart skipped a beat. Claire placed her hand on the door, ready to push her way in. However, she stopped herself when she saw them kissing. Was she just assuming the worst?

Claire grabbed a small bag of chickpea snaps and opened it, needing something to busy her hands. The door slid back open and there was a shift in the air.

"He's decided just to go to the club for lunch, meet up with some buddies," Margot said, her voice strained.

"Is everything all right? Should Zachary and I leave?"

"Oh no, no, no," she said almost too strongly. "Not at all. Jeffery's glad to have an excuse to go to the club. He hardly ever gets to go. Sundays he's usually stuck here with us."

"Stuck here?"

"No, he loves it. Family day is his favorite. He's wrapped around Ari's little finger. But he rarely gets a day to himself, so he's taking it today."

"Oh," Claire said. "We could leave if…"

"No! The kids are having too much fun. Maybe we'll order a pizza! Does Zachary like pizza? Gosh, I can't remember the last time I had pizza."

Everything about the interaction was strange. Margot went to stand on the ledge of the porch and called out to the children.

"Who wants pizza?"

"Um, maybe Zachary and I should go," Claire said.

Margot shook her head. "Oh, no, please don't. I'm sorry. I get anxious. I just want you both to have a good time."

She sat back down, her knees bouncing.

"Are you sure everything is all right? Did…did something happen?" Claire darted her eyes inside, as though they could be being watched, but no one was there. "You can talk to me."

"No," Margot replied, though her hands tightening together in her lap told another story. "What kind of pizza do you and Zachary like?"

"Listen," Claire said quietly. "You can talk to me. I can help you."

The moment she said those words, Margot stood and acted like she hadn't heard her.

"Pepperoni fine? Or should I get just cheese?"

"Sure, either one," Claire replied. Margot pulled out her phone and made the order. Once she was done she smiled down at Claire.

"We're very happy," she said. "Very."

And that was that. Claire didn't mention it again. She had learned pushing didn't work; it only made the person resistant to help.

By the time the pizza arrived, Margot seemed less anxious. They ate outside. Pizza was Zachary's favorite meal, so he downed two slices easily. Ari exclaimed that it had been forever since she'd been allowed to have it, to which Claire picked up Margot making a low sound and then forcing a smile.

When they finally left, Claire sat in the driveway for a long moment. Something was off, but she couldn't quite pinpoint what. Well, outside of the husband. He was definitely controlling, that was for sure.

"Aunt Claire?"

"Yes, bud?"

"Can we go home now?"

"Absolutely."

Chapter 12

Margot

Margot hid the pizza boxes at the bottom of her trash bin, under some piles of trash. She closed the lid right as she spotted Jeffery's car pulling into the driveway. It was probably silly of her to even hide the boxes. Jeffery wouldn't really care, would he? It's just that he preferred they eat healthier for lunches and dinners.

She unlatched the gate to walk out and greet him.

"Hi," she said, opening his door for him. "How was the club?"

"Fine," Jeffery answered. He got out of his car and shut it behind him. His eyes looked past her and into the backyard. "Have they left?"

"Yes, about an hour ago. Ari is inside doing puzzles with Nanny Fay."

"Good," Jeffery said. "I don't want her coming around again."

"What? Why on earth not? She's so nice! And Ari really enjoyed playing with Zachary."

"I hear Claire gets in women's heads and makes them leave their husbands." Jeffery ran his fingers through his lush locks. "I don't like it."

Margot shook her head. That wasn't what this was, was it? Had Claire come over in an attempt to change her mind? *No*, she told herself.

"Claire has an organization helping domestic abusive victims. The women she helps are victims. That's not the same as—"

"I said I don't like it," he repeated firmly. "And I don't like you making plans on family day. It won't happen again."

"It wasn't supposed to be today. We had plans for yesterday, but Zachary..."

"It. Won't. Happen. Again," he said, emphasizing each word.

Margot inched back. Jeffery had never hit her, so she didn't know why she was so frightened. There had only been that one time with her wrist, but that had been an accident. He hadn't meant it.

Thankfully, Ari skipped outside. The moment Jeffery spotted her his entire demeanor changed. He bent down and reached out his hands for her to run into. He lifted her up and spun her around before putting her on her hip.

"Guess what, Daddy?" Ari said.

"What's that?"

"We had pizza for lunch! From the store! Not homemade!"

"Oh you did, did you?" Jeffery's voice stayed sugary sweet, but he cut his eyes right to Margot in such a way that it made her stomach lurch.

"Well, you know me, I can't cook," Margot attempted to say playfully. "And everyone was hungry."

"But darling, that's why we have a chef. He could have whipped you all up something better, even pizza."

"Right. I wasn't thinking. Silly me."

"Ari, go back in with Nanny Fay. It's about time for your bath anyway." Jeffery set Ari down and she ran back inside, leaving Margot and Jeffery alone.

Lately, he'd been more intense, even for him. His brows creased tightly and his shoulders were squared.

"Are you okay?" he asked her, throwing her off guard. She'd been expecting more berating for the fast food and changing of their weekly schedule. He took her hands within his own.

"What do you mean?"

"Your anxieties. Are they acting up? Perhaps we should call Dr. Shawl and see about getting your meds adjusted."

"No, no, I'm fine," Margot insisted.

"I think we should set up an appointment anyway," he said. "You're not acting like yourself. I'll have my assistant call and set it up for later this week during a time I can come along as well."

"Okay," Margot said, knowing agreeing with him would put an end to all of it.

"Good. It's settled then." He rubbed his hands on her upper arms before bringing her close and into a hug, settling his head on top of hers. "I love you, Margot, and I want you to be healthy."

She did have issues with her anxiety and seeing things in a different way than they actually were. Had her behavior been because of that? Perhaps going to the Taylor Foundation fundraiser had started this, her seeing things that weren't there.

"Yeah," she whispered. "You're probably right."

That evening, Jeffery tucked Ari into bed as Margot watched. He was always so patient with Ari, reading however many stories she asked for him to read. Once the final book was over, he kissed the top of her head and turned off the light.

"Are you ready for bed?" he whispered to her as he walked up. His hand grazed against her lower back, causing tingles to run up her spine. She grinned.

"Yes," she answered.

In bed was where they really shined. Jeffery knew how to make it about her and her needs before his own. He'd never been selfish in bed.

Her fingers locked with his as they walked down the hallway to their bedroom. Her toes dug into the plush carpet, her one request when they'd been building this house. Jeffery made most of the plans, and she hadn't minded.

Once they entered the room, Jeffery closed the door, locking it behind him. He picked her up and laid her down on the bed, making her hair spread out around her head.

"I love you," he murmured before capturing her lips with his own.

"And I love you."

His hands started undoing the buttons of her silk pajamas when a buzz from his phone made him stand. He groaned. In the past, he would have just hit the silent button, but he didn't today. He grabbed the phone and brought it up to his ear.

"Yes?" he growled.

Margot sat up, curious. She fixed the buttons on her top as he went over toward the bathroom and disappeared. Her brow rose. She tiptoed out of the bed and to where her husband was, listening in from the doorway. Though there was nothing she could make out. Jeffery's voice was low, but urgent.

He came back out a moment later, nearly knocking her over.

"Is—is everything all right?" she asked. He nodded, heading to the closet. She watched as he pulled out a pair of pants and a button-up shirt. "Are you going out?"

"I have to. There's a problem with a client." He shucked off his pajama pants and threw them into the laundry chute, even though he'd only worn them for less than an hour. But that was Jeffery. He deemed things dirty no matter how short of time he wore them. Everything had to be washed right away.

Margot sunk back down on the bed. She didn't understand his job. What could he possibly be doing where there was an emergency late at night? Why couldn't he just tell them to wait until tomorrow? "Will you be back this evening?"

Jeffery looked up from putting on his black socks.

"I don't know," he answered. "Don't wait up."

"I won't." Margot tried not to show her disappointment. He grabbed his keys and wallet, stuffing them into his pockets. Then he gave her a quick kiss.

"I'll call you when I can," he said.

"Okay."

Once Margot was alone, she grabbed one of her books from her bedside table. It's what she often did when she was alone in the evenings and Ari was in bed. It was only eight. She sighed.

She reached for her phone, randomly wondering if Claire was in the middle of nighttime routines with Zachary. From their meeting today, Margot found she really liked her. Yes, Margot had friends. She had Victoria, Jenna, and Abby. But their relationship was on the surface. They never really spoke about the real things, the things that mattered. Claire was real. Even in the short time Margot had spent with her, she knew that Claire wasn't the type to just skirt around the issues. And Margot needed that. She needed a real friend.

The issue was Jeffery. He didn't like Claire. He had a preconceived notion about her, and usually once he was decided on something like that it was hard to get him to change his mind. But perhaps, overtime, she could get him to see. She had changed her opinion on Claire. For right now, they would have to meet when Jeffery was at work. He said he just didn't want her around the house, so they could meet somewhere else.

She grabbed her phone and typed a quick message to Claire before she could talk herself out of it.

It was nice spending time with you today! Would you like to meet for lunch sometime this week?

She placed her phone back on the bedside table, not expecting a response right away. She opened her book and started reading. A few minutes later, she got a text.

We had fun today too. Zachary talked about it all of dinnertime. I have lunch every day from 12:00–1:00. We could meet somewhere near my workplace.

Margot grinned. She waited a beat so she wouldn't sound too needy.

That sounds great. Pick the place and the day this week. I'm free every day but tomorrow. She knew it would take at least a week before a meeting with her therapist could be scheduled. She was always booked. Also, if she was lucky enough, Jeffery would forget he wanted to make the appointment. Of course, that was just hopeful thinking. He wasn't one to forget stuff.

Great. Let's do Tuesday. I'll send a link to a restaurant.

Perfect!

Jeffery hadn't come back that night. It was a first in a long while that he stayed out all evening. Whatever was going on at work must have been major.

But with Jeffery not home, Margot was in charge of breakfast. The chef usually didn't arrive during the week until afternoon to prepare dinner. He had prepared some snacks for the week, but that wouldn't suffice for breakfast.

Margot stared inside the fridge. They had yogurt and fruit. Perhaps that would do?

"Let me handle this," Nanny Fay said.

"Yes please." Margot was happy to hand the breakfast reins over to Nanny Fay. She ignored the look of disproval in Nanny Fay's eyes. Margot wasn't stupid; she knew Nanny Fay, as well as Jeffery's entire family, felt he could have done better.

Before Jeffery, she lived off takeout and easy meals. She never thought twice about a frozen waffle popped into the toaster. It made for an easy and simple breakfast. But now her life consisted of quinoa and oat milk. All foods were freshly prepared and always healthy. Even the ice cream shop they took Ari to was all organic. The one caveat that Jeffery allowed to his rules was pizza, and that was also rare.

Sometimes, Margot would sneak a candy bar or some chips when she was near a convenience store, eating it quickly and then hiding away the evidence. Only once she'd been caught. Jeffery laughed before going into a tirade about that food being terrible for her, that he only cared about her health. She felt so guilty that she didn't touch fast food for months. Since then, she'd learned how best to hide it. She wondered if she could sneak out now and get a McGriddle from McDonald's.

"Daddy!"

Margot jumped. She turned, finding Jeffery entering the kitchen. He smiled brightly, drawing Ari into his arms. He didn't look like a guy who had been out all night for work. He appeared well rested. There was nagging in the back of her mind that something was out of place, but she couldn't pinpoint what it was.

"Good morning," he said to her. He walked over to Margot, placing his arm around her shoulders and kissing her cheek. "Looks like I made it just in time to make breakfast. Good thing too, right, Ari? Mommy isn't really all that good in the kitchen, is she?"

"I'm not," Margot replied with a forced smile. "Nanny Fay was about to figure something out."

"Well, I'm here now. Nanny Fay, why don't you take Ari upstairs to get dressed and ready for school? I'll handle this."

With Nanny Fay and Ari gone, the kitchen grew quiet. Jeffery pulled several ingredients out, while simultaneously adding notes to the fridge pad for groceries needed. Jeffery handled all of that. A lot of the time, Margot felt like she had so little to oversee in their family. They had a nanny, they had a chef, and they had a maid. Jeffery told her that her job was to socialize and always look nice. She often wondered what her purpose was. Sometimes, not that she would admit it, she missed the life she had before, especially her job.

"Could I help you with something?" Margot asked.

"No, go on and get yourself ready for today," he said.

Margot looked down at her jeans and T-shirt.

"I wasn't planning on going anywhere today. I just thought I'd chill around the house and maybe do some reading."

Jeffery paused the knife mid-cut into a tomato. He sat it down before turning to face her.

"What if someone stops by?" he asked.

"Like who?"

"The mailman? A salesman?"

Margot tucked her hands into her pockets. "I need to be dressed up for them?" She laughed, but only to ease her nerves. By now she knew what Jeffery expected.

"Presentation is how the world sees us, Margot. Don't you want our family to be viewed well? You don't want them to think we just wear whatever, do you?"

"No, of course not." She didn't know what made her wear this in the first place. She guessed she'd been hoping he wouldn't be home until dinnertime. It was silly, really. He asked for so little. He provided her with everything she ever could have wanted and more. So why couldn't she just wear what he wished of her? "I'll go upstairs and change."

Chapter 13

Claire

E ver since seeing the tension between Margot and her husband the day before, Claire had been in a funk. She called her parents and asked if she could drop Zachary off after school, promising to pick him up after dinnertime. She was so grateful how willing they were to always help her at the drop of a hat.

Now at home, she stood anxiously by the doorway with her phone in her hand. She peeked through the blinds and saw Max coming up the walkway.

"Finally." She opened the door. When he got to the doorway, she grabbed the lapels of his shirt and pulled him inside, shutting the door behind them. Immediately, her lips met his.

"What's this?" he asked, gently pushing her away.

"I just...I need this," she told him. She kissed him again and was glad when he kissed her back. Her fingers tugged at the bottom of his shirt, pulling it out from his pants. They stumbled back and moved up the staircase with her walking backward up the stairs.

By the time they reached her bedroom, both of their shirts had been discarded somewhere on the stairs. Max's hands ran up her bare back and to her bra.

"See, I knew this is what we needed, to get back to this," Claire said.

Max's hands dropped from her skin. He took a step back, running his fingers through his hair.

"We can't do this," he said. "I can't believe..." He shook his head.

"What's wrong? We're good at this."

"We agreed we would go on dates, that we would be more than just sex," Max said. "Why did you call me today?"

"Hm?"

"When you called and said you needed to talk, that's not what you actually wanted, was it?"

"Of course it—"

"Something upset you and you just wanted your bit of comfort."

Claire wanted to say something to dispute what Max was saying, but she couldn't. He was right.

"Max, I..."

"Do you want to be with me?" Max asked. Claire inhaled sharply. She told herself to speak, but nothing would come. Max nodded. "That's what I thought." He sighed. "It's never going to change, is it?"

"Change?"

"Us, you and me."

Claire tapped her toe, not knowing how she wanted to respond.

"So...so that's it?" she asked. "We just end it?"

Max's jaw dropped. Claire covered her lips. She had to make this right. She couldn't have just said that.

"There's nothing to end," Max said. "You've made it clear you and I are nothing more than friends with benefits."

"But we're still friends?" She made sure not to give away any vulnerability as she spoke. Because if his answer was no, then he could no longer see that part of her. Only few people ever did.

"Of course we are," Max said. "But that's all."

"Right, absolutely," Claire replied. Disappointment bloomed in her chest, but she didn't let it show on her features.

"You know," Max began, "we could be more. You don't have to do it on your own, Claire. You've stopped your life for four years, and I get it, I do. But Taylor would not have wanted that for you."

A lump formed in the base of her throat. Tears stung her eyes. She blinked several times to keep them at bay.

"Lunch this week?" Claire asked, wanting to pretend Max hadn't just said those words. The words that could change everything for her, for them.

"I can't," Max replied, regret in his voice. "I'm on a case right now. Big one."

"Right," Claire said, hating how small her voice sounded. She shook it away. "Then next week we'll do lunch."

"Sure."

Claire stood there for several seconds waiting for something else from him. What, she wasn't sure. It didn't come. Instead, he turned and exited her house. As she watched him walk out to his car, she felt the tears sliding down her cheeks. Why couldn't she just let him in?

Claire stepped into the restaurant to find Margot standing at a table and waving her over. Again, she was dressed up from head to toe. Claire appreciated a nice outfit. She had always been a fan of dressing up and wearing nice things, but something about Margot's outfits bothered her. It was like she was trying too hard, that the clothing wasn't really her.

"Hi!" Margot said a bit too cheerfully.

"Hi," Claire said. They both took their respective seats. She didn't quite know why she'd agreed to this meeting. But it wasn't like she had a lot of friends that she could hang out with now with Zachary. Those relationships had kind of become a basis of see one another maybe once or twice a year. While she tried to enjoy nights out with friends, instead she often chose to enjoy the quiet of being home alone when Zachary stayed over with her family.

"I'm so glad you agreed to come," Margot said. "Ari keeps talking about Zachary. She had a lot of fun on Sunday."

"Yes, Zachary did too." Claire took the pitcher of water and poured it into her glass. "We'll have to have another playdate soon."

Margot shifted oddly in her seat, as though she was hiding something, before looking up at Claire with a bright smile.

"Sure! How about on Saturdays after their soccer games? We could head over to the park right next to where they play."

"Sure," Claire replied. The waitress came up to the table. Claire lifted her menu. She hadn't had the chance to look at it. "You go ahead," she said to Margot. Margot nodded.

"I'll have the cheeseburger with fries, and a chocolate milkshake on the side," Margot told the waitress.

"Um…" Claire quickly scanned the menu. "I…I guess I'll do the same." She handed her menu to the waitress. As she returned her attention to Margot, she saw her still staring at her with that same bright smile.

"You like milkshakes with lunch too?" Margot asked.

"I do," Claire replied. "Zachary especially loves a good milkshake. He'd live off them if I let him." She chuckled.

"It's so nice to have someone else who will have a milkshake. But don't tell Jeffery," she said, still smiling. Claire narrowed her eyes.

"What do you mean?"

"Oh, he's just a health nut. Only healthy foods. Milkshakes are a once a year treat for him. When we go out for ice cream, he always gets a smoothie instead. It's nice though. He makes sure we stay healthy."

"Huh," Claire muttered. She rose her brows, but decided against saying anything as she tapped her fingers against the table. She hardly knew Margot, and her one attempt to say something had caused her to get yelled at. She was not getting involved. She had decided long ago to help people from the sidelines. Getting involved meant there was a higher chance of getting hurt again.

"It's sweet, really," Margot continued to say. "That he makes sure we only eat the best."

"Sure," Claire said. It was hard, biting her tongue. Claire wasn't one not to speak up. Before she could stop herself, she asked, "So what would happen if he found out you had a milkshake today?"

"Oh, nothing," Margot said, a clear lie. "He'd probably just laugh it off. But"—she grew serious—"he wouldn't like it."

"So if you eat sweets you have to hide it?"

"Kind of," Margot replied. "This whole meal, really." She laughed it off.

Claire's mouth tightened. There was so much she wanted to say.

"It's all because he loves me," Margot continued. "You see, I have really bad anxiety and he's helped me manage it with food and therapy. Before him, I really struggled."

"But weren't you a well-accomplished pharmacist before you met him?" Claire asked.

"Well, yes, but…" Margot was cut off by the waitress bringing their milkshakes. All the red flags were there. Claire shifted uncomfortably in her seat.

"How do you do it?" Margot asked her a moment later, drawing Claire from her thoughts.

"Do what?"

"Raise Zachary all on your own when you didn't even plan on raising a kid?"

Claire stared at Margot, who had gone from bright and bubbly to anxious, spinning her straw around in her milkshake.

"I'm sorry. I don't know why I asked that. I do that sometimes, ask totally inappropriate questions when I shouldn't." She bent her head, taking a long sip of her milkshake. Then she sat back. "I'm sorry," she repeated.

"No, it's fine," Claire said. "I don't mind it. It's hard," Claire told her honestly. "But I have a good support system with my family, and Zachary is a good kid. And I love him, and I loved his mother. I do it for her."

"That's beautiful," Margot replied. "Really."

"I guess." Claire's stomach growled. She should have had more for breakfast than the leftover crackers Zachary left on his plate. "I don't regret it. I love him. I do everything I do for him." It was part of the reason why she kept pushing Max away. How could she know for certain it would be what was best for Zachary? Sure, they got along fine now, but would they always?

"I get that. It's how I feel about my Ari. She's my everything," Margot gushed.

They fell into an easy rhythm after that, talking about the children and their lives. By the end of lunch, Claire was actually sad to see that it was time to go. She could hang out with Margot again.

Chapter 14

Margot

Margot stood at the window of her bedroom, staring down at their driveway where Jeffery paced and spoke on his phone. While she couldn't make out what was being said, she could tell by the way his shoulders were tensed that this was a stressful conversation.

"Mommy?"

Margot jumped. She placed her hand on her chest and turned to face their daughter. Her hair was in two braids, done by Nanny Fay every evening before bedtime. She held a book in her hand.

"You're supposed to be in bed," Margot said lightly. "Bedtime was over an hour ago." She walked over to her daughter, lifting her up into her arms. Ari rested her head on her shoulder, a clear sign that she was tired. Margot rubbed her back as she sat down on the plush chair next to the window. She peeked through the blinds, but Jeffery was no longer there.

"I couldn't sleep," Ari said, her voice heavy. Margot kept rubbing her back. With her free hand she took the book from Ari and placed it next to them. It had been a while since Ari had come into their bedroom at night.

"Did you have a bad dream?" Margot asked.

"I don't know."

"Is something bothering you?" Margot worried from time to time Ari might have inherited her own anxiousness.

"No."

"Well, Mommy's got you now," Margot said. She kissed the top of her head. She could already feel Ari growing heavier in her arms, letting her know she would be asleep soon. Margot cherished this, since these moments were rare.

"She's supposed to be in bed," Jeffery's voice boomed. Margot jerked her head up. Jeffery stood in the doorway, looking a mess. His tie was undone and his shirt untucked. She wasn't sure she'd ever seen him this unruly, even when he'd come home from work.

"She couldn't sleep. She—"

Jeffery was now in front of her, lifting Ari from her arms. She fussed momentarily until Jeffery placed his hand gently on the back of her head. Margot stood.

"What's…?"

"She needs to be in her bed," Jeffery just said. Margot watched helplessly as he took Ari back down to her bedroom. After a beat, she followed behind them, making sure Ari was all right. Not that she thought Jeffery would ever hurt her. He was always so gentle with her. He put Ari into bed, kissed her head, and then left the room. Thankfully, Ari just turned to her side and went back to sleep. Jeffery closed the door behind him.

"What is wrong?" Margot asked. This was completely out of the norm for him.

"Nothing," he replied. He took her hand, leading her back into the bedroom. As they entered, he closed and locked the door. His hand skimmed over her collarbone before pushing the sleeve of her robe off her shoulder. "I just wanted some time alone with you."

After Jeffery fell asleep, Margot climbed out of the bed. She grabbed her silk nightgown from where she'd folded it and put it on her chair, throwing it on. Then she grabbed her robe. As she stepped forward, Jeffery made a sound. She paused, trying to stay as quiet as possible. She turned her head to look at him, but he was still asleep. She put on her robe before exiting the bedroom. The door creaked and she worried that she'd wake him, but he was out.

Once she was downstairs, she felt a sense of relief pass over her. She'd made it. She went right down to Jeffery's office and searched for more information about what was going on. She had a feeling this had something to do with his work. It was what took up most of his time. If she knew, perhaps she could make it better.

Her hand skimmed over the desktop. It was hard to see without the light on, but she would manage. She opened his top drawer. Nothing was there. It was completely empty. Her hands went inside, shocked. She opened the next drawer. It was the same. And the next, and the next.

The light flipped on.

"What are you doing in my office?" Jeffery asked.

"I—I—" Margot blinked, not sure what to say to explain herself in this situation. She'd never done anything like this before, but Jeffery also had never acted like this before either.

Jeffery stepped forward. Margot stepped back. Her heart raced and her entire body's temperature warmed.

"Why are you in my office, Margot? Are you snooping around my things?"

"No, I was... You were asleep and I didn't want to wake you. You've been so tired and stressed." Margot shook her head. "I was trying to figure out what was wrong so I could help," she squeaked.

Jeffery stopped his steps. He brought his hand up, running it through his hair.

"You are too cute," he said. "I'm not upset."

Margot chewed on the edge of her thumb. Had she been imagining things?

"I am worried about you, though," he said, now standing right in front of her. "You have been acting very strange lately."

"I have?" Jeffery took her hand away from her mouth.

"Yes. The pizza, inviting that woman over on our family day, and now snooping through my stuff. Has something happened?"

Margot shook her head. "I...I don't think so." She rubbed her head. "Maybe I'm just tired."

"Perhaps." Jeffery didn't sound so sure. He pulled her close to him. "It's all going to be just fine. You'll be at the therapist tomorrow."

"I don't think I need..." She was surprised he'd been able to book an appointment so soon.

"Tomorrow."

When Margot woke up the next morning, Jeffery was sitting on the edge of the bed with a cup of tea. He handed it to her as she sat up.

"How are you feeling today?" he asked her.

"Fine," she answered. She took a sip before setting it down on the bedside table.

"Are you sure?"

"Yes, I'm fine," she repeated. "I was only worried about you."

"Hm," he said, his eyes bearing into her. "And here I am worried about you."

Margot pushed the covers off her and stepped out of the bed.

"I promise it's nothing." And it really was nothing. He had been the one acting off last night, not her. This had all started back on that day when he left the bruise on her wrist.

She recalled his anger from that night. She had left the cap of the toothpaste unscrewed. He had grabbed her wrist and dragged her into the bathroom, insisting she fix it right away. Immediately, he'd realized what he had done and dropped her wrist. He'd never hurt her before that moment, and hadn't hurt her since. But the craziness in his eyes as he held on to her that day still haunted her dreams. Since that moment, Margot had noticed Jeffery becoming more intense. Had he always been this way?

"When I set you up an appointment with your therapist, I mentioned how odd you've been acting."

Margot inhaled, moving her eyes to the window. She didn't want to look at Jeffery right now.

"I'm going to start breakfast and make sure Ari is up and ready for school. Don't take too long upstairs." He came up behind her, placing his hands on her upper arms and kissing the back of her neck. "Love you."

"Yeah," she murmured. "Love you too."

Chapter 15

Claire

Claire stared at her reflection in her visor's mirror in her car. She twisted her curl so that it fell perfectly over her right cheek and then ran her lipstick over her lips. Once she was sure she looked perfect, she stepped out and walked up the stairs to Max's PI firm.

They'd made plans for lunch. That's what friends did. They had lunch. The plan was to meet up here and then walk across the street to the new pizza place that had opened just the month before.

She entered the firm. The front was empty. Max's new receptionist must have already been off at lunch.

Claire headed back toward Max's office, walking right past Liliana's workspace. She did a wave, but didn't say anything, ready to see Max. Today would make things right between them again. She just knew it.

"He's not here," Liliana said, now up in her doorway. Her cheeks and nose were bright pink from her vacation the week before.

"He's not?" Claire asked, trying her best to hide her disappointment. "When...when did he leave?"

"Um," Liliana hummed. "Probably about an hour ago. He got a lead on a case."

"Oh. So, he should be back soon then," Claire said hopefully.

"Oh no, not likely. He had to head about an hour north of here."

"Oh," Claire said again. She forced a smile on her lips. "Of course. Well, I guess I should get going then. Um, Zachary has an early pick-up day today. So, um, I should go anyway," she lied through her teeth. There was a heaviness on her chest that she forced herself to ignore. She wouldn't let Liliana see how upset she was.

"How is Zachary?" Liliana asked. "You haven't brought him by lately." She bounced on her heels. The twenty-three-year-old still held a lot of her youthful glow, even working at this job. Sometimes, Claire missed that part of herself. But she'd never been quite as bubbly as Liliana was.

"He's great. He broke his arm, but he hasn't let it get in the way. Doing wonderful in school. He loves school. Definitely doesn't get that from me," Claire said with a little chuckle. She just wanted to escape this conversation. "But I should go."

"I'll tell Max you stopped by."

"No," Claire said, shaking her head. "Don't bother him. I'll call him later."

She dashed out of the small house that Max had turned into his PI business before the tears threatening to escape finally did. She got into her car, clenching her jaw. She would not cry. There would be no more tears shed for Max.

Zachary ran right past her and into her parents' house with his bag slung over his shoulder. Claire's eyes widened and she called out after him, "Do I not get a hug?"

Zachary paused, turned around, and ran right back into her arms. She held him for a long moment, kissing the top of his head.

"Can I go now, Aunt Claire? Anthony is out back on the playset!"

Claire let him go and nodded.

"Yes, be good for Grandma and Grandpa, all right? And be careful!"

"I will!" He ran off outside, dropping his bag by the back door. Claire stepped into the house where her mother still stood by the door. Ever since Zachary had moved in with her and she became his legal guardian, her parents took him in as their own grandbaby. He was treated just the same as their other grandchildren, which included inviting him to the grandchildren sleepover nights. These occurred about once or twice a month, whenever her mother got the itch to have the kids over and spoil them rotten. Zachary always came back home the next day thoroughly exhausted, with several candy bars in his overnight bag and stories of how much fun he had.

Claire's eyes fell to a new picture framed on the table that sat in the foyer. She picked it up, her breath catching in her throat.

"Where did you get this?"

"I found it on my computer looking at old pictures. I thought it could be nice for Zachary to have a picture of his mom here too. I know you have several pictures up of Taylor at your place, but…"

"I love it," Claire murmured. She couldn't take her eyes off the photo. It was her and Taylor on Christmas Eve the first time she visited the house. They sat next to one another on the couch, sipping something out of a mug, probably hot chocolate. Their eyes were on the camera with bright smiles. "It's a great picture."

"I think so too."

"Don't keep him up too late," Claire said, putting the photo down, even though she could have stared at it for hours. "Thankfully, tomorrow is a bye week in soccer, so he doesn't have a game in the morning. But still..."

Her mother rolled her eyes. "Sure. I'll make sure he's asleep before the sun comes up."

"Mom," Claire growled.

"Oh come on, the kids stay up as late as they want at our house. You can go ahead and take him home with you if you wish," she said, raising her brows.

"No, I need this night off. Fine. How about you keep him until Sunday then?" she asked teasingly.

"Sure. We're happy to."

"Seriously?"

"Absolutely. Nora is coming tomorrow night to stay over. Mila worried that since she's still a baby, she wasn't quite ready for cousin night."

"But you'd be okay with Zachary too?" Two nights off from parenthood sounded amazing.

"Yes. He's a great kid. You've done a good job with him, Claire." Her mother patted her shoulder.

Those words meant more to Claire than her mother would ever know, especially since she questioned her own job at raising Zachary. She told her mother goodbye and headed out the front door. But before she went to her car, she walked around the side of the house and peeked over the fence to get one last look at Zachary, smiling as she saw how much fun he was having.

Usually on her childfree nights, Claire stayed in. But she hadn't last night. She ended up at a singles bar downtown, and this morning she was paying for it. Her microwave beeped and she touched her temple, groaning. She opened up the microwave and pulled out the breakfast sandwich, hoping it would quell her uneasy stomach. However, she knew it wouldn't fix her poor decisions from the night before.

She took a bite right as her doorbell rang.

"Shit," she mumbled. She dropped her sandwich on the counter and adjusted the belt of her robe. Who on earth was coming over to her house at this time in the morning? She wondered if she'd forgotten an Amazon package she'd ordered.

But when she opened the door, her heart fell to her stomach.

"M-Max," she stuttered. "What...what are you doing here?"

"I felt bad about missing our lunch date yesterday, so I thought I'd surprise you today to take you out for brunch." He wore a bright smile on his face.

"You never told me you were going to leave. You never even called," Claire said. The anger bubbled within her.

"I know. I'm so sorry! I've been dealing with this crazy case. But as soon as I remembered, I wanted to make it up to you. Plus, I know Zachary is with your parents right now, so I know you're free."

Claire crossed her arms over her chest. "How do you know that?"

"You told me," Max said, chuckling. "Look, I know you're angry with me, but it was an honest mistake."

Claire didn't know what to say. She stepped forward and into the threshold, bringing the door partly closed behind her.

"Look, I'm really tired today..."

The door swung open. The shame covered her as Max took in the man who opened the door.

"You have a guest," Max said. His face gave way to no expression, but his eyes said everything.

"Who are you?" the guy said.

"Go get dressed," Claire interjected, pushing him back as he stood there only in his undershirt and boxers.

The guy ran up the stairs.

"It wasn't like—"

"I don't need to know," Max replied, his voice steady but his jaw jutting forward. "You don't owe me any explanation, Claire. You're a grown woman. You and I are *not* dating, as you've made *absolutely* clear. You can do whatever you want."

"It was just...a night."

Max put his hands up. "I don't need an explanation."

"Hey, Claire! Where's my shirt? Is it downstairs?" the guy called from upstairs. Claire tightened her hands at her sides.

"I don't know," she called back, though as she turned she spotted it on the edge of her couch. She spun back to Max and found him already walking away back to his car. She ran after him, barefoot. "Max!"

Max waved his hand in the air. He paused and looked at her.

"It's fine, Claire. But I should go. I'm interrupting your time with your new boyfriend."

"Boyfriend," Claire scoffed. "It was nothing. Honestly."

"Look, I'm happy for you. Looks like he's a nice guy, maybe." Max pulled a face.

"I don't need your judgment," Claire snapped.

"No judgment here."

They stared at one another, neither one making the next move. Claire's chest rose and fell, anger simmering beneath the surface. She knew it was her go-to move, get angry instead of facing the truth of the situation. Max's throat bobbed as he swallowed. Claire took a step forward. She needed to say something, anything. She had to make this right. However, Max stepped back, away from her.

"Have a good rest of your day, Claire," he said, emotionless, before getting into his car. Claire watched helplessly as he drove off. Tears prickled her eyes. She sighed and went back into her house to find the man now dressed in his clothes from the previous night.

"So, can I have your number?" he asked. He cocked his head to one side and ran his hand languidly through his thick, mahogany locks, almost as though he was waiting for his picture to be taken for the cover of a magazine. That's when she remembered he was a model. He'd told her that the night before.

"Absolutely not," Claire answered. "You can go now, I want to say...Derek?"

"Glen."

"Glen?" Claire sighed. "Okay, Glen. Well, you can go now."

"What about a date? Tonight."

"No." She opened the door. Thankfully, he headed out, but not before giving her a hopeful glance.

"Tomorrow?"

Claire shut the door, making sure to lock it behind her. She turned, allowing her head to fall into her hands. What had she done?

Chapter 16

Margot

Margot couldn't believe her luck that Claire had invited her out for some shopping therapy. She'd never been invited for such a thing before. She spent over an hour trying to figure out what she'd wear. Claire always looked flawless and cool, but in an easy way. She oozed coolness. Margot knew at forty-six she was too old to be worried about how cool she looked, but she feared that next to Claire, she would appear boring.

When she got to the outlet mall, she felt overdressed in her purple dress and silver heels. Claire wore only jeans and a T-shirt, but she still looked amazing. She fit in with everyone at the mall. Jeffery always made Margot feel as though wearing something so casual would have her judged, but Claire wasn't. She was dressed appropriately for their day out, whereas she stood out like a sore thumb.

"Wow," Claire said, "I love that dress on you." Her words were sincere.

"Thank you. I guess I wasn't sure what to wear." She bit on the inside of her lip.

"I like it. Own it." Claire winked. "Now come on, I need to do some serious shopping therapy. I haven't done this in a long time, but felt like it was needed today."

"Oh?" Margot asked. They walked past a shoe store where Claire paused by the window.

"Yeah, I just messed up any chance to get with the only man I probably could ever love." Claire's brows furrowed.

"Do you want to talk about it?"

"No." Claire shook her head. "I just want to put more money on my credit card." She opened the door to the shoe store and went right in. She passed the rows of women's shoes and headed right back to the children's shoes, lifting a pair of Spider-Man light-up shoes. "God, I've become that woman."

"What woman?" Margot asked.

"The woman who shops for her kid instead of herself." She dropped the shoe back in its place. "I told myself I wouldn't change, but I have."

"Yes, children do change you."

Claire's lower lip trembled, but just as quickly as her vulnerability slipped it disappeared. She cleared her throat and headed back over toward the women's shoes. Claire grabbed a pair of red high heels.

"Do you think I could pull these off?"

"Yes. But I am sure you could pull anything off."

Claire turned the heel in her hand. Margot picked up a different one.

"Let's both try them on," Claire suggested. Margot put the shoe back.

"No, that's all right. Jeffery doesn't like red shoes."

Claire made a disapproving sound.

"It's not that..." Margot tried to explain herself.

"Try them on. I bet they'll look great on you."

"No," Margot said again. She gave a small smile. "But you should try them on. Jeffery just has a thing about the color red. It's all his mom ever wears, and he associates it with her. So he prefers that I don't wear it. Of course, he'd let me if I really wanted."

Claire slipped her shoes off her feet, not bothering her anymore about the shoe, though Margot could tell it bothered her that she wouldn't try on the red shoes because of Jeffery's opinion of them. She should have kept her mouth shut. She didn't need to give Claire any more reasons not to like her husband.

"Ow," Claire muttered, taking her foot out of the shoe about as quickly as she'd put it on. "Those pinch. Never mind." She plopped the shoes back into the box. "But I do think I'll get Zachary those light-up shoes. He'll love them."

When they entered the next shop, Margot was drawn toward the graphic T-shirts. She lifted one with Coca-Cola bottles on the front.

"Do you like that one?" Claire asked. Margot tried to discern the tone of Claire's voice. Was she judging her choice? But as she met Claire's eyes, she saw there was no judgment.

"I don't know. Isn't it a bit silly for me to wear?"

"Silly? Why?"

"Well, it's a graphic T-shirt and I'm forty-six."

"So?" Claire took the shirt out of Margot's hands before holding it up against Margot's front. "It's cute. You should get it."

"Oh, I don't know." Margot shook her head. "I don't think Jeffery would like it. He isn't really into the T-shirt look."

"Who cares what he thinks?" Claire grabbed another couple of shirts from the pile. "Now, which ones do you like best? You should wear what makes you comfortable. Be you. Tell me right now, what you would wear out of everything in your closet that would make you feel the best?"

"Really?"

"Yes, go on."

"Okay." Margot only had to think for a moment. "My Taylor Swift concert T-shirt with my faded jeans."

"You're a Swiftie?"

"Yes."

"Which album is your favorite?"

"*1989.*"

"I'm a *Reputation* girl myself." Claire smirked. "But I do have a soft spot for her album, *Evermore.*"

Margot laughed, feeling such at ease with Claire. She had this personality that she felt magnetized to.

"I see it," Margot said.

"Well, get some of these shirts," Claire said. "At least the Coca-Cola one! You went right to it."

"No, I couldn't. Jeffery wouldn't approve."

Claire rolled her eyes and huffed, but she put the shirts back in their place.

They grabbed pretzels to munch on since there was no time to sit and eat. It was so different than what she was used to, and she loved it.

By the end of Claire's lunch hour, she'd ended up with multiple bags of clothing and shoes, but only one item for herself. Margot convinced Claire to get this one silver dress. It looked stunning on her. But Margot bought nothing. She didn't shop for herself normally. Jeffery had people for that.

"I wish you'd gotten that shirt," Claire said. "You really liked it." She checked her watch. "I have a few more minutes before I have to go back to work. Let's go back."

"No, that's okay," Margot replied. "But I appreciate you inviting me along. This was fun." And she meant it.

"It was fun," Claire agreed. "Let's do it again sometime."

"Definitely."

Claire leaned forward, giving Margot a hug. It was so different than the hugs she received from her other friends. It felt genuine, kind, not just a superficial thing one did to say hello or goodbye, but like Claire really did enjoy spending her time with her.

"Therapy? You went to therapy?" her mother asked into the phone.

"Yes."

"But I thought you didn't need therapy anymore."

Margot chewed on the edge of her thumb.

"Mom, everyone can benefit from therapy," she said.

"Well, yes. How...how did it go?"

"Good. She could tell my anxiety has been higher, so she adjusted my medicine."

"Oh," her mom said on the other line. "Still the same ones?"

"Yes. Mom, I used to be a pharmacist. The meds I'm on are exactly what I need. They help me."

"Well, I'm glad of that, at least. So, going back to therapy, did you decide that or Jeffery?"

"Me," Margot lied. She knew her mother wasn't fond of Jeffery. She never said it outright, but some of the comments she'd made over the years made it pretty obvious, like how she felt he didn't let Margot make any decisions for herself. It was why she and Ari often went to visit her in Colorado than her coming here to visit.

"Okay. Well, I hope it goes well for you. How's my granddaughter?"

"She's good," Margot said.

"Beautiful. She looks so much like you as a child. I love the new pictures you sent."

Margot smiled. She was a proud mother. Her daughter was beautiful.

"She misses you," Margot told her. "Maybe we could come and visit you soon."

"Or I could come there. I've been thinking about moving closer."

"Oh?" Margot felt conflicting emotions. She loved her mom. They'd never been the type to go back and forth with one another. Even as a teenager, they hadn't really argued. She wished they could see her more often. The two of them had always been close. But her mom plus Jeffery could be an interesting combination.

"Yes, well, I miss so much of you and Ari over here, and now with your dad gone..."

Margot's heart clenched. She hadn't realized how lonely her mom was. Her dad had passed away just two years ago.

"Well, I know Ari would love seeing you all the time."

"And you?"

"Yes, me, definitely." Margot missed her mom. She missed having her comfort and her love. It would be nice to have her near. "When would you move?"

"I'm not sure," her mom said. "I'd need to sell the house first, but maybe by January."

"That's so soon. Do you think you could sell the house that quickly?"

Margot peeked outside to check on the soccer lessons Ari was doing. She still wasn't too keen on the whole idea. Ari was only seven. She didn't want the extra pressure to make her burn out at such a young age.

The front door opened. Margot turned, surprised to find Jeffery coming inside the house.

"Mom, I have to go. I'll call you back tomorrow." She said her goodbye and placed her phone in her pocket right as Jeffery came up to her, cupping her cheeks and giving her a kiss. "This is a surprise."

"I wanted to see how practice was going," he said. He skirted past her, and went out back. Margot followed behind. Jeffery placed his jacket over the chair and went down to play along.

"Daddy!" Ari joyfully ran toward him. Jeffery gave her a quick hug.

"You're going to play in that?" Margot asked, shocked and amused. Jeffery shrugged. He kicked the ball toward Ari, who kicked it back. Then the coach gave them both some tasks. Margot sat down on one of their chairs to watch. She grinned. She could get used to Jeffery being home more on the weekdays like he had been at the beginning of their relationship. Ari always brightened around her father.

After the time was up, Ari came to Margot, ready for some water and a snack.

"Oh come on, Ari, we can still play for a bit," Jeffery called out after he gave the coach a handshake and led him over to the gate for him to leave.

Ari climbed into Margot's lap.

"I'm tired," she murmured.

"Come on! Let's play."

"Jeffery, I think it's time for dinner," Margot said. "Ari's tired."

"Oh, you're not tired, are you, Ari?" Jeffery came up to Ari, bending down to her level. "Daddy came home just to spend this time with you." His white button-up shirt was soaked through with sweat around his collar and beneath his armpits. Again, this was a surprising look for him. Never in her wildest dreams would she have expected him to play in his work clothes.

"I am," Ari responded. Her eyes grew wide. "I've been playing for hours!"

"Yes. She had already been going for nearly forty-five minutes when you got home. Let's go in and eat. It's already six thirty. By the time we eat and she takes her bath, it'll be bedtime."

Jeffery gave a look showing he wasn't pleased, but he nodded, patting Ari's head.

"All right. We'll go in for dinner."

Stepping out of the shower, Margot heard Jeffery on his phone in the bedroom. She wrapped her towel around her middle and went to the door. The moment she opened the door between their bedroom and the bathroom, Jeffery's voice got lower. She knitted her brows in confusion.

By the time she stepped through the doorway, Jeffery was off the phone and sitting on the edge of their bed.

"I thought you might join me in the shower," Margot said, drying her hair with a different towel. "I waited for a while."

"Oh, I actually have to go back in to work." Jeffery jumped up. Margot noticed he was in a new suit. The sweaty one laid in a pile on the floor.

"What is going on?" Margot asked. "This isn't like you. The phone calls. The playing in your nice clothes. Leaving your clothes just in a pile on the floor."

"Dammit, Margot! Why are you nagging me so much?! Do you know what I do for this family?"

Margot froze. Before she knew it he was up in her face, his hand on her upper arm.

"I do everything for you! You have this beautiful house! Those beautiful clothes! A beautiful daughter, who has everything she could ever ask for. Why must you nag and nag all the time? Nothing I do is ever enough."

His hand unlatched from her arm and he turned. She rubbed her arm, but she didn't think it would leave a mark. He hadn't held her too tightly.

"I'll be back later." He left their bedroom, closing the door behind him, being careful not to make a sound. Margot stood there in shock, though should she be shocked? It wasn't the first time he'd held her as he screamed at her.

She wiped her brow and dropped her towels into the laundry basket inside her closet before grabbing her robe and throwing it over her shoulders. She sat in the chair at her vanity, picking up her comb to brush her wet hair. As she stared at herself in the mirror, tears formed in her eyes. She blinked them back, refusing to cry. Everything was fine. She was fine. They were fine.

Chapter 17

Claire

"Aunt Claire?" Claire yawned, half asleep. Ever since everything had gone down with Max last week, she hadn't been able to sleep.

She sat up to find Zachary standing in the doorway, dressed in his soccer uniform.

"Oh shit!" She jumped up from the bed.

"I get a dollar in the swear jar!" Zachary said with a smile. He'd just lost a tooth the night before right up front. She remembered then that she'd also forgotten to put money under his pillow.

"Shit," she murmured again.

"Two dollars!"

"Yes." She patted his head. "Two dollars. Um, I forgot that the Tooth Fairy messaged me and said she's running behind."

Zachary gave her a look.

"You know I don't believe in the Tooth Fairy, Aunt Claire."

"You don't? Since when?"

"Since forever. She's not like Santa. She's fake."

"Right…" Claire said. "And why is she fake?"

"I dunno. She just is. But Santa is real, right?"

Claire rubbed her temple. This was too big of a question for her at this time in the morning. She never knew how to navigate these moments. Taylor would have known.

"You believe he is, right?" Claire asked.

"Of course."

"Then he is." She yawned again.

Zachary grinned. "You need to get dressed. My game starts soon."

"Yes." She checked her watch. There were only thirty minutes until the game began. "Shit."

"That's three dollars. I think I have fifty dollars now. Can we go shopping after the game?"

"After we do our playdate with Ari at the park, we can. Now go downstairs and get yourself a Pop-Tart or something."

Zachary ran out of the room. She could hear his feet going down the stairs. Claire had fortunately picked out her outfit the night before, so it didn't take her too long to get ready. She put some product in her hair, deciding it would have to be enough for today.

By the time she was downstairs, she saw Zachary munching on the cake she'd made earlier in the week. She gave him a look. His eyes shot up at her before giving her the cutest grin with his missing tooth.

"What? You said 'or something'."

"I mean, I guess, all the quick options are straight sugar. Grab an apple to eat in the car at least."

"All right!" When he smiled up at her, all she could see was Taylor staring back at her. It was odd how that would happen. He didn't always look like Taylor; he often looked like his own little person. But there were times when he'd smile up at her and all she could see was Taylor in his face. Those moments always stole her breath away, reminding her that she'd been trusted with such a precious gift of Taylor's.

Zachary didn't complain once about his broken arm. He played right along with the game, not letting it get in the way. Claire cheered him on, so proud of him. Today, her brother James and her parents had made it to watch. All three of them stood with Claire, cheering.

"Go, Zachary!" He turned to face them, giving them two thumbs-up. Then he went back to playing.

As they called the first half and Zachary ran over to get water and say hello to his family, Claire told him she was proud. She then went over to where Margot sat chatting with some of the other women. Upon noticing Claire, she got up from her seat.

"Oh, Claire!"

"Hi," she said. Claire glanced around at the other women. She recognized some of them from the year before but she couldn't remember any of their names. They were cliquey, like all of the other parents at soccer, and Claire had never been about cliques. Margot was the only one with a sincere bone in her body.

"Want to sit with us?" Margot asked.

"I can't. My family is here." Claire pointed over at her family, grateful she had an excuse. "I just wanted to say hi."

"And we'll meet up afterward?" Margot asked quietly. Claire nodded and winked, patting her shoulder.

By the time she was back over by her family, Zachary was playing again.

"So which one of you ruined the Tooth Fairy for Zachary?" Claire asked her parents and James.

"What?" her mom asked.

"This morning, he told me he doesn't believe in the Tooth Fairy."

"He didn't hear it from us," her dad said.

"It was me," James said. He rose his shoulders. Claire narrowed her eyes. She knew it.

"Why would you tell him that?"

"He was asking me all sorts of questions, saying the other kids at school said it was babyish to believe in it. What did you want me to say?"

"Tell me about it to handle it," Claire spat. "That's my job. Not yours."

"He was over at Mom and Dad's at the time. You were out doing God knows what…"

Claire's chest heaved. "Just because you've decided to give up on life and love doesn't mean you take away his childhood innocence. Taylor would be so disappointed in what you've become." She knew it was harsh to say that, but her patience with her brother was waning. He was stuck in life, not moving forward, not trying to really live. Sure, he showed up for Zachary, but otherwise he did so little. Claire knew he usually just went to work and then sat at home or their parents' house, drinking his sorrows away.

"Claire!" her mom scolded her.

"You know I'm right," Claire said in response. James tucked his hands into his pockets.

"I'm leaving."

"Don't leave," their mom said to him. "Zachary will be disappointed."

Claire just stared at him, daring him to go, prove her right. He growled and turned away from her, watching the game.

"I'll stay for him," he gruffly said.

He stayed until the very end, giving Zachary a quick high five before heading off to his car and not saying another word to Claire or their parents. Her dad led Zachary over to where snacks were being passed out by another teammate.

"You need to be kinder to your brother," her mom said as soon as Zachary was out of earshot. "You and James used to be close. But now you both fight like cats and dogs."

Claire huffed. "You need to stop coddling him."

"He's depressed. I thought you, out of everyone, would understand that the most and be empathetic." Claire didn't respond. She did understand, but it wasn't fair. She'd lost Taylor too. She had been her best friend, and now she had to move forward. She didn't have the luxury James did to wallow in her depression.

She walked over to where Zachary stood holding the snack bag he'd gotten from his teammate. They were gift baggies with several snack options, two drinks, and some little toys.

"That was fun," Zachary said as he waved to all his teammates walking away. He gave Claire's father a hug and then her mother. "Thank you for coming!"

"Of course, we'll come next week too."

Claire gave them both a quick peck on the cheek. "We'll see you next weekend."

She took Zachary's hand, now way too familiar with his sticky hands that she already had wipes in her purse. They walked across the street to the playground. Ari and Margot were already there. The nanny wasn't with them. Margot sat on a bench by the park while Ari climbed up the climbing wall. Claire noticed she'd changed into regular sneakers.

"Crap. I need to run to the car to grab your sneakers."

"That's fifty cents, Aunt Claire. You're cursing a lot today."

"Crap isn't really a bad word," she said.

"But it's not a nice one. That's why it's fifty cents and not a dollar." He squished up his nose. She tapped it with her finger.

"Can you watch him while I run and grab his shoes?"

"Sure."

By the time Claire arrived with Zachary's change of shoes, he was sitting on the bench with his soccer cleats beside him, swinging his legs back and forth while he chatted with Ari. Margot stood nearby but also far enough away to give them space. Claire walked up beside Margot.

"They're cute," Claire said.

"I think they'll be the best of friends," Margot replied. She wore a T-shirt and jeans, making Claire think she looked more comfortable in her skin. Claire guessed Margot had snuck out of the house with it on.

"I love your outfit."

Margot glanced down at her top, the tops of her cheeks turning pink.

"I don't look stupid?"

"No, not at all," Claire said. "You look beautiful. You should try wearing more outfits like that. It suits you."

Margot twisted her lips, tucking her hair behind her ear. Something about the look on her face made Claire think she probably wouldn't, at least not often.

"I'm sad soccer is almost over."

"Oh?" Claire tapped her fingers against her thigh. "I'm not really. I hate getting up early on Saturday mornings for games. Maybe when he's older and the games are later. Why are the little kid games so early?"

"Because little kids like to wake up earlier."

Claire shrugged. "I guess. I am not a morning person."

"Oh, me neither, but I don't mind it that much."

"Mornings were one of the hardest adjustments when I started raising Zachary. He was up with the sun, every morning, no relief. And I was grieving. And it was just...hard. But then he got a bit older and I was able to convince him to entertain himself in his bedroom until his little clock beside him turns green. That was a lifesaver."

Margot chuckled. "I think Nanny Fay got one of those for Ari, but she doesn't use it. I've always been a pushover with her. If she wants me, she gets me."

"So the nanny doesn't get her in the mornings or anything?" Claire asked. She didn't quite know how nannies worked. Her parents had never had one. How, she wasn't sure with both being successful lawyers with five small kids. Though, Claire did remember her grandparents being around a lot when she was younger. That was probably how they pulled it off.

"Oh she would, but..." Margot shrugged. She leaned in closer to Claire and added, "I honestly don't even know why we still have a nanny. It was nice when Ari was little and didn't sleep through the night, but now... I mean, she is family. She was Jeffery and his brothers' nanny when they were little. And I love her, I do. I just..." Again she shrugged.

Claire rose her brow, interested. "Oh, so why not let her retire? She must be tired of caring for kids."

"No, Jeffery would never allow that."

Again with the *never allow*. Claire hated those words. She rolled her eyes.

"But does she still want to nanny?"

"I think so. She adores Ari, and Ari really loves her too."

"She can still be a part of your family if she's no longer working for you, can't she?" Claire asked.

"Of course. She definitely could be. I don't know. It doesn't matter. She probably doesn't want to leave anyway." Margot sighed.

"Where is your nanny today?"

"She took the weekend off to visit her family up in New York. I'm pretty excited with her being gone for the weekend. That sounds awful, doesn't it?"

"No," Claire said.

"It's just nice to have a purpose for the weekend. I get to be the one in charge of my family. Most days I'm not sure what my purpose is, you know? We have a house cleaner, a chef, a nanny. What am I supposed to do?"

"Work?"

Margot laughed. "I wish."

"Do you? Do you wish you were working?"

"Sometimes."

"Then why don't you?"

Margot opened her mouth, but Claire interrupted, knowing exactly what was about to come out of her mouth.

"Jeffery would never allow it?" she asked, raising her brow. This reminded her so much of Taylor. Dylan had never let her work either.

"When you say it like that, it sounds awful. Jeffery just likes taking care of me and Ari. He wants what's best for us. It's why we have all the best people working in our home, so I don't have to lift a finger if I don't want to."

"Right," Claire said, trying her hardest not to go on a rant. Biting her tongue wasn't her specialty. "Well, as long as you're happy."

"I am, definitely."

"Great," Claire clipped. Thankfully, Margot didn't seem to notice.

That night when Claire went into Zachary's room to read him his goodnight story, she found him sitting at his desk by the window. He worked diligently on the paper in front of him with his colored pencil. She stepped behind him, glancing down at the paper. To her, she thought he was an artistic genius. Of course, she knew little about color theory or what was typical for this age. When he realized she was standing there, Zachary glanced up.

"It's really beautiful," Claire gushed.

"It's a picture of our family," he said. He pointed to the small figure. "That's me. And that's you." She smiled. "And that's Mommy. She's up in heaven."

"That's right." She mussed his hair. "And who is that?" She pointed to the figure that stood beside her.

"Max," Zachary said. "You know, the guy who's always here but you pretend he's not."

Claire's jaw dropped. It seemed Zachary was more perceptive than she gave him credit for.

"Well," she said when she gathered her wits about her, "he won't be here, not anymore."

Zachary touched the figure on the paper.

"But why? He always seemed to make you happy."

Unexpected tears stung her eyes, making Claire blink to keep them from falling.

"This is why I tried to keep him hidden, Zachary. Grown-up stuff can get messy, and I don't want to involve you in it."

Zachary did a little click of his tongue before turning back to his drawing. He lifted a corner of it, tearing off the part of the picture where Max was. Claire gasped. He handed it to her.

"Here," he said. "It's for when you're missing him."

Claire held the drawing in her hand. She glanced back at Zachary and then back to the paper. That worry seeped in again, the worry that she wasn't good enough for him, that she needed to do better for him. Her mother told her that was natural, that all mothers felt like that from time to time and that it was a sign she was doing a good job, but she wasn't so sure.

"You know," Zachary spoke up again, turning in his seat to look at her. "You can get him back. He's not in heaven like Mommy, so you can always have a second chance."

Claire reached out and caressed Zachary's cheek.

"I'm not so sure about that. Now, clean up your drawing stuff and pick a book to read for bedtime."

Zachary quickly did as he was told, like he always did. As he looked through his bookshelf for a book, Claire stared back at the drawing. Her finger rubbed over Max's face. Could she just call him up? Before Claire could debate on it any longer, Zachary was up in his bed with a book ready for her to read with him. She folded up the drawing and stuck it in her back pocket, deciding it was better not to think about it at all.

Chapter 18

Margot

*T*he kids had so much fun Saturday, Claire said in a text to Margot.

Margot smiled. She hadn't spoken to Claire since the park two days ago and was glad to get a new text from her today.

They did. What will we do after soccer? This week is the last week.

Weekly playdates? Claire suggested.

Absolutely.

Margot placed her phone down on her vanity. She brought her fingers up to her cheeks and pushed them back. Most of her friends had at least Botox by now, and sometimes she felt like she needed it. But she hated needles, and Jeffery told her she was beautiful as she was. She dropped her hands.

She got out of her chair and checked the time on the clock by the bed. It was nearing ten. She rubbed her eyes. She was tired, but she wanted to wait until Jeffery was home to go to bed. As she made her way over to the dresser, she noticed paperwork on top. It was a little odd for paperwork to be left upstairs and not in his office. Of course, last time she was in his office, no paperwork was in there.

Jeffery didn't like things left out. He liked order. She grabbed the paperwork and took it into the office, setting it in the little desk tray on the corner of the desk.

While she was downstairs, she popped into the library to grab another book off her TBR. She looked at each of the books, trying to decide which book she wanted to read the most. Finally she picked one that looked like a nice, simple read. Tonight, she wanted something easy and fun. Once she made it back up the stairs, she got into bed and started to read, hoping Jeffery would be home soon.

"Where is it?!"

Margot turned her head, her eyes heavy from sleep. She yawned, trying to connect the dots. Had someone just yelled? As her eyes opened, she closed them back. The room was bright.

"Where is it?!" the voice repeated.

"Where is what?" she sleepily asked. She'd fallen asleep mid-book. She heard her book plop on the floor as she turned to her side. "Jeffery, it's the middle of the night. Come to bed."

She attempted to get comfortable, too tired to think about what Jeffery was going on about. Right as she tucked her hand under her pillow, she was jerked up and off the bed by Jeffery's hand on the back of her neck. She nearly screamed out, as her hands reached back to try and remove Jeffery's fingers from her skin. He dragged her over to the dresser where the papers had been. With his free hand, he touched the spot.

"Where. Are. The. Papers. Margot?"

"I...I..." She tried to escape. Never had she seen him this angry before. Her heart raced.

"Where did you put them? Those were mine!" His voice rattled in her ear.

"I put them in your office!" she stammered. "I was trying to help!"

"Help," he scoffed. He threw her back against the bed. She scurried back, so that she was all the way on the other side, away from him. He stood there, eyes wild and chest heaving. "You need to stay out of my business."

She cowered behind the bed. She heard his footsteps, but realized they were going away from her instead of toward her. When she gathered the courage to glance over the bed, she saw he was no longer in their room. She got up and rushed down to Ari's room, glad to find her still fast asleep.

She pressed her hand against her chest, not knowing what to do. What did one do when their husband woke them up and grabbed them by the neck? Her first thought went to the number she'd hidden, the one Claire had given her that night at the fundraiser. She shook that thought away. He didn't mean what he'd done, right? She found herself trying to find an excuse for his behavior, just like she had when he bruised her wrist. However, she found she couldn't come up with one. Could there be a good enough excuse for what he'd just done?

She decided to go into Ari's bedroom and lie in the bed with her. There wasn't enough room, but she felt safer in here, and she wanted to also know that Ari was safe. In the morning, she would figure everything else out.

"Mommy, you're in my bed," Ari said with a bright smile as she awoke the next morning. Margot nodded, giving her daughter a weak smile in return. She'd hardly slept. Every time she got to sleep, all she could see was Jeffery's intense, angry face staring back at her.

"I am. I thought maybe we could go do something fun today. What do you think about that?"

"But I have school," Ari said. Her lips curled into a frown. Margot tucked some of Ari's stray hairs behind her ear. She was trying her best to keep it together, not sure how exactly her life had gotten to this moment. She needed time to sort all of this out. Her husband had been violent last night, so violent that she'd been frightened. She was finding it hard to justify his actions. She wished she could figure out what had made this change. Was it something to do with his work?

The door to Ari's room opened, making Margot shoot up. There in the doorway stood Jeffery, his eyes solemn. He took a step forward; Margot instinctively placed her arm in front of Ari. However, Ari, unaware of everything that had happened, ducked beneath her arm and ran to her father.

"Daddy!"

Jeffery lifted her up and onto his hip.

"Good morning. How did you sleep?"

"Good! Mommy slept in my bed with me!"

"Yes, I know. Wasn't that fun?"

Ari nodded.

Margot sat, frozen. Scenarios ran through her mind of what she needed to do, to grab Ari and run down the stairs. But she found herself unable to do it. She didn't want to scar her daughter. The less she knew of the situation, the better. And Jeffery wouldn't harm Ari, would he? He loved her.

"I thought we could go out to breakfast," Jeffery said. "What about the pancake place down the road? It wouldn't hurt if Ari was a little late to school, would it?"

Margot remained in her spot on the bed, unable to speak.

"Daddy, you don't like that place. You said it's unhealthy."

"Ah, but every once in a while it's all right."

He was trying to placate her, take her somewhere he knew she'd like to make her forget about his behavior the night before.

"I think Ari should just go to school," Margot said, her voice raw. She got up and walked over to Jeffery, taking Ari out of his hands. She kept her head ducked down, knowing if she looked him straight in the eye she might give in.

His hand snaked around her upper arm. Her back straightened.

"I think we should go to breakfast. Ari is only seven. I doubt she'll miss much from school."

Margot couldn't make out if his words were a warning or not.

"Please, Mommy! I want pancakes!"

"They have chocolate chip pancakes," Jeffery told her.

"Oh Mommy, please!"

And here she was trapped.

"Okay," she whispered. "We can go to breakfast."

Jeffery unlatched his fingers from her arm. He planted a kiss on the top of her head before bringing his lips to her ear and whispering, "I'm sorry."

"Come on, Ari, let's get you dressed."

Inside, she was panicking again. After they dropped her off at school, the two of them would be alone in the car. What did she do then? As she turned to look at Jeffery, she saw he still had those same pitiful eyes staring at her, begging her for her forgiveness.

She pointed outside Ari's room before following him out there and closing Ari's door.

"I do not forgive you," she said, surprised at herself for speaking up. Even though she tried to stay strong, her words shook and her voice was weak. "And I don't know what this is that you're pulling, but it is *not* okay."

"You're right," he said. He reached out to touch her, but Margot stepped back. "I was just stressed. Work last night, it—"

"I don't care about any of that," she said, unable to meet his eyes. She brought her arms around her chest like a hug.

"I know. I...I don't know what came over me. I didn't mean—"

"Mommy! Can you help me with my shirt?"

Margot sighed. "Sure! I'll be right there," she called back.

Breakfast had been awkward, but manageable. Ari kept her from having to make a lot of contact with Jeffery. However, now the two of them sat alone in the car in the school parking lot. Margot tried to remain steadfast, but she could feel her resolve fading. The anger from before was dissipating. At breakfast, she was reminded how good Jeffery was with Ari, and how much she loved and adored him. He always made his time with Ari all about her, asking her about her life, and making sure she got all the attention she deserved. She'd been tired, half asleep when it all happened. Had the night before been *that* bad, or had she been imagining it?

Her hand rubbed over the spot on her wrist where the bruise had been. She'd forgiven him then. Could she forgive him now? Should she?

"I'll understand if you can't forgive me, Margot," Jeffery said. Margot faced him. He had tears in his eyes. "I'm not sure I'll ever forgive myself."

"I don't know," was all Margot could get out. A lump formed in her throat. She loved her husband. She loved her life. Was she ready to throw it away over a few rare moments?

"You don't have to know right now. I'll give you some space. Let me take you home. I'll...I'll sleep in the guest room for the next couple of nights."

She didn't respond.

By the time they reached their house, she was in a daze. Never before in her life had she felt so confused. She walked inside, watching from the window as Jeffery drove off to work. Then she sat. She just sat. Her fingers went to the back of her neck, rubbing against the sore skin where some of her hair had been pulled. There wasn't a bruise, but it ached.

She immediately thought of Claire. A girls lunch might be just what she needed.

"Well, this was a lovely surprise," Claire said, kissing Margot's cheek. She sat back down at the table and Margot took the seat across from her. She'd been glad when Claire said she would be thrilled to meet for lunch.

"I just thought lunch could be fun."

"Oh, absolutely." Claire lifted the menu. Margot didn't need it. She'd already eaten here many times and knew what she liked. But she picked the menu up anyway. It was easier to stare at a menu than to think about all that had transpired in the past twenty-four hours.

"So, you work a lot with domestic violence victims, right?"

"No," Claire said, placing the menu down. "I just fundraise. Why?"

"Oh, no reason," Margot replied. She looked back at the menu. However, Claire's hand came over the menu, forcing Margot to look up at her.

"Why?" Claire asked again. "Has something happened?"

"Happened?" Her voice squeaked.

"I knew it," Claire said. "All right, what did he do?"

"He? Do? What are you talking about?"

Claire's eyes rolled. "I'm not playing games with you, Margot. What did Jeffery do?" Her arms crossed on top of the table and she leaned forward. Her perfect, dark curls framed her face.

"He's just been acting differently is all. But it's not anything bad, really. He's a good man." Margot closed the menu, sitting it back in front of her. As she met Claire's gaze again, prickles ran up her spine. Claire's deep brown eyes bore into her, saying everything that Margot knew. Margot couldn't tell Claire what had happened. She couldn't share that. If she did, there would be no turning back. But there was a large part of her that wanted to tell her. Her chest tightened. She pushed that want away.

"Right," Claire said a second later, her lips tightening. "They're all so good," she bit.

"He really is," Margot replied, heat rising up her chest. "You just don't understand."

"You're right. I don't." Claire stood, pushing her chair into the table.

"What...what are you doing? We just got here."

"Look, I get it, okay? It takes time for women to leave their abusers—"

"Jeffery is *not* an abuser."

Claire cut her eyes at her before adding, "Sure he's not. Today, I just...I can't do this."

Nothing else was said. Margot watched helplessly as Claire walked away from her and the table, confused.

Chapter 19

Claire

Her finger lingered over Max's name in her phone as she sat a block away from his PI office. All she had to do was call him or go up to his office and go inside. There was no reason to make such a big deal out of this. But she dropped her phone in the cup holder.

"Shit." She turned on her engine, hot tears stinging her eyes. She'd lost two best friends—Taylor, and now Max. He was who she would go to about this, but she couldn't anymore. She'd ruined that. There were no other friends she could vent to about this situation with Margot. Really, she was angry with herself. She knew it was a bad idea to get involved. She'd seen the signs, but here she was.

Deep down, she knew she should have stayed and tried to help. That's who she was, but it had been too similar to what she'd experienced before.

When she reached her parents' house, she parked her car next to her brother's. Getting out of the car, she spotted Zachary on the front porch petting her parents' dog. James sat on the bench beside him. His shirt was stained, and he had an unlit cigarette dangling from his lips. Claire wanted to snatch it away. She hated him being like this around Zachary.

"Aunt Claire!" Zachary waved at her but stayed down by the dog, scratching its ears. "When can we get a dog?"

"Um..." Claire tapped her fingers against her thigh, trying to come up with a new excuse for why they couldn't have a dog right now. "I'm not sure. Probably in a few years. Why don't you go tell your grandparents goodbye and grab your backpack?" Her mom had picked him up from school.

"Okay!" He hopped up and ran inside the house, the dog following after him.

"You look ridiculous," Claire snapped once Zachary was out of earshot. She pointed to the cigarette in James's mouth. "I don't like you doing that around Zachary."

"I wasn't smoking. It's not lit."

"I still don't like it. And you don't clean your clothes anymore?"

James glanced down at his top. "It's just mustard from my lunch."

"Sure."

Zachary ran back out with his bag over his shoulder. He went over to James, giving him a big hug. Then Zachary gently took the cigarette out of his mouth.

"You know, that's really bad for you, right?"

James took the cigarette and threw it over the side of the porch.

"You're right."

"So no more," Zachary said, pointing his finger at him.

"No more," James agreed, giving him a wink.

"All right, Zachary, we have to go." She took Zachary's hand, only giving her brother a small wave.

As they reached the bottom of the stairs, Zachary glanced back up at where James sat and then to Claire.

"I wish you two didn't fight."

"Fight?" Claire asked. "We don't fight. We're siblings, Zachary. They just act like that sometimes."

She opened the back door for Zachary, who got in right away. He sighed. His little face pinched up with what looked like worry. But before Claire could ask him about it, he grabbed the door and closed it.

When Claire sat in her seat, she stared at him through her rearview mirror. He sat back in his seat with his arms crossed over his chest.

"I don't want you to worry, Zachary," Claire said. "James and I get along fine. You're supposed to only worry about kid things, all right?"

"I just worry about you," Zachary said, his voice innocent and sweet. "I want you to be happy. You're not happy, Aunt Claire."

The air rushed out of her lungs. She turned to him, taking his hand into hers.

"I am happy, Zachary. I have you. And it's not your job to make me happy. My job is to make sure you're happy and well taken care of. Your job is to be a kid, got it?" A tear slipped down her cheek. Sometimes she felt like she was failing him. She swiped the tear away, hoping he hadn't seen it, and gave him a wobbly smile. "I love you so much."

"I know. I love you too. Can we visit Mommy?"

"Sure, of course we can."

They visited Taylor's grave every so often. Zachary only asked to visit once in a while, so Claire always made sure to do it when he asked. They ran by the store to grab some fresh flowers and then went to the cemetery.

It always caused chills when Claire stepped in front of her grave. Memories flooded her of Taylor, and there were too many what-could-have-beens that would go through her mind. At Taylor's grave sat another fresh batch of flowers. Claire bent down, inspecting them. There was a card.

I miss you. – James

Her heart clenched. She knew how much her brother loved Taylor, how their short, tragic love affair had changed his life. That little sound of guilt whispered in her ear that she'd been too tough on her brother all these years. She shook it away.

"Put your flowers next to those," Claire instructed Zachary. He did.

"Do you like them?" he asked the grave. Claire stepped back, allowing Zachary this time with his mother. He pulled one lone flower out of the batch and placed it on his baby sister's grave next to Taylor's.

No matter how many times Claire had been here, it always overwhelmed her. She would never get used to the fact that her best friend was dead, and that she'd been murdered.

Her fingers twisted in front of her before she closed her eyes. Sometimes, she could feel Taylor here with them. But today was not one of those days. Disheartened, Claire reopened them. Zachary returned to her side.

"I think we should get ice cream," he told her. "Mint chocolate chip, just like you and she used to eat together. It was her favorite, right?"

Claire smiled down at him. "You're correct. And I think that sounds like a good idea." She checked the time on her watch. It was time for dinner. "Ice cream for dinner it is."

"Yay!"

They went to the ice cream shop just down the road. Zachary stepped forward and then took Claire's hand before they crossed the street. When they got inside, Claire blanched. Max sat over in the corner with someone she'd never seen before. A woman.

"Claire, isn't that Ma—"

"Shh," Claire interrupted Zachary. "Let's quickly get ice cream. We'll eat in the car." But as they stood in the short line, she couldn't help but look over at Max and the woman. Her back was to Claire, so she couldn't get that good of a look at her. She just knew she wasn't Liliana, because her hair was nearly black, long, and silky. Max was grinning. He hadn't noticed Claire and Zachary yet, and Claire hoped it stayed like that. Had she not promised Zachary ice cream, she would have left already.

Finally, they made it to the front of the line. Claire ordered their ice cream, tapping her fingers against the counter as it was made. When Zachary's scoop was handed to her, she turned to give it to him, but he wasn't there. Her eyes scanned the room. Her heart sunk. There Zachary stood next to Max, chatting with him. Max's eyes met hers. She wished she could just fade away right then and there. Once her ice cream was given to her, she walked over to where Zachary was and handed him his. She looked to Max and then the woman with him. She didn't recognize her.

"What a surprise to see you here," she said a bit too happily.

"Yes, it is," Max replied. Claire eyed him, trying to see what he meant with his words, but he was doing too good of a job keeping his face neutral.

Zachary scooted himself next to the woman, making her slide closer to the window. Claire's eyes widened.

"Zachary, come on, it's time to go." Claire reached for his hand.

"But I haven't seen Max in ages!" Zachary declared. Claire stared at him, her jaw slack. He and Max rarely ever spent time together. This was some plan of his. She'd let him watch *The Parent Trap* a few times too many.

"Oh, it's all right, you two can eat with us. Come on, sit." Max patted the spot next to him.

Claire's eyes darted between Max and Zachary. Zachary's lips curled up slightly as he rose his shoulders and gave Claire a small wink. She took her time sitting next to Max, trying to see what the woman across from Max thought without making it obvious. When that didn't work, she decided to look right at her and ask outright. Clearly, Max wasn't going to say it first.

"So..." Claire awkwardly began. "I don't think we've met."

"I'm Stacy."

"She's my cousin," Max filled in.

"Oh," Claire replied. She bit the inside of her lip to keep herself from grinning too much. "Are you in town visiting?"

"Yes," Stacy answered. "I'm staying at my aunt and uncle's house. Max offered to show me around the area."

"That's nice," Claire said. She dug her spoon into the cup, spinning her spoon around in the ice cream. She glanced at Max from the corner of her eye, but her stomach fell when she saw him peering into his own ice cream and not looking at her.

"So, um, who are you?" Stacy asked.

"Just a friend," Claire answered.

"She's Claire," Zachary spoke up. "My aunt Claire."

"Oh, *Claireeee*." Stacy dragged her name out in a sing-songy voice, her eyes shooting over to Max. "I finally get to meet the famous Claire."

"We're not—" Max started. His lips pursed tightly, and he shook his head.

"He talks about you all the time," Stacy told her.

"I do not," Max contradicted.

"Oh?" Claire asked, hating the hopefulness in her voice.

"Yes. It's so nice to finally put a face to the name."

"We're not like that," Max said under his breath at Stacy. Claire swallowed hard.

"He's right. Just friends." She blinked before standing. "Come on, Zachary. We should head back home. You have school tomorrow."

Zachary took her hand. They stood there momentarily. Max refused to look up at her; Claire inhaled sharply.

"Nice to meet you, Stacy. Hope you have a nice visit."

Zachary fell asleep that evening right as his head hit the pillow. Claire poured herself a glass of wine before settling on her couch to watch TV.

Deciding not to think about Max, she started thinking about Margot. All she kept seeing was the shocked look on Margot's face when she stood and left lunch without any explanation. It hadn't been fair of her, taking out her own trauma on Margot.

Claire grabbed her phone. Should she call her?

She pressed Margot's name and held the phone to her ear. It was late. She probably wouldn't even answer.

"Hello?" Margot answered.

"Oh, hi," Claire said. She brought her feet up under her and placed her wine next to her on the side table. Now that she was on the phone with Margot, she wasn't sure what to say. Apologizing had never been her strong point. "I just wanted to say—"

"It's okay," Margot said into the phone. "You don't need to apologize."

"But I do," Claire replied. "I took my personal issues and put them into your situation."

"But maybe you were right." Margot's voice was low, and Claire had to strain to hear her.

"What?"

"He's sleeping in the guest room. He offered. But..." There was a sigh on the other end of the line. Claire thought she heard a hiccup. "I love him. But..." Claire remained quiet. She couldn't intervene, no matter how much she wanted to. Margot had to come to her own conclusions to make that step. "He was never like this before."

"Like what?"

"Like this," was all Margot gave Claire. "If I left him, how would I even start? And can I even? I mean, he's a great guy. Wouldn't that make me crazy to leave him?"

Claire sat up. This was her moment. She couldn't screw it up and say the wrong things. Even though she wanted to stay out of it, she couldn't do that anymore. Not with her asking these questions. "No. It would not make you crazy."

"But everyone loves him. Everyone tells me how perfect of a family we are."

"Screw everybody else. They don't know what goes on inside your household."

"True," Margot murmured.

"Why don't you come over tomorrow and we can discuss this in person? I can give you some resources."

The line went silent, until finally Margot whispered, "Okay."

Chapter 20

Margot

Margot sat down on the plush couch before taking in Claire's living room. There were several nice paintings on the wall mixed in with framed drawings likely by Zachary behind the couch. The other walls were covered in framed photographs. In many of the frames were pictures of Claire, Zachary, Claire's family, and Taylor. The room was clean and organized, but there were some toys spread out across the floor and a large Hot Wheels set taking up about a third of the room. Jeffery would never be okay with that. Toys were only allowed in the playroom and in Ari's bedroom. Even then, they were supposed to be cleaned up the moment she was done playing with each item. Thankfully, Ari liked to keep her stuff organized, so that made it easier on her and the housekeeper.

As she shifted in her spot, she felt something hard against her hip. She moved over and found a small, metal car. She picked it up and set it on the coffee table in front of her.

"Oh, sorry about that," Claire said, entering the living room with two cups of coffee in her hands. As usual, she was effortlessly beautiful. She wore short black shorts and an oversized sweatshirt. Her tight curls were pinned back out of her face.

"It's no problem," Margot said.

"I find those all over the place. Those and his action figures," Claire chuckled.

"Thanks for taking this morning off to talk with me. You didn't have to do that," Margot said, shifting the conversation.

Claire waved her words away, taking the seat next to her.

"Okay, so you're ready to talk about possibly leaving Jeffery?" Claire asked.

"I...I think so," Margot replied. "I mean, yes. He..." She glanced down at her pants, finding a piece of fuzz that she attempted to brush away.

"Are you safe?" Claire asked. Margot popped her head back up. She nodded.

"Oh yes, of course," Margot told her. "I'm not worried about him doing anything to me, not anything *that* bad."

"But he has gotten physical with you," Claire prodded. Margot scooted uncomfortably in her seat.

"Only once. Or, well, twice. And the first was an accident. And the second..."

"Showed you the first wasn't an accident," Claire said, matter-of-factly.

"Yes," Margot said.

Claire sat up.

"Then you aren't safe, Margot. Not at all. He's gotten physical with you, and he will again." Claire pressed her fingers firmly against the coffee cup in her hand. Margot could see the skin around her nails tightening from the force she had on the cup. "The most dangerous time for someone is when they are leaving their abusive partner."

Margot shook her head. "Well, I'm not leaving him yet. I'm just talking about if I did. And Jeffery isn't like that. He's not abusive. One time isn't—"

"Two times," Claire corrected. "And abuse isn't just physical. In just the short time I've known you, I see how controlling he is of you and your life. He controls every aspect."

Margot sat back against the cushions. She didn't have a retort to that.

"You'll need to be careful," Claire said a moment later. "Controlling people are some of the most dangerous. The more control they lose, the more dangerous they become." She sighed, tapping her fingers against her cup. "You should probably go to a lawyer first, and also someone who deals best with this just to have a plan in place for when you are ready to make that decision to leave him."

Claire got up. She placed her cup on the coffee table before disappearing through a doorway closer to her front door. Margot could hear papers being shuffled around and drawers being opened and closed. Claire came back out a few minutes later with two business cards in her hand. She sat back down across from Margot and handed her the first one.

"That's my sister Mila's card. She's a lawyer, a great one at that. Call her, meet up with her. She specializes in messy divorces."

"I don't think it would be messy. And should I see a lawyer? I haven't even made that decision yet. I'm just..."

"Yes, see a lawyer. Learn your rights. The more knowledge you have, the easier it will be when the time comes that you choose to leave."

Margot nodded. This was all overwhelming. She wasn't sure she had what it would take to leave him. Claire seemed sure of it though.

"And this is Stevie Jones," Claire interrupted her thoughts. "She works with women leaving abusive marriages. She can give you advice on the best steps to take moving forward. Of course, the best abusive husband is a dead one."

Margot did a double take. Claire lifted her coffee cup to her lips, raising her brow. Then she slowly lowered it to her lap.

"It works best if there's no body. So, like, make sure he either disappears or is cremated. Of course, I'd help, but I'm at my limit for murders," Claire said. Margot stared at her for a moment before cracking a smile. Claire and her dark humor.

"Funny," Margot replied. "I definitely don't want him dead. He's a great father. He loves Ari. So I'm not worried about that."

"He may be the best dad to her now, but you have to protect her too. You don't know what he's capable of. Hopefully, he'll never hurt her, but you can't be so sure."

Margot shook at the weight of those words. Her eyes shut and the memory of Jeffery grabbing her by the neck flooded her. What if he did do something like that to Ari? Or worse?

"I guess you're right."

"How are you financially?" Claire asked in a careful manner.

"Fine."

"Do you have money you can access without him knowing about it?"

"Yes," Margot said. "About fifty thousand."

"Oh," Claire replied, seemingly impressed. "Yes, that will do. You're already in a better place than most women trying to escape. That will work nicely."

"Well, my mom set up an account for me to put money in. She always thought it was important to have a secret account in case it was needed. I always felt it was kind of silly, but now..." Margot tucked a stray hair behind her ear. "Jeffery has never watched our finances closely, nor has he cared about how much money I spend. He doesn't check. That check I was going to donate to the foundation, I added it to my secret account like you suggested."

"Well, that's good at least. But still, you should be careful. Doesn't mean he won't now. You can't let him know your plans. Even now when you're just exploring ideas, you have to keep it a secret. If he gets wind of any of this, it could get more dangerous for you."

"I won't," Margot said. Her hands squeezed together in her lap. "It all seems surreal, me even thinking about leaving Jeffery."

Claire reached across, taking Margot's hands in her own and then meeting her eyes.

"It's scary. But you wouldn't be doing this if it wasn't what's best for you and your daughter. I won't lie to you, it isn't going to be easy. Once he finds out, he'll probably try to convince you to stay, or he could get more violent. Likely both. You may even change your mind."

Margot chewed on the inside of her lip. She removed her hands from Claire's and stood, turning her back to her and walking over to the window that looked out onto the street. A mother walked by on the sidewalk, pushing a stroller.

She wasn't sure if she could do this, but here with Claire, she did feel surer of what she could accomplish. It was just such a huge step. The flashes of Jeffery in his anger kept flooding her.

"At the very least, I need a plan," she said to herself. But Claire heard her as well.

"You do."

Stepping back into her home, Margot felt like an intruder. She slipped off her shoes, placing them in the spot where all their shoes were kept. Then she walked down the hallway. A door slammed. She jumped.

"Margot?" Jeffery's voice rang from the back of the house.

"Y-yes?" She remained in her spot. His footsteps came toward her and he walked up with a big smile on his face. "Shouldn't you be at work?"

"I came home to surprise you, but you weren't here." He bent over, giving her a kiss. "I thought I could take you to lunch."

"Oh." Margot's lips quirked into an awkward smile. "I just...this is a surprise."

"I know. You're still angry with me. If you don't want—"

"I don't know," she said. She needed time to process everything she and Claire had talked about. Yet, as she looked at her husband's face, she could feel more of her resolve fading. Had it really been that bad? Bad enough to even think about leaving him? She had been so sure about it just an hour ago, but here with him she didn't know.

She glanced down at her outfit. Jeans and a T-shirt. She'd been wearing this combo more whenever Jeffery wasn't around her. Her eyes met his, ready for him to say something about needing to change.

"Don't change. You look nice." His hand landed on the small of her back before drawing her closer to him. "You look beautiful. I love your hair like this."

She brought her hand up to her hair, remembering she'd braided it into a French braid that morning.

"But you've always said—"

"Come on. We'll be late for our reservation."

Margot realized she'd never actually agreed to going with him to lunch. Even so, he led her out of the house. He kept his hand on her lower back the entire walk to his car. There he opened her door, helped her into her seat, and then closed the door behind her.

Jeffery got into the car. He grabbed her hand, giving it a loving squeeze.

"I'd like to start over," he said. "You and me against the world. Remember that?" He brought her hand up to his lips, kissing the skin. "Work has had me all over the place and stressed, and it made me forget what is most important: you and Ari. Why don't we go to therapy? I'll do anything not to lose you. I love you more than anything in this world, Margot. Anything."

Margot sat there, dumbfounded. Did he know about her secret meeting that morning with Claire? Was this sincere? He was saying all the right things. She nodded.

"Therapy could be good," she said.

"I agree," he replied. "I'll stay in the guest room for a little bit longer."

"No," Margot said, surprising herself. "I miss you in bed with me." A light flickered in his eye.

"I miss it too."

When Margot woke up, Jeffery was still sleeping. She grinned, inching herself closer to him and placing her head over his bare chest. His hand came up to her back. He kissed the top of her head.

"Good morning." His voice was gruff.

"Morning."

"Last night was great."

"It was," she agreed. Everything felt as though it had fallen back into place. Once again, she felt safe in Jeffery's embrace. However, that didn't stop the little voice in the back of her head telling her to run. It sounded a lot like Claire. She shook it away.

"What if we went away for the weekend?" Jeffery suggested. Margot maneuvered her head so she could look at Jeffery.

"The weekend? Where would we go?"

"I don't know. A nice hotel. We could even do a staycation. Just stay somewhere nearby but with a nice indoor pool."

"Ari would like that," Margot said. Jeffery placed his hand on her cheek.

"I thought just you and I would go. Ari will be fine here with the nanny. It'll be good practice for when we go on our anniversary trip. It's only a couple months away."

"But..." Jeffery shushed her by bringing her in for a kiss. As they pulled apart, she gave him a small smile. "I guess it could be nice. I do need to get used to being away from Ari, and one night wouldn't be too bad." He smiled back before climbing out of bed and walking into the bathroom, turning on the water for the shower.

Margot grabbed her phone next to the bed. There was a text from Claire. She held her breath as she opened it.

How is it going today? I made you an appointment with Stevie at noon tomorrow. Her address is on the business card.

Margot read over the message several times. What did she say? How could she tell Claire that she and Jeffery had patched things up? He seemed to want to make things right. Another message popped up.

Mila can't meet with you until next week, but she said she'll let me know what date and time by the end of the day.

Okay, thanks. Margot sat her phone back down. She no longer wanted to go and speak with either of them, but Claire had gone out of her way to make the appointments.

Since the appointment was already set, Margot decided to go to the first one. It wouldn't hurt anything to just go and see what the woman had to say.

Stevie's office was smaller than Margot expected. The walls were bare and painted an ugly yellowish color. Stevie remained at her seat as Margot came in, typing something on her computer. When Margot sat in the torn pleather chair, Stevie glanced up.

"So, you're thinking of leaving your husband."

"Well, no, I mean—" She sighed. "I'm looking into resources, just in case."

Stevie pulled down her dark-rimmed glasses before sliding them completely off her face and onto the computer desk.

"Just in case what?" Stevie asked, raising her eyebrows.

"In case he gets violent...again." Just saying it made her wince. Was this really her life?

"That's smart, because he likely will. Do you have a safe place to go?"

"No."

"What about your parents?"

"My mom lives states away. She's thinking about moving closer, but that won't be for a while." Margot tapped her foot against the floor. "This is silly, isn't it? I...I shouldn't be here, taking up your time."

She went to stand, but Stevie put her hand out and then motioned for her to stay in her seat.

"You're here because you know deep down you need to leave him. You're not ready yet, and that's okay. But having a plan for when you are ready is smart."

"What if I'm never ready?" Margot asked.

"You will be," Stevie said. She shuffled through some papers on her desk. "I suggest finding an apartment. Something in your name that he doesn't know about. That gives you and your daughter a safe place to move when you're ready."

"An apartment?"

"Yes. Have it set up with things you need. So when he gets dangerous again, you and your daughter can move out. Don't let him know where the place is or that you even have it. Claire said you have some funds, so this is possible for you to do, right?"

"Yes."

"Good. We have places available, but we like to keep them for people who cannot afford them."

"It just seems kind of unnecessary."

"Having a safe place to go is never unnecessary. Your husband got violent with you, correct?"

"Well, yes, but—"

"Then the odds of that happening again are high. Here." Stevie handed her a pamphlet. "Read through this. Make a plan. I'm happy to assist in that plan, but you don't seem ready for it. I'm here for when you are."

Margot took the pamphlet, folding it and then stuffing it into the bottom of her bag. She'd have to find a place to hide it when she got home.

Chapter 21

Claire

This was brutal. Claire checked the time on her watch. It had only been ten minutes. She glanced back up at the stage where the children continued singing some song about a pumpkin and a bear. She checked the program. There were still five more songs until Zachary's class's turn.

"It's so cute," her mother gushed next to her. Claire rubbed her temple. Cute was not how she would describe it. Of all the parts of parenting she'd taken on when she got custody, this was probably her least favorite.

Her entire family had shown up for Zachary's fall performance. They took up two full rows. James sat as far away from Claire as possible, and she was sure it was on purpose. Not that she would blame him. Her nine-month-old niece pulled at her necklace from her mother's lap. Claire took her necklace off and let her hold it.

"You can't just give a nine-month-old a necklace with small pieces on it," Mila whispered harshly beneath her breath, pulling the necklace out from between Nora's little fingers.

"Sorry," Claire muttered.

"Also, your friend, she canceled."

"What?"

"Shh," their father hushed them.

"Yeah, she called and said she didn't need me anymore," Mila whispered as she handed her daughter an age-appropriate toy.

Claire huffed, crossing her arms over her chest. Not that she was actually surprised. She knew how this worked. It was never as easy as just leaving him. And Margot wasn't even ready yet. She probably pushed her too much. She'd have to be patient, something she wasn't good at.

This was too close to what she'd gone through with Taylor, and she found that she wished she could just separate herself from it all.

Finally, about twenty minutes later, Zachary's class was up on stage. He waved at all of them, and all their phones came out to record and take pictures. His class sang some song about the leaves changing colors. Claire couldn't keep her eyes off Zachary. He was the most adorable one up there.

When the next song came on from a different class, Claire noticed that James's seat down the aisle was empty. They were all supposed to go out to dinner together, and she assumed he didn't want to be there with her. Fair enough.

They only had to sit through a few more songs before the program ended. Zachary ran right up to them all after it was over.

"Thank you for coming!" Zachary said. He was the sweetest child. Claire bit back the tears. These were the most difficult moments. Moments where Taylor should be here, experiencing this with her son. He was so much like her.

Zachary was up unusually late for a school night, playing with his Hot Wheels and eating his second bowl of ice cream while Claire watched one of her favorite sitcoms. She didn't have the energy to get him ready for bed. Maybe they'd both play hooky tomorrow. Or at the very least, she could take Zachary in late. He hardly ever missed school.

Zachary finished his bowl of ice cream, setting it on the coffee table. Then he curled up on the couch next to her. Instinctively, Claire brought her arm around him.

"Do you think she can see me?" Zachary asked with a yawn.

"Who?"

"Mommy."

"Oh yes, definitely," Claire told him.

"I hope she liked my performance."

"I know she did."

His eyes fluttered closed. Claire kept watching her show until she also dozed off on the couch.

The next morning when she awoke, she regretted it. Her neck ached. She rubbed it, sitting up. Zachary wasn't next to her.

"Zachary?"

"In here! Making breakfast!" Claire scrambled to her feet and rushed into the kitchen, relieved when she saw he'd only pulled out some cereal and was eating it plain. She checked the time. It was already nine.

"We're late," Zachary said.

"Yes, I know." Claire took the seat next to him. "What if we just stayed home today?"

"But I have school, and you have work. You have to go to work," Zachary said, raising his little brow. Claire groaned. He was right.

"You're too smart," she said, ruffling his hair. "Well, I don't have to be in until eleven today. I'll bring you a little before that."

She pulled her phone from her jacket pocket to see she had missed a call from Max. Her heart skipped a beat. He had called just a little before she'd woken up. She stood, walking out of the kitchen before calling him back.

"Claire?" he answered before a full ring could even go through.

"Hi," she said, breathless. "You called?"

She heard fumbling on the other end before Max's voice came back on. "Oh, I guess I did. I'm sorry. That was an accident."

Her heart dropped.

"Of course."

"Is everything okay?" Max asked.

"Sure it is. With you?"

"Yes."

"Good. Glad to hear it." Claire hit her forehead with her palm. She sounded so stupid. "Well, I'll let you go. Goodbye, Max." She hung up the phone before he could say anything else.

She hated therapy. Not the purpose of it. Just for herself. After Taylor died, her parents had insisted on putting both her and Zachary into therapy. Zachary went once every other week. He handled it better than she did. It probably helped they'd started him early. It had been wonderful for helping him process what he'd been through. Not that it was always an easy road, but Claire did have to admit she was grateful her parents had suggested it.

Claire had managed to get hers dropped to once a month. She wanted to cancel her therapy completely, but her parents and therapist insisted she at least try monthly. So here she was, sitting in the office, not knowing what to say to the woman in front of her.

"This is stupid," Claire finally said, breaking the silence. Her therapist chuckled.

"You say that every time you're here."

Claire tilted her head. "Then why do you make me come?"

"You don't have to come. No one is forcing you," the therapist said. Claire rolled her eyes.

"Sure," she said beneath her breath.

"We can just sit here if you'd like. There's nothing new to talk about? What about Max? Are you two still friends with benefits?"

"No," Claire answered, upset with herself for telling her therapist about him. "We're not talking."

"I see." She scribbled something in her little notebook. "And Zachary, how is he?"

"Good."

"Good." More scribbles. "What about the new friend you made? Um..." She flipped through the pages of her notebook. "Margot?"

"Staying with her abusive husband," Claire said, offhandedly.

"Oh." The therapist placed her book on the table and leaned closer. "And how does that make you feel?"

"What does it matter? It's not my life." Claire shrugged. Sometimes in this office, she felt much younger than she actually was.

"Are you feeling helpless? Is it bringing up your past trauma with what happened to Taylor?"

"I run a charity to help women like Taylor. I deal with that trauma all the time."

"Yes, but this is different. This is the first woman you've gotten close to. With your charity, you help from afar. You don't interject yourself into their lives."

"So, are you saying I'm a bad person?" Claire asked, her lips tightening.

"Not at all. I think what you're doing is amazing. I'm saying this situation with this woman is different. It has to be affecting you."

"Well, it's not," Claire said. "I'm fine. And it's not like Taylor. She has the financial means to get away if she wants, and she has support. She has a mom that's alive."

"Okay," the therapist said, her voice unsure. "It's okay to feel things, Claire. It's okay to not be strong."

Claire's eyes rolled, again.

"Yes, you've told me this before. Thank you for that knowledge. So glad my parents pay hundreds of dollars an hour for you to tell me that. I'm all cured."

The therapist did not look amused, but she was used to Claire's antics by now. She had been going to her for four years at this point.

"You and Max just went no contact because you're cured then, I guess?" the therapist bit back.

"Yep. Oh look, time's up," Claire said and stood.

"You've only been here ten minutes."

"Yeah, well, we'll call it good," Claire told her with a wink. "See you next month."

Chapter 22

Margot

Margot stayed up all night long, unable to sleep, thinking about leaving Ari without her for the weekend. When Jeffery had first mentioned it, she was caught up in the moment. However, as it got closer, she couldn't do it.

"I don't want to go away this weekend," Margot said the moment Jeffery woke up.

"What?" Jeffery asked mid-yawn, rubbing his hand over his face.

"I don't want to leave Ari," she said. She bit the inside of her lip. His hand came up to cup her cheek.

"All right," he said.

"All right?" she asked in shock. He never changed plans if he made them. Maybe he really was changing.

"Yes, all right. We'll wait a little bit longer. Push it back a month? Give you more time to get used to the idea?"

"Yeah, okay. That sounds good. And then maybe take Ari with us to Paris?"

Jeffery laughed. "No, but there's plenty of time to worry about that. It isn't until January."

Margot nodded. She then drew herself away from Jeffery's touch and went into the bathroom to start the shower. Jeffery was right. It was just her anxiety getting in the way.

He walked up behind her, bringing his hands around her middle. Their eyes met in the mirror.

"I love you," he said.

"I love you too."

"Thank you for giving me a second chance, Margot. Words cannot express how much it means to me." He kissed the crook of her neck before leaving her alone in the bathroom.

As she waited for the water to warm, she opened the small drawer in the bathroom which held some of her more simple pieces of jewelry, trying to decide which one she wanted to wear today. She lifted the charm bracelet Jeffery had given her, taking the time to admire each piece he'd chosen that represented Ari. Her favorite was the cluster of emeralds, Ari's birthstone. As she touched it, her brows furrowed. Part of it was pulled apart from the rest. She brought it closer to get a better look. Then she tugged on it just a tiny bit, shocked when the charms slid off, and she saw that it was a cover for something. Attached to the bracelet was a small USB.

"What?" she murmured to herself. She heard Jeffery coming back toward the bathroom and quickly covered it back up, plopping the bracelet into the drawer.

"Oh, you should wear that," Jeffery said, spotting the bracelet sitting on top of the rest of the jewelry pieces.

"I thought you wanted it to stay here."

"No, that's not what I meant," Jeffery told her. He lifted it back up and brought it around her wrist. "Look at that—beautiful."

"It is beautiful," Margot agreed. She traced the piece with the hidden USB with her finger. Jeffery pulled her hand away, bringing it up to kiss her knuckles.

"Don't lose that," he said with a wink.

"I-I won't."

The moment she knew Jeffery was gone for work, Margot grabbed her laptop from its spot on her table and brought it over to the bed. She opened it and slid the USB drive into the port. For several seconds, she waited. Finally, the little pop-up showed. She clicked it. But when she did, the USB drive asked for a password.

Margot sat on her bed, pondering what the password might be. She typed Ari's name, her full name, and her date of birth. When none of Ari's information worked, she tried typing in things about herself and their anniversary date. They didn't work either. She tried a few more words, but everything came up wrong before something flashed across the screen: *Too many password attempts. Files closed for twenty-four hours.*

In a panic, Margot shut down her computer and pulled out the drive. She slid the cover back on and reattached the bracelet around her wrist. She didn't want Jeffery to know she'd found the USB and tried to open it. So for now, she would keep this close.

Her heart raced. She rubbed the charm between her fingers. This had to be important, but how did she find out what was on it?

Margot went to Claire's work the next day.

"I didn't expect to see you here," Claire said, not looking up from her computer where she typed. Margot stood in the doorway of Claire's office, trying to decide if she should walk farther in or stay put.

"I... You're angry." Margot remained in the doorway. Claire's sister must have told her she canceled her appointment. She probably should have been the one to do so.

"No, I'm not." Though Claire's incessant typing on her keyboard said differently.

"You are," Margot playfully prodded, hoping to lighten up the room. Claire removed her hands from her keyboard and turned her chair so she was facing Margot completely.

"I'm not," she said again. "I understand how this works. It's not that simple. God knows if it was, more people would leave. But, I do worry about you."

"Why?"

"I saw what it did to my friend. I know how it can end." Claire's voice grew grim, her eyes downcast. But just as quickly as she showed a sign of weakness she popped her head back up and shook it away. Margot tightened her hands together, remembering what all she'd read about Taylor and her death. Jeffery would never be like Dylan. He'd never go that far.

"I understand how it can end. I know that's hard what you went through. What Taylor went through. It's just..." Margot touched her wrist where the bracelet was. She unclipped it, hesitating for a moment before laying it down in front of Claire. Claire stared at the bracelet.

"Thanks, but this isn't really my type of jewelry."

"No. Jeffery gave me this. And it was an odd gift, because he usually gets me really expensive, designer type jewelry." Again the hesitation bloomed within her, but she pushed past it. "Then I found this." She pulled off the cover to reveal the USB drive. Claire's back straightened.

"Oh my God," she murmured.

"I know, right?"

Claire lifted the bracelet. "What's on it?"

"I don't know. It's password protected."

"Hm. That's suspicious."

"That's what I thought," Margot said.

"And he gave you this as a gift?" Claire plugged the drive into her computer. "Why would he give this to you?"

"I don't know."

"He didn't say anything about it?"

"No. He just bought it, and he didn't really want me to wear it."

"Well, of course he doesn't. Still odd that he'd give it to you if he wanted to keep it a secret."

"Maybe it was the best way he could think to hide it," Margot suggested, though she'd wondered the same since she'd found it.

Claire made a face as she typed quickly on her keyboard. Then she chuckled and shook her head.

"I don't know why I think I can figure this out. It's locked until later today, and I'm not some spy who can solve riddles." She chewed on her bottom lip before tapping her fingers against her desk. "But it is curious." She withdrew it from her computer, handing it back to Margot. "What do you want to do about it?"

Margot shrugged. "I want to know what's on it, but I'm also terrified to find out. Perhaps it would be best just to put it back in the drawer it was in."

"Perhaps," Claire agreed.

The bracelet felt heavy in her hand. She dropped it into her bag, no longer wanting to have it touching her fingertips.

"Do you know anyone who could help me figure out what's on it?" she asked.

Claire's lips twisted. She made a small sigh before nodding. "I do."

"Who?"

"Um, he's a PI. His name is Max. His hourly rate is expensive, but he's good at what he does." Claire scribbled his name, number, and address on a Post-It note, pulled it off, and then gave it to Margot. Margot glanced at it.

"How do you know him? Your foundation?"

"No," Claire answered. She darted her eyes back to her computer screen. "Be careful."

"I will."

Claire met her eyes again.

"Be careful."

"I don't want to go to bed," Ari complained as Margot brought the blankets up and over her.

"Yes, but you must," Margot said, kissing the top of her head.

"But I haven't seen Daddy," she whined.

"You never see Daddy at bedtime during the week."

"I know, but I miss him."

"I know you do." She turned off the bedside light. Ari's spinning nightlight lit up the room. Mermaids and starfish filled every wall. "I'll tell you what, I'll have him come in as soon as he gets home to give you a kiss on your cheek. How does that sound?"

Ari tapped her finger against her chin. "I guess that will do."

"Good. Now sleep. I'll see you in the morning."

"Keep the door open!" Ari called out when Margot started closing it.

"I always keep it open partway," she reminded her daughter, making sure to keep the door open by a few inches. Jeffery should be home soon enough. Ari had managed to stay up later than normal this particular night.

Although she'd put the bracelet back in its spot in her drawer, she checked it once more, making sure the USB was in its place.

She pulled up Amazon on her phone, searching for mini USB drives so that Jeffery wouldn't notice the other one was missing. After scrutinizing each one, she found a close copy that looked the most like the one in her bracelet, hoping it would work in its place. It could arrive by tomorrow.

"Mommy?" Ari's voice came from her bedroom doorway.

"Yes, darling?" she said, walking back to Ari's bedroom. Ari had her hands on each side of the doorframe, grinning up at her. "Why are you out of bed?"

"I'm not tired," Ari exclaimed.

"It's nearly nine at night. You're supposed to be in bed by eight."

"Can I sleep in your bed?"

"No," Margot said. She touched her daughter's hair, spinning one of her braids with her finger. "You need to sleep in your own bed. You're seven."

"But Mommy," Ari cried. She grabbed onto Margot's arm with all her might, tears now streaming down her face.

"Oh, just for tonight," Jeffery's voice rang up the stairs.

Ari's face lit up. She dropped her grip on Margot and ran toward her father. Margot's gaze followed her. Jeffery took Ari's hand and came up to Margot with her. "Please Mommy, just for one night."

Margot stared at Jeffery. Her mind went back to the USB drive in her drawer. What was on it? What was it hiding?

Jeffery gave her a pitiful face. "Please, Mommy?" he repeated. Margot stood there, shocked. It was always him who insisted she sleep in her own bedroom. She didn't know what to think. What was going on with him? She sighed.

"Fine," she conceded. "One night."

"Yes!" both Ari and Jeffery said in unison. Jeffery kissed her.

"It'll be fun," he said. "We'll watch a movie."

"Yay!" Ari jumped up and hugged Jeffery's middle. "A movie!"

"It's late."

"Oh, it'll be fine." Jeffery picked Ari up and the two of them headed to the bedroom. And now he was okay with her staying up late to watch a movie? Jeffery turned back to face her. "Are you coming?"

"Yes. I'll be right there."

Chapter 23

Max

Max arrived at the office earlier than he'd planned. When he walked in through the front door he saw his sister sitting in her old spot up at the welcoming desk. His brow rose.

"Well, this is odd," Max said.

"We kept getting phone calls and the receptionist has the morning off." Liliana shrugged.

She stood, swiping her long blonde locks off her shoulders. "You're early."

"Not by much." He checked the time on the clock on the wall, remembering he still hadn't changed the battery on the back. He should really do that soon.

"Thirty minutes," Liliana said.

"Has anyone been by yet?"

"Nope. I've just been working on this new cheating case like I have been for the past several days. I'm not as good at this as you are." Liliana rubbed her temple.

"Sure you are. You've solved some big cases. Want me to take a look?" He circled the desk to see the laptop his sister was working on.

"I've done everything you told me to do."

"Did you check for extra profiles online? Dating website?"

"Yes," Liliana said, annoyed. "Of course I did. I'm not stupid."

Max rolled his eyes. He turned the laptop toward himself and typed in a few key terms in his software.

"What about that?" He pointed to a link that had popped up with the person's name.

"What about it? It's just a job link."

"Yes, but I thought he worked in finance. That's a grocery store down the road."

"He could do finance at the grocery store," Liliana said.

"Well, have you checked it out?"

Liliana made a face. "No," she pouted.

"Do that next."

Max turned the laptop back toward his sister and walked into his office. Before he could sit, the front door dinged.

"Hello, I'm looking for Max Evans," he heard a voice ask.

"Back here," Max called. He glanced out the door to see a woman standing there. She appeared uncomfortable. It wasn't anything new to Max. More often than not new clients looked like this on their first visit, never guessing they'd ever hire a PI.

The woman walked up toward him, holding a bracelet between her fingers. She kept rubbing one piece with her thumb.

"Hello," she said, shifting awkwardly between both feet. "Um, Claire sent me."

"Oh?" Hopefulness bloomed in his chest. He missed her.

"Yes, she said you're the best PI there is and could help me."

His face fell.

"Come on in." He moved out of the doorway and motioned for her. He stepped around to the other side of his desk, waiting for her to sit before taking a seat of his own. "So," he began. "What do you need help with? A cheating spouse?"

"Oh, no," she said. "Not a cheating spouse. This."

She placed the bracelet on his desk. He leaned forward, perplexed.

"I'm not sure what you want me to do with this, Mrs...."

"Lewis, Margot Lewis. You can call me Margot or whatever you want," she said, her words jumbled together as she said it quickly.

"Mrs. Lewis, what do you want me to do with a bracelet?"

She grabbed it back, pulling one end of one of the charms, showing him a tiny USB. Both of his brows rose. Okay, now this was interesting.

"My husband gave me this bracelet, and I found the drive just the other day. Weird, right?"

"It's definitely unusual." He took it from her hand, holding it up to examine it. "May I?" He pointed to the computer.

"Go ahead. It is password protected though, so you won't be able to see anything."

Max plugged it into the computer, waiting for it to ask for a password. He typed in a few common phrases that some people used. Unsurprisingly, none of them worked. He assumed someone smart enough to hide information in a bracelet would know how to choose a decent password.

"I can get this figured out," he told her. "Is that what you want?"

Margot nodded. "I want to know what he's hiding on there. I need to know if I should leave."

"Him?" Max asked for clarification.

"Yes."

"I have someone who can do this for me. It shouldn't take him long. Are you sure this is what you want? I'm not cheap."

"Yes, I know. Claire told me." Margot fiddled with the strap of her purse, but her eyes stared confidently at him. Hearing Claire's name caught him off guard even though she'd told him that's how she knew to come to him. He'd accidently called her the other day, and when she called back he wished he'd said something else. He missed her, but he didn't know what happened now. She'd slept with someone else. And while he'd meant what he said about her not owing him anything, it did make him question what they'd had all these years. Had they meant nothing?

"Okay. Well, I can do this. I should be able to get the password by tomorrow. I'll have the files copied over to a disk, and then give you back the original one to put back in its place."

"Will you look at the files?"

"If that's what you want."

"I do. I think it's safer that way, if you look through them. But you really think you can have it back to me by tomorrow?"

"Yes," Max said confidently.

"Good. I bought a replacement to put in the bracelet, but I am worried about what would happen if Jeffery realizes it's the wrong one."

Max's stomach clenched. "You think you could be in danger?"

"Oh, no," Margot said, though her voice shook slightly with her words. She gave him a small smile.

"You know, Claire has resources of people you can go to if you don't feel safe."

"I know. I'm fine. It's probably something silly on that anyway, like a will or something." She shook her head like she was trying to convince herself of that.

"Well, we'll see," he said. "As I said, give me a day. I'll get this back to you tomorrow." He handed her a card with his cell phone number on it.

"Perfect."

Margot turned to walk away, but she paused in the doorway and looked back at him. "How do you know Claire?"

Max looked at the woman before him. It was a complicated question. He just shook his head. "I helped her with a case once."

Chapter 24

Claire

"Oh! Aunt Claire!" Zachary said, pulling her arm and tugging her over toward a large box full of kittens outside the grocery store. Claire peeked into the box. Five small calico kittens meowed at her.

"Yes, I see." She looked at the cats before looking at Zachary's hopeful expression. A sigh passed through her lips. She was going to have to break his heart. There was no way she could handle a kitten on top of a child.

"They're free," Zachary pointed out. The woman sitting behind the box nodded.

"They are. My cat, Whisky, had them. I need to find them homes," the woman told them.

"Well, good luck," Claire said. She began to walk away, but Zachary held her hand a little tighter, refusing to leave his spot. "Zachary," she said, bending down to his level. "We can't get a cat."

He glanced down as his shoulders sunk.

"I really am sorry," Claire murmured. It was rare she told Zachary no. His little downtrodden face made her heart hurt, but this was something she couldn't give in on. No pets had been her rule from day one. She knew what she could and couldn't handle.

"It's okay," Zachary said, finally meeting her eyes. "But what about James? He's lonely."

Claire furrowed her brows. "James? What do you mean?"

"Well, he loves cats, doesn't he?"

Claire chuckled. "Yes, he does, but we can't just gift someone a kitten, Zachary."

"Why not? Also, it's his birthday tomorrow!"

Claire tapped her fingers against her thigh. She knew the reasons she could give him, the most important being giving a pet as a gift isn't a good idea unless you know the person wants the pet and has the means to take care of them. And yet, she stared at the kittens inside the box. James had always loved cats, and maybe he needed a pet to care for, something to give him joy every day.

"Hi, James," Zachary said, bouncing up the stairs of James's house. He sat outside on his front porch.

"Happy birthday," Claire said. She stood in front of her brother now with Zachary next to her. Her sunglasses covered most of her face.

"Happy birthday!" Zachary echoed. He pushed the small present they'd brought for him into James's hands. Their bigger surprise sat in Claire's running car, waiting to be revealed.

"Thanks, bud," James said. He avoided Claire's eyes.

Whatever, Claire thought.

James dug through the bag, dropping the tissue paper by his feet. Zachary quickly picked up the pieces and folded them between his arms and his body.

"So, do you like it?" Zachary asked, his eyes wide and hopeful.

James's lips quirked up as his eyes glistened with tears. He lifted the small drawing Zachary had made.

"I love it," he said sincerely.

"I drew that just for you. That's me, and that's you," he explained, taking the seat next to James. "And Aunt Claire had it framed so you can put it on your desk."

"And that's exactly where it's going to go," James promised.

"There's also a gift card at the bottom of the bag," Claire added. "I didn't know what to get you."

"Aunt Claire says I'm as talented as my mom. Do you think I am?" Zachary asked, inching closer to James to look at the picture and then back at him. The little spot between his brows was creased as he studied the expression on James's face.

"Yes," James said. "I think you might be."

Zachary beamed.

"Now?" Zachary asked.

Claire sighed. She couldn't believe she was doing this. If James said no, then she would be the owner of a kitten. She hoped this went well.

"Yes, now."

"What are you talking about?"

"Your other surprise! Come on!" He motioned for James to follow him out to the car. Claire held her breath. She had already prepped Zachary that James might not want a cat and that pets usually weren't the best gifts to give others, but he still hoped he would be pleased with their gift.

Claire opened the back door and lifted out the cat carrier.

"What's all this?" James asked, an amused look on his face.

"It's your new pet, Callie." Claire handed the cat carrier to James. He took it, though he kept his eyes on her, suspicious. "I mean, you can change her name. Zachary named her since she's a calico cat, but I told him you might decide to change it."

"Yes, it's okay if you change it, James. I won't mind," Zachary spoke up. "Though Callie is a good name!"

"You got me a kitten?" James stared at the cat in the carrier.

"Yes."

"Why?"

"Zachary insisted," Claire said.

"I did! Isn't she cute?" Zachary asked.

"Let's go inside," James said. Claire grabbed some of the cat items after turning off the car. She handed Zachary a small bag of toys to carry inside. There, James opened the door of the carrier, taking the kitten into his arms. She immediately settled against his chest.

"So, will you keep her?" Claire asked.

James sat on his couch, rubbing the back of the kitten's neck. Claire took the seat closer to the window, moving the blinds over to let some natural light in. Zachary stood next to James to pet the cat's head.

"I bought food and some toys for her. She's had her shots. Oh, and there's a litter box in the trunk. I forgot that."

"I'll keep her," James said.

"Yay!" Zachary clapped his hands. "See, Aunt Claire? I knew he would!" He looked to James. "Can I hold her?"

"Sure." James handed the kitten to Zachary.

"I thought the cat could be good for you. I'm worried about you, James. And maybe this kitten could make you happier. I miss the old you."

James nodded, looking over at Zachary with the kitten before looking back to Claire. "And I miss the old you."

Claire inhaled sharply. "The old me? I don't think I've changed at all."

James scoffed. "You don't let yourself be happy."

"I'm not sure what you're implying, James. I am very happy."

"How's Max?"

Claire huffed, crossing her arms over her chest. "I don't know. Will you keep her name?"

"No changing the subject," James said. "Why do you keep ruining it with him?"

Tears formed in the corners of her eyes. She didn't know how to answer that question.

The cat left Zachary's arms and went into James's. It was a good look for him.

"I'm sorry I've been such a bitch," Claire said. James laughed loudly. Zachary gave her a pointed look, which meant he expected payment for it. Claire couldn't help but grin.

"I mean, it's you. I expect it."

Claire reached across and playfully hit his knee.

"Are you keeping her name?"

James scratched behind the cat's ears, earning purrs.

"Of course. Callie is a good name."

"It is," Zachary agreed. "Can I get a glass of water?"

"Sure, go on," James told him. Zachary disappeared into the kitchen. Claire was grateful. She reached over to pet the cat.

"How do I know that they'll get along? That it's a good thing for Zachary?"

"What, Max and you?"

"Yes."

"That's just an excuse," James said.

"It's not," Claire argued. "Is it fair to Zachary? Shouldn't my whole world be about him?"

"No," James said. "Your entire world can't be about Zachary. You deserve happiness, and Zachary deserves for you to be happy, Claire."

"Maybe," she replied.

"I'm right. He does. You have to stop pushing him away." The cat meowed in James's arms. Claire stared at Callie. Then she met James's eyes.

"I'm not sure I deserve him," she quietly admitted a moment later.

"Why not?"

"I'm not good enough for him."

"That's not true, Claire. He loves you. He wouldn't have stuck around for this long if he didn't."

"Yeah, I guess," Claire sighed. "What about you? Will you try to find some happiness? I think the cat could help."

James placed the now sleeping kitty on the small bed Claire had brought in for it.

"I think she could," James agreed. "I found a support group I've thought about going to."

"What type of support group?" Claire asked. "Is it like therapy?"

"Yes, but in group form. It's for people who lost a loved one."

"So, you'd have to, like, listen to other people's problems too?" Claire asked.

"Yes," James said.

"I don't think I'd like that. I hardly like talking about my own problems."

"Yeah, I don't see you doing well in a group therapy setting," James said, sticking his tongue out at her.

"But it does sound good, for you. I'm proud of you, James. I'm happy that you're working on yourself."

James nodded. "Now it's your turn."

Claire knew her brother was right. Her heart still hadn't healed from her own trauma. She'd just done a better job of covering it up. She let that heartbreak ruin the most important relationship she'd ever been in. For the past four years, she'd pushed Max away, only letting him close when she needed comfort. It hadn't been fair to her or him. It was time to make some changes.

"Thanks for seeing me on such short notice," Claire said, taking a seat in her therapist's office. After being at James's, she decided she needed to come right away. She called and had an appointment booked in just a few minutes. James was keeping Zachary for her.

"I was surprised you called," her therapist replied. "Is everything all right?"

"I think you and I both know I haven't been all right in a long time." Claire crossed her right leg over her left. "But I want to be."

Her therapist's eyes grew. "Oh? What changed your mind?"

"I screwed up with Max. I've watched my brother drown in his own sadness and I want better for him. So I..." She paused. "I just think maybe I do deserve more than what I've lived for the past four years."

"You do," her therapist said.

"But...it's hard. I have all these thoughts and feelings that aren't okay," Claire admitted. A stray tear slid down her cheek and she made no attempt to wipe it away.

"Like what?"

"I sometimes wish Zachary didn't exist, because if he wasn't here, Taylor would be. She was going to leave Dylan, but then she found out she was pregnant. She was nineteen and scared. But Zachary was her whole world. She loved him more than anything. *I* love him more than anything. How could I think something so terrible?"

"Because you're human, Claire. That doesn't make you a bad person. It makes you human. It doesn't mean you love Zachary any less. I know you love that boy."

More tears came.

"It's okay to be vulnerable, Claire. Not just with me, but with those you love too. What you went through was traumatic. No one expects you to be perfect."

"I do."

"I know you do," her therapist said pointedly. "What happened with Max?"

"I slept with someone else."

"Who?"

Claire shrugged. She couldn't remember his name. She'd done everything she could to try to forget that night, even though her mind wouldn't let her.

"Is it someone you liked?"

"God no."

"Then why did you do it?"

Again, Claire shrugged. The therapist kept her eyes on Claire, making her uncomfortable.

"You know why you did it."

Claire wiped the tears off her cheeks, but more still came. "Self-sabotage."

"Yes," the therapist agreed. "You do that, Claire. And you need to stop. You deserve love. You deserve happiness."

Claire wondered if she could go to Max and talk to him. But it was probably too late. She screwed it up, and she doubted Max would give her another chance.

"Maybe I should start coming in more often," Claire said.

"Yes, I think that could be good for you."

Chapter 25

Margot

Margot paced the hallway between her room and her daughter's room. Then every few minutes she would pause to check her phone to see if she'd heard back from Max about the flash drive. She kept the bracelet on her wrist, afraid if she left it somewhere else, Jeffery would randomly decide to check the USB and see if she'd changed it out.

Right as she went to check for a message, her phone rang in her hands. She jumped, nearly dropping the phone onto the floor. She caught it just in time and answered it.

"Hello?" Her other hand clutched against her beating heart.

"Margot, are you all right? You sound out of breath," Jeffery's voice said on the other end.

"Oh, yeah. I...I...um, I was running up the stairs when you called." *Bad lie*, she thought.

"Oh good, you're home. I need you to bring me your bracelet. You know, the one with the charms. You've been wearing it a lot." Margot swallowed hard. "I need it by one. Do you think you could do that?"

This couldn't be happening. Margot checked the time on the clock on the wall. It was ten in the morning. She had three hours. Three hours didn't seem long enough. What if Max didn't have it ready in time?

"Yes, sure. Why?" She hoped she sounded calm and nonchalant, even as her cheeks turned red and beads of sweat formed on her brow.

"I'm running it over to the jewelry store during my break. I found a new charm for you."

"What kind of charm?" she asked. She descended the stairs, grabbing her coat from the hook by the door and throwing it on. It was a rare cool day. Her mind raced, mulling over all she had to figure out.

"I can't tell you. That would ruin the surprise."

"Right." She headed out to her car, spotting Nanny Fay sitting on the bench by their flowers in the front yard. She ducked her head, hoping she wouldn't try to say anything to her. She didn't have it in herself to make small talk.

Once she got into her car, she said, "I have to go and meet the girls for brunch to celebrate Jenna's pregnancy, but I'll bring the bracelet by one."

"Have fun with your friends. Margot, I love you," he said. "You know that, don't you?"

"Yes, of course. I love you too."

When she got off the phone, she started her car. There was a brunch today for Jenna's pregnancy, but she had lied to them about being sick to miss it. She'd gotten a little too comfortable with lying in such a short amount of time.

Driving down the road, she asked her phone to call Max through the Bluetooth. He answered almost immediately.

"Is it ready?" she asked.

"Not yet," he answered.

"Jeffery wants me to bring it to him," she said. "By one."

"One?" Max went silent for a moment before adding, "Crap. Okay, let me see what I can do."

"I'm on my way there."

"You can't come to my office. I'm not there. I'm at this guy's place who works on these, and he doesn't like visitors. Meet me at my office by twelve thirty. He'll have it done by then."

"And if he doesn't?"

"He will."

Margot pulled into the driveway of the closest fast food restaurant and rested her head on her steering wheel. Every inch of her body ached as the adrenaline from the fear pumped through her.

Slowly, she lifted her head. She'd have to trust that Max could do this. She had no other choice. She stepped out of her car and walked into the restaurant. It was too early for a burger, so she took a breakfast muffin instead and walked to the farthest corner booth so no one would notice her. For extra protection, she lifted the hood of her jacket up and over her head. Then she munched on her muffin, waiting impatiently for twelve thirty to arrive.

She arrived at Max's office ten minutes before twelve thirty. No one was there. There was a sign dangling on the door that said, *Out of office, be back soon*. It also included a phone number to reach one of them if it was an emergency. Margot sat on the top step. She checked the time again. It was only 12:21.

Her phone rang. It was Jeffery. Her heart nearly leaped out of her chest.

"Y-yes?"

"Don't worry about bringing it to me. I'm heading home now."

"Now?" she croaked. She stood. "But I'm still out with the girls. I'm not home. It would be faster if I just brought it to your office."

"Where are you eating with the girls? Normal place?"

"Um, no. Somewhere new," she lied. She tapped her foot against the step.

"Just come home and bring it here. This is important, Margot, very important."

"Oh, okay. I can leave, sure. We've already paid."

"Good. Get home now. You should be there in, what, fifteen minutes?"

"Closer to thirty."

She heard Jeffery growl on the other end. "Just get home, please. I'm trying to do something special for you, Margot."

"I know," she said, chewing on the inside of her lip. "I'll be there."

The line was disconnected between them. Only a minute had passed. Margot was seventeen minutes from her house. If Max didn't show up when he said he would, she was going to be in so much trouble. While Jeffery had been more lenient lately, he was starting to show aggressive signs again.

Fortunately, she spotted Max pulling into the parking lot just a minute later. She rushed down the stairs, meeting him at his door as he stepped out of his car.

"Do you have it?"

Max stuck his hand into his jacket pocket before showing her the small USB drive. Margot reached for it, but it slipped from her fingers and onto the muddy ground. Max was quick to dive down for it, swooping it back up into his hand.

"That won't do. It's filthy!" Margot declared.

"I have something inside that will clean it. Come on."

Margot followed behind him. While she did, she pulled the fake USB out of its spot on her bracelet, dropping it into the trash bin in Max's office building. Max grabbed a can that said it was a keyboard cleaner. She watched as he sprayed the air over the USB, happy as most of the dirt flew off and onto the desk. He took a small tissue and wiped the rest before spraying it one last time. He rubbed it against his shirt and then held it up for Margot to see.

"Good as new."

"Thanks," Margot said, breathless. She attempted to put the USB back in its spot on its charm, but her fingers shook too much. Max stepped in, gently taking the USB away from her and sliding it in its place with ease. "Thank you," she said again, now with sincerity. "Were you able to see what's on it?"

"I have it on here," Max told her, pulling out a larger USB from his other pocket. "I'll start looking through the files tonight, if that's still what you want."

"I do." Margot had to know what was on this drive and why her husband was hiding it in a piece of jewelry.

Max went around his desk, placing the USB next to his computer. Margot felt like she could breathe again with the USB back in its rightful place. But just as quickly as she felt at peace, she panicked again.

"I have to get home."

At the house, Margot spotted Jeffery sitting out on the same bench with Nanny Fay. The two of them were talking about something.

What, Margot didn't know. But she could see that Jeffery was smiling. He always had a childish smile on his face when he was with her.

Margot parked and got out of her car. She waved when Jeffery looked at her. His smile slid off his face. He kissed Nanny Fay's cheek before making his way to her.

"You're late," he said.

"There was traffic." It had only been by a few minutes, but Jeffery hated when anyone was late. He touched her cheek, stroking her skin.

"Well, I'm glad you're here. Where is the bracelet?"

Margot lifted her wrist, showing it to him. He undid the clasp before turning the bracelet in his hand. He inspected the charms, taking an extra second on the one where the USB was hidden. Her heart skipped a beat. Could he tell that she'd found it? That she'd messed with it and taken it out? Would he be able to notice that the files had been copied?

He placed the bracelet into his pocket before looking at Margot and giving her a wink.

"I'll have this back to you tonight," he promised. He leaned forward, kissing her cheek.

"I look forward to it. Can you give me any hints about the new charm?"

"No." He took her hand into his own and gave it a loving squeeze. As he stepped back, he kept her hand within his until they were too far apart. When he dropped her hand, he blew her a kiss before rushing to his car.

Margot let out a loud breath of air. She'd done it. She'd actually done it.

"He's a good boy," Nanny Fay said, walking up behind her. "You are so lucky to have Jeffery as your husband. He takes such good care of you and Ari."

"I know," she said with a tiny nod.

"So whatever you're up to, you better stop." Margot froze. She turned to face the nanny.

"I'm not up to anything."

"Oh honey, I wasn't born yesterday." She patted Margot's upper arm. "You would be nowhere without Jeffery. Nowhere. Remember that."

Chapter 26

Max

The adrenaline rush was one of his favorite parts of his job. Max loved nothing more than that last-minute rush to get something solved. The tighter the time limit, the better. He worked best under pressure.

Now that Margot had her USB again, he sat back at his desk. A chuckle left his lips. He did it.

Clasping his hands together, Max slid his chair up and closer to his computer. It was time to see what was on this secret USB. He hoped it amounted to something. He needed something to dig into to distract him from thinking about Claire.

He put the copied USB into its spot and waited impatiently for the little box to pop up. It did. He clicked it, and as the file opened, several documents filled the page. Each file had been given some sort of fruit code name. Weird, but whatever. He clicked on the first one.

Knock. Knock.

He glanced up to find Claire standing right in his doorway. His heart leaped in his chest. Claire was here. He hadn't seen her since they'd run into one another grabbing ice cream. Of course, he'd thought about her every day, but he hadn't had the courage to do anything about it. He'd been too afraid of more rejection.

As he looked at her carefully, he realized that, for the first time in his life, she looked timid.

"Hi," she said.

"Hi." He forgot all about what was on his computer and made his way over to her. He kept a good distance between the two of them, not wanting to frighten her away.

"I really messed up," she told him, a tear slipping down her cheek. Max reminded himself that he wouldn't fall back into this again. He knew he had a hard time whenever he saw her cry. He hated seeing her unhappy.

"Claire..."

She wiped below her eye, shaking her head. "Just let me talk for a minute, please?" Her words were soft.

"Okay."

"I shouldn't have slept with that guy."

"Claire, we weren't together. You don't owe me—"

She put her hand up. "You know it's hard for me to be vulnerable. You said you were going to let me talk."

Max brought his fingers over his lip in a zipping fashion and pretended to throw away the key. Claire rolled her eyes, but she continued.

"I did it to hurt myself," she said. "I knew that it was the only way I could completely break away from you. And I wanted to do that because I don't deserve you, Max. You put up with so much from me. You need more than that, but..."

"No." Max couldn't stay silent. "No, Claire. I don't."

"You know, I'm pretty messed up. Um, survivor's guilt is what my therapist calls it, and I think she might be right." She wiped her cheek again. "And then there's Zachary. I worry that I'm not good enough for him. And if I get with you, that makes me feel selfish, like I'm taking something away from him. I don't know." She tugged against her sleeve that had ridden up, bringing it back to her wrist.

"You aren't selfish, Claire. You care for that boy more than anyone could imagine."

"I do," she agreed. "My therapist says I like to self-sabotage. I think she's right about that too. I'm seeing her again, weekly. I'm going to do the work." Max's heart felt lighter. Claire was actually going to do the work to get better. He never thought he'd see the day. "And..." she continued as she stepped closer to him. "I know that I have screwed up, and that I don't deserve any more chances. I don't expect anything from you. I need you to understand that before what I say next."

"I understand."

"Max," she began, "I...I love you. I have, I think, since soon after I met you. And I just had to tell you that. But again, please don't feel like you have to say anything back."

Max stood still, unable to speak. Had he just heard what he thought he'd heard?

"All right," Claire said, a shaky breath leaving her lips. "I'll let you get back to work."

Her eyes searched his face for a split second before she turned. Max shook himself out of his stupor, following behind her and taking her upper arm in his hand to stop her from leaving.

"Please don't go," he begged. She faced him again. They were so close that their noses almost touched. He took a small step back. "I love you too, Claire. But I think you already know that. Why else would I stick around for four years?" His lips tugged upward as his thumb rubbed against Claire's skin.

"Can we make this work?" Claire asked, her voice small. It was so rare to see her like this, so vulnerable before him. "Like, really make it work?"

"I think so," Max said. "I mean, yes, we can. We're Max and Claire. What *can't* we do?"

He earned a genuine laugh from her. "Go an hour without arguing." She rose a brow.

"We've made it several hours without arguing."

"While we were asleep," she said. He grinned. "Do we start over? Do we go on a date? How exactly does this work?"

"I think we do whatever we want to do. We're Max and Claire," he repeated.

"Claire and Max," she corrected.

"Claire and Max," he agreed.

Chapter 27

Margot

Margot lay in Ari's bed until she fell asleep. It was their new normal, since Ari still was having trouble sleeping. She inched out of the bed, hoping none of the sounds woke her back up. Once she exited the room, she made her way down the hallway into her bedroom. She walked to the window, willing Jeffery to be home already. She knew he could work really late, but she hoped that wasn't the case tonight. There was no way she could sleep tonight without knowing what he added to the bracelet and if he could tell that she'd copied what was on his USB.

She'd messaged Max to see if he found any information yet, but he told her he hadn't, that it would probably take him a few days to make it through all the files on it. Margot was both curious and frightened about what he might find. Sometimes, she wished she was the Margot before she found that USB. But at the same time, she didn't. She couldn't be that Margot anymore, the one who really wasn't happy with her life.

Jeffery's car lights shone in the driveway. Margot rushed back and into the bed, throwing the comforter and blankets up over her legs. She turned on the lamp on her side table and grabbed the book that sat there. Flicking to the page where her bookmark was, she tried to immerse herself in the pages. Or at least, look as though she was.

By the time she heard Jeffery's footsteps, she'd read over the same sentence at least twenty times. She kept her nose in the book until Jeffery knocked on the frame of the door. When she looked up at him, he smiled.

"You're still awake," he said.

"It's not even nine," she replied. She placed the bookmark back in its spot before plopping the book on the table.

"You haven't gotten very far in that book. You usually finish books much faster. Is that one not good?"

"Just hard to get into, I guess. But I've heard it's worth it in the end," she lied.

Jeffery came over, sitting on the edge of the bed next to her. He pulled the bracelet out of his pocket and placed it in her hand. Immediately, she searched for the new charm. There it was, a small locket with Ari's initials on it. But that was when she noticed the other charm was now gone, the one with the USB.

"Where's the one with the emeralds?" she asked, trying not to sound too curious.

"Oh, that one was broken," he said. He grabbed the bracelet from her before showing her the new one. "But this one is much prettier, don't you think?"

"Uh, yeah, it is. I did like the emerald one too."

"Well, we'll get you another," he promised. He brought the bracelet around her wrist, securing it into place. Then he pulled her in for a kiss. His forehead rested against hers as his hand held her cheek. "Why don't we go downstairs? I brought you dessert."

"Dessert?" she asked, surprised. "What kind of dessert?"

"You'll have to see."

Margot took the hand he held out for her as he stood. The two of them went downstairs. There she found two pints of ice cream on the countertop. Real ice cream, with all the delicious sugar.

"What's this about?" she questioned. She reached out for the pint of chocolate chip before pulling her hand back. What if this was some sort of test? Could he be checking her loyalty? Or was this part of his apology for his two violent outbursts?

"It's not about anything," he said. He grabbed the pint she'd been reaching for and then took it over to where the ice cream scoop was. He pulled a bowl from one of the cabinets and dug out a few scoops into the bowl. "Here."

"Are you not having any?"

"No," he said. "But you should. I think we should treat ourselves a little more often, don't you think?"

Margot uneasily nodded. She'd love to think this was some new change with Jeffery, but there had been so many changes in him lately that it was hard to keep track knowing which one was the real him.

They sat on the couch. Jeffery turned on the television, choosing a show he knew she liked. Out of habit, Margot cuddled up beside him. Desperately, she wanted to be wrong about everything. Yet, despite it all, the voice inside her nagged that she wasn't.

Jeffery's arm came around her shoulders. She tensed before allowing herself to get comfortable in his touch. It was getting harder to be relaxed around him. He kissed behind her ear as his hand cupped her cheek, turning her to face him. His eyes searched hers. Her breath hitched in her throat. Before she knew it their lips touched. Then he took her upstairs.

Margot was in a deep sleep when Ari woke her up. She stood at the foot of their bed with her stuffed unicorn in her hands. She had her thumb in her mouth, a habit Margot thought they'd squashed years ago.

"Ari, is everything all right?" she asked through a yawn. Ari walked over to her.

"I'm scared," she said.

"Oh sweetie," Margot said. She lifted Ari into her arms before looking over her shoulder. Jeffery was still fast asleep. Margot adjusted Ari on her hip and then walked her back to her room. Ari fussed the moment Margot sat her back into her bed.

"I want to stay with you!"

"Shh," Margot soothed as she sat down next to her. "It's all right. I'm right here. Now, why were you scared?"

"You and Daddy. You've been fighting." Ari sucked her lower lip between her teeth. Margot's heart clenched. She thought she and Jeffery had kept their issues well hidden from their daughter, but apparently she had been wrong. She wondered just how much Ari knew. Had she heard it the other night when he threw Margot across the room? Nothing had happened today, but perhaps Ari could notice the tenseness that Margot felt. Apparently, things hadn't gotten as back to normal as she had hoped.

"We aren't fighting," Margot said. She rubbed the back of her hand against Ari's cheek. "Everything is just fine, I promise."

"Please don't leave me alone," Ari begged. She clung to Margot. "Please."

"I won't. Just close your eyes."

It took a little while, but Ari finally settled back into the bed. However, her fingers still dug into the skin of Margot's arm. When Margot was sure her daughter was asleep, she carefully pulled away each finger until she was no longer holding on. Margot stood. She stared down at Ari. Tears stung her eyes. What all did Ari know? How did she protect her from this point forward?

After standing there for close to a few minutes, she went back into her room. Quietly, she climbed back into the bed. Jeffery turned closer to her. His arms came around her as he spooned her body. His lips kissed the crook of her neck.

"If you ever leave me," Jeffery whispered in her ear, "I will get Ari."

Margot's body tensed.

"What?"

Jeffery sat up so that he now looked down on her. Even though it was dark in the room, she could see the whites of his eyes. She tried to sit up, but he put his hand on her shoulder. He bent down so that his lips were against her ear.

"I will get Ari. If you ever leave me, she's all mine. No court will ever give you custody, not after what happened after she was born. Don't you forget that, Margot. Don't you forget who you really are."

"But..." Her throat grew dry.

"Nanny Fay, the doctors, everyone will be on my side. They'll speak up for me and against you. Remember that if you ever think of leaving."

Jeffery lay back down beside her, bringing her into his arms. His head rested against her back. As he fell asleep again, Margot found that she couldn't. She lay there until the sun came up.

Chapter 28

Claire

Everything was perfect. Claire had never felt so at peace with Max's arms around her in her bed. The sun had risen a while ago, but she was just enjoying being here with Max. Even his snoring in her ear didn't annoy her.

Soon Zachary would be awake, and she would have to get up. But not until then. The two of them were happy. It was such a strange feeling. They hadn't even slept together the night before. Instead, they'd stayed up late, talking and laughing and then watching TV until they fell asleep.

Max made a weird snore-hiccup sound before jerking behind her. His arms slipped away from her body. She turned to face him. He was awake.

"Good morning," she said.

"Good morning," he repeated. "Should I go out the window?" he teased.

"No. It's the final day of soccer. Do you want to join?"

"I get to go to soccer?" Max asked, a glimmer in his eye.

"Yes. It's the final game."

"Well, of course I'll go."

Claire kissed the tip of his nose and got out of bed. She grabbed her robe off the hook by the door and slid it on.

"Oh shit!"

Max sat up, his brows knitting in concern. "What?"

"Goldfish. I forgot Goldfish. I'm supposed to bring snacks for after the game, and I forgot the Goldfish."

"Goldfish?"

She laughed. "You really don't know much about children, do you?"

"No."

"It's all right. I didn't either. You'll learn. But right now I have to look through my pantry to figure out what I can whip together for the game."

"I could run to the store," Max offered. Claire felt that familiar flutter in her chest.

"We have to leave in an hour. Do you think you could be back in time? I have goody bags to get together."

"Sure. It's right down the street. Anything else you need?"

"Um, maybe grab a chocolate bar for my friend, Margot." Claire knew how much Margot loved chocolate and how much Jeffery kept her from eating sweets, so it might be nice to bring her the treat.

"Margot? As in Margot Lewis?"

"Right, I gave her your info. What did you find on that USB?"

"I can't answer that," he said with a wink. "Not your business."

"I'd argue it is. She's my friend, and I'm your...girlfriend?" Claire hedged, and Max grinned. "Also, I suggested you to her."

"That's not how it works." Max's grin grew, his hands on her hips. "But also, I don't know what's on the USB yet. I have several files to go through."

"I bet he's into something bad. I get horrible vibes from him."

"You do read people well."

"Yes, it's my blessing and my curse." Claire gave Max a kiss, easily melting into his embrace. Then she remembered Max had to run to get the snacks, so she pulled away. "You have to run to the store. Goldfish."

"Right." Max slid on his jeans. Once he threw on his shirt, he sat up and gave her a quick peck. "Where will I find those?"

"Cracker aisle. You can't miss them." She watched him as he exited her room.

Claire grabbed her phone from the charger, seeing she had three missed calls from Margot. Her stomach tightened. She dialed Margot back.

"He knows," Margot said in a strained whisper. "And now..."

"Wait, hold on," Claire said. "Are you in danger?"

"No. No, I'm—I'm fine. But Claire...you don't know, and I won't...he'll take Ari from me!"

Claire did her best to make a soothing sound.

"He won't. We won't let him."

"But—"

"Come over to my house after the game. We can talk more then."

Zachary looked cute standing with the little medal in his hands. His team hadn't won the game, but it didn't matter. Zachary was excited.

Claire took several pictures of him to send to her parents and James. They were unable to make the game today. Her parents went on a trip, and James was starting his new therapy group this morning.

It was nice though, for it to be just her and Max together at the game. It gave Claire a moment to see what family events could be like with Max, who had been supportive of Zachary the whole game. Claire had to admit it was nice to see Zachary light up and wave to Max every time he spotted them.

Margot had been distant the whole time, but Claire decided not to bother her. She didn't know what had happened, or if Margot was in danger. She would wait to talk with her at the house where there wouldn't be any prying eyes or ears.

"Are you ready to go?" Claire asked Zachary.

"Is Max coming back to the house?" Zachary questioned in return. He glanced up at them both with a wide grin.

"That's a good question," Claire said, facing Max. "Are you? I mean, can you? I know you have work to do."

"I can come over. I have my laptop. I can do work and watch Zachary while you talk with Margot."

"Really? You wouldn't mind?" Claire asked.

"Of course not. It sounds fun."

When Margot arrived, she appeared as though she hadn't gotten a wink of sleep the night before. She had dark circles under her eyes and her hair was pulled up in a messy bun. Ari hadn't come with her to the house—she went on a playdate at Victoria's house—and Claire thought that was probably for the best.

Margot gratefully took the cup of coffee Claire offered her as she sat in a chair on the back porch. There was a nip in the air this particular fall day so Claire turned on the small heater she kept outside for mornings like these.

"Okay, so tell me what happened," Claire said the moment she sat down. Margot sipped on her coffee for a minute. Her breaths were sharp, as if she was trying to keep herself from crying.

"He told me that if I tried to leave him, he would make sure he got Ari. He told me I would never get custody of her."

"Pfft," Claire said, rolling her eyes. "He's just trying to scare you, Margot."

"But he's probably right. I don't have any income. I'm fully reliant on him. The judge will probably think…"

"No," was all Claire said in response to that. "He can't use that against you. He'll try, but it won't work. My sister's dealt with plenty of cases like that."

"Maybe, but you don't understand," Margot said. Her hands trembled as she put the coffee cup on the table in front of her. She covered her mouth with her hand before a sob escaped her lips.

"What? What don't I understand? You're a wonderful mother. That girl adores you. No judge would take her from you."

"Yes, they would. They would." Margot was becoming hysterical.

"My family will make sure they don't. They will represent you. And they don't back down."

"They can't save me from what I've done." Margot's voice went grim.

"What you've done? What does that even mean, Margot?"

She hiccupped. "I…Claire, I almost killed her when she was a baby!"

Claire's eyes widened. "What? That…what do you mean?"

"After Ari was born, it was…it was bad. I struggled with severe postpartum depression. I had horrible thoughts about harming her and myself. Jeffery kept telling me it would get better. Nanny Fay took over on nights so I could get more sleep. I was never left alone with her. Except for one day..." A shaky breath left Margot's lips.

"One day what?" Claire asked.

"I put her in the bathtub. I was obsessed with cleanliness, and she had spit up all over herself. I put her in—clothes and all—and turned on the water. I just put the small little baby into the tub. And..." Margot looked away. "I don't remember what else happened. Except that Nanny Fay happened to come into the bathroom and find her almost under the water. Apparently, I was just sitting there, not doing anything. Next thing I remembered was being in the hospital. I was hospitalized for a month."

Claire took this all in. "So, they left you alone with the baby when they *knew* you were struggling?" she clarified.

"I almost killed her!"

"But you didn't. She's absolutely fine. And you are fine now, right?"

"Yes. But—"

"Where were they when this happened? They knew you were struggling! We can use it against them!" Fire raged through Claire.

"Jeffery was at work. And Nanny Fay went for a quick walk. Ari had been asleep. She didn't think—"

"Yeah, she didn't. And now he's trying to hold it over you? Rich." Claire rolled her eyes. "And this is how Jeffery thinks he'll win custody? Over something that happened seven years ago? When you clearly had postpartum depression? I don't think it works like that, Margot."

"I've never forgiven myself. I can't lose her! She's my whole world."

"You're not going to lose her, I promise." Claire grabbed her phone and typed a message to her sister, Mila.

"What are you doing?"

"Setting up a meeting with Mila. I'll go with you. We'll settle this once and for all."

Claire found Max and Zachary in the former guest bedroom that she'd recently turned into her new office, since her old office space had become a space for Zachary to create in. In her old office, all of his pictures and drawings were hung on the walls and she'd bought an easel for him.

But even her new office still wasn't completely hers. She'd learned those were a rarity with children. The only spaces she had that were her own were her bedroom and bathroom.

One side of the office had a desk where she'd work on her laptop, while the other side had two shelves covered in toys. Zachary sat over there playing with his LEGOs. He didn't even seem to notice Claire walking in. Max, however, did. He glanced up from his laptop and grinned.

"Can I ask you the hugest favor?" Claire asked, biting on her lower lip.

"Yes," Max said, reluctance in his voice.

"Could you watch Zachary for a bit longer? I have to take Margot to my sister's office. And I can't take him along."

"Sure, no problem. We get along just fine, don't we, Zachary?"

Now Zachary looked up. He shrugged before going back to his LEGOs.

"Great, thanks." Claire bent over and kissed Max's cheek. "I owe you."

"I'll make sure to remind you of that," Max said with a wink.

Claire then made her way to Zachary, kissing the top of his head. "Be good for Max. I won't be gone too long. I'll bring you back something for lunch."

"Okay. Tell Mila hi from me!"

"I will," she promised.

As she reached the doorway, she paused. She glanced back at Max and Zachary both busy with their own things and thought, *This is easy*. She wondered why she'd ever thought it wouldn't be. With a smile, she exited the office. Zachary was in good hands with Max.

"Wait, is that Max Evans, the PI?" Margot asked. "I thought I recognized his car outside. Is that why you recommended him?" She stood at the end of the small hallway between the downstairs guest room and the living room, waiting for Claire.

"Um, yes," Claire said.

"So, you're...dating?"

"Yes," Claire replied, pleased with how easy the answer came out. "We are."

Chapter 29

Margot

Mila Donahue-Miller's office was in the same large office building as the rest of Claire's family. It was perfectly put together with no personal mementos except for one small picture on the corner of the desk of a baby, who Margot assumed was Mila's baby. Claire had told her on the way over that Mila had a baby girl.

Mila looked a lot like Claire with her rich brown skin and almond eyes. She was a little shorter than Claire and she kept her hair in braids. She also had a tight expression on her face. According to Claire, Mila had a hard exterior but was actually quite loving. To Margot, she sounded a lot like Claire.

"All right," Mila started, sitting in her nice leather desk chair. Fleetingly, Margot thought about how Jeffery would like that type of chair in his own office. "So, you want to leave your husband? Is that right?"

"I...I think so." She hated how unsure she sounded. There were still so many what-ifs up in the air, like the USB drive.

"She thinks he will get custody," Claire filled in. "But I told her with you, that would never happen."

Mila took a measured pause. Her eyes moved between Claire and Margot before she slid forward.

"I do win custody cases. Though really, the children win. I do what's in the best interest of the child."

"Her husband is threatening to take full custody of their daughter if Margot tried to leave."

Mila rose her brow. "He's threatening you?" She grabbed a notebook that sat beside her on her desk before scribbling something down. "Has he ever been violent?"

"Not really—"

"Yes," Claire cut in. "And controlling."

"Hm." Mila scribbled some more in her notebook. "What is he threatening you with?"

"My—"

"Her past. She had—"

"Claire, shh. Let Margot talk," Mila said sharply. Next to her, Claire's eyes rolled as she crossed her arms over her chest, but she stopped talking and sat back in her chair.

"I had bad postpartum and ended up in the hospital after almost drowning my daughter. It wasn't on purpose. She got dirty and I put her in the bath, but I guess I lost it and I just let the water rise and rise."

"That's it?"

The *that's it* shocked Margot. That moment haunted her until this day and for it to just be dismissed as nothing surprised her.

"I mean, I almost killed her."

"You had a psychotic break. But you were hospitalized, and I'm guessing nothing else like that ever happened again?"

"Never."

"And how old is your daughter now?"

"Seven."

More scribbles on the paper.

"Are you on any medication?"

"Yes, for my anxiety."

"Okay. Do you see a therapist?"

"Yes."

"Yeah, there's no way he's getting full custody. Most likely it will be fifty-fifty. Do you do most of the childcare?"

"Me or the nanny."

"Ah, you have a nanny. Does she do most of the childcare?"

"No. I'm always with Ari. The nanny mainly helped when she was younger."

"Okay. But still, fifty-fifty is what you should be expecting. He'll try to scare you, and let him. Keep track of it. It'll be useful in court."

"What if I'm not ready to file for divorce?" Margot asked. She refused to look at Claire, because she knew exactly what she would want to say. Hopefully she wouldn't cut in again.

"You said he's been abusive?" Mila directed the question to her.

"Just twice, yes," Margot admitted.

"There's no *just* when it comes to abuse, Margot. Well, I wouldn't file until you had somewhere safe to go. Leaving is one of the most dangerous times, as I'm sure my sister here has told you."

"She has."

Mila tapped her fingers against the wood of her desk. It was oddly comforting how she and Claire used the same motions.

"How much does your husband know about you wanting to leave him?"

"I don't know. Maybe he knows something," Margot said. She had been wondering this all night. Did he know she'd found the flash drive? Did he know about her talks about leaving him? "He just told me last night, in the middle of the night, that if I ever left him, he'd get Ari in the divorce."

"Controlling move," Mila said under her breath. Next to her, Claire cleared her throat. She sat up as though she might add something, but didn't. Margot found it funny how the only person who seemed to keep Claire from speaking her mind was her older sister. "He may not have any idea, or he might. Has he ever said anything like that before?"

"No," Margot told her. "Never."

"How did he act when you were put in the hospital?"

"Lovely! He took such good care of me. He made sure I was never stressed. He's made sure I've been taken care of since." Margot tightened her hands together in her lap. This was a bad idea, talking to a lawyer. If Jeffery found out...

"I'm sure he has," Mila broke her thoughts. "I suggest you find somewhere safe to go. Have a plan before we file anything, if you decide," she added. "I know this is difficult, Margot. I know you don't want to break up your family and that you want the best for your daughter. But you have to think if staying really is what's best. You say he's been violent with you twice. Is there any record of that?"

"Record?"

"Police report?"

"No, no, I never...I never told anyone. Well, until recently." She wondered if she should mention the USB drive, but decided against it until she knew what was on it.

"Next time, you call the police. Have it on record."

"But the police don't listen," Claire broke in. Margot turned to face her. Claire's cheeks were pinched in and her hands were in fists at her sides.

"Claire, you know I need reports. It helps with the case. But my sister's right, don't expect them to help. You could get lucky, but odds are they'll just write something down. Not much can be done unless it gets really bad or it's too late. Be careful."

The meeting with Claire and Mila had been overwhelming. Ari would need to be picked up from Victoria's soon, but she found herself sitting in the front room of the house where all the books were. She could send the nanny to pick her up from Victoria's, but that would mean talking to her, and Margot had avoided her since the day before when she'd warned her as well.

This was all too much with the flash drive, thinking of leaving Jeffery, both Jeffery and Nanny Fay warning her, and everything else. She wasn't sure she could handle it. She thought about calling her mom to see what she thought. However, it was well known her mother didn't like Jeffery. She wouldn't be able to get an unbiased response from her.

Realizing she had to leave now or she would arrive later than the discussed time, Margot made herself get up. As she walked toward the door that led to the garage, she stopped. A chill ran down her spine. She looked over her shoulder. Nanny Fay stood in the corner of the hallway, sipping on a cup of coffee. They stood there in a standstill, neither removing their eyes from the other. Finally, Nanny Fay walked away. Margot let out a deep breath. Her hand was still on the door handle. She exited into the garage, closing the door swiftly behind her, feeling much better on the other side of the door.

Chapter 30

Claire

Claire arrived to a spotless and quiet home. She dropped her keys into the bowl next to the door. The living room had every item put up and away. All of Zachary's toys were in their correct baskets against the wall, the blankets that usually scattered the couches were folded up and placed on the back of each couch, and all of Zachary's papers that usually littered the coffee table were gone. Claire narrowed her eyes.

"Zachary? Max?" There was no response. She walked to the edge of the stairs and called up louder. "Zachary? Max?!" Again, nothing. She headed into the kitchen to find the breakfast dishes no longer all over her countertop. They must have been cleaned and put away. She wondered if this was Max trying to impress her or if he was always this neat and tidy. His office surely wasn't. And she'd only been to his apartment once, years ago. "Zachary? Max? This isn't funny."

If he was trying to impress her, this wasn't working. Not knowing where Zachary was was *not* okay with her. She grabbed her phone from her back pocket, ready to call him.

Bam! She jumped. A soccer ball had hit the kitchen window. Heading over to it, she spotted both Max and Zachary looking at the window. Upon seeing Claire, Zachary waved sheepishly. She laughed.

When she made it outside, Zachary ran up to her. His arms wrapped around her waist.

"I missed you! Max has been teaching me new soccer moves."

"Oh? I didn't know you played soccer." Claire realized there was still so little she knew about Max's life outside of the small things they'd talked about over the years.

"He played through college!" Zachary said with a little jump. "He played until he messed up his knee. Think I could play like him?"

"If that's what you want," Claire told him. Zachary skipped off toward the ball, leaving Max and Claire alone. Max ran his fingers through his dark blond hair. Sweat soaked the front of his shirt, despite the cooler weather outside. "Thanks for watching him. This was easier, having you here to help when an emergency popped up."

"It's almost like what I always said it would be," Max teased. Claire rolled her eyes. "He's a great kid," Max added. "A lot of energy."

"Yes. He has a lot of that," Claire chuckled. "Were you able to get any work done?"

"Not really."

"Sorry."

"No, it's fine. How was your meeting?" he asked.

"Hard," Claire said honestly. "A little too close to the past for my comfort."

Max reached out and touched her shoulder. Instinctively, she started to pull away, to push him away from her vulnerability, but she knew she couldn't do that, not anymore. For the two of them to work, she had to let that part of herself shine through.

"Do you want to talk about it?"

"Maybe," Claire said. "But I'll probably do that with my therapist."

"Will you actually talk with her about this now?"

"Yes." Claire rubbed her hands together. "It's hard to talk about, but I need to. I can't push it down anymore."

"Yeah."

"As horrible as it sounds, part of me wishes I'd never gotten involved," Claire admitted. "I just keep thinking about Taylor."

"It doesn't sound horrible. But that wouldn't have been you to not get involved."

"Yeah, why am I like this?" Claire asked with a groan.

"You're a good person, Claire. You care." He cupped her face. "But I should go now, get back to the office."

"Like that?" Claire pointed to the large sweat stain.

"I'll probably head home to shower first."

"You could shower here if you wanted," Claire offered.

"I don't have extra clothes."

"Right, of course."

"I think tonight is going to be a long night," Max said. "But perhaps tomorrow we could do a date?"

"I'd like that," Claire said. "However, I don't know if my parents will be free to watch Zachary."

"Bring him along," Max offered.

"On our date?"

"If we're going to be together, he's part of the package, right?"

"Well, of course, but..."

"Tomorrow night. Pizza?"

"Pizza sounds great."

Max kissed her cheek. He ran over to Zachary and gave him a high five before going into the house. Zachary walked back over to Claire and placed the soccer ball into her hands. Her fingers touched dirt. She had to control her facial expression to keep from showing her disgust.

"Max was fun! Can he come over again?"

"Of course," Claire said with a smile.

"Wanna play, Aunt Claire?"

"How about we have ice cream instead?"

"Okay!"

Claire was grateful that was acceptable to Zachary. She'd never been the get-in-the-dirt-and-play-rough type. Though she was glad Max was. That would be good for Zachary.

Inside, Zachary kicked off his shoes before picking them both up and putting them at their spot where they went by the front door.

"Since when did you put up your shoes?"

"Max and I worked really hard cleaning up for you!"

"Oh you did, did you?" Claire put her hands on her hips. "What about when I do the work to make it clean for you?" she teased. Zachary pursed his little lips, tilted his head, and copied Claire's motions by putting his own hands on his hips.

"I do!" he responded. "I'm always keeping things clean."

He wasn't wrong—not in his mind, at least. He did put things away, in a sense. Just as well as a seven-year-old thought was clean. Many times after Claire would ask him to straighten up his room, he'd call for her saying it was all done. Claire would come in to find toys stuffed under the bed or thrown into boxes and his drawing stuff shoved into drawers. Not that she minded. She'd never been strict about any of that.

"You are," she said with a wink.

After Zachary was in bed for the evening, Claire called Max hoping for an update, both about what was on the USB drive as well as them. She was giddy about the prospect of their date night coming up and then was surprised by her giddiness. She, Claire Donahue, did not get *giddy*. She and Max had been together for four years, but not *together*. She hadn't been in a relationship since Taylor died, and that one had ended abruptly.

No answer. She placed the phone by her feet and turned on the television. Her mind drifted to Max sitting with her watching television after Zachary went to bed and cuddling up with him. She actually wanted that to be her new normal. She wasn't going to screw this up this time.

Knock. Knock.

She sat up. Her brows creased. There was another knock.

Slowly, she got off her couch and headed to her front door. She peeked through the blinds to find Margot outside. She opened the door.

"Sorry," Margot said. "I know it's late. This was just when I could get out of the house for a bit. Ari is asleep and I told Nanny Fay I needed to go on a drive. Can I come inside?"

"Sure." Claire let her in. "Would you like anything to drink?"

"No." Margot clasped her hands together in front of her before rocking on her heels back and forth. "Sorry, I shouldn't have come."

"Don't apologize. Let's sit."

Even though she sat down, Margot remained standing.

"I don't want to lose my daughter," Margot said.

"You won't," Claire assured her. She stood back up.

"She's feeling the pressure. She's not sleeping well. She knows we're fighting. Maybe I've gone about this all the wrong way."

"Please sit," Claire said. "Let me get you something to drink."

Margot finally sat this time. Claire went into the kitchen and got them both a glass of white wine. She had just made cupcakes with Zachary that evening, so she popped a few on the plate, making sure to leave the ones with little fingerprints on the cake stand.

She took them into the living room. Margot's face brightened at the cupcakes. She immediately took one.

"Parenting is hard," Claire said, taking the seat next to her. She set the plate and wine glasses on the coffee table in front of her before picking up one of the glasses of wine to sip on. "You question every day if you're doing the right thing."

"But this isn't a small thing like if it was okay that I let her have a sucker before school. This is leaving her dad."

Claire nodded, even though she couldn't relate. "And that's hard," Claire validated. "It really is."

"What do you struggle with? You don't strike me as someone who struggles much in their decisions. I picture you as someone sure in everything."

"I'm good at appearing that way," Claire said, okay with the change of topic. "I question every day if I'm doing right by Zachary. Everything I do, I worry that it's the wrong thing. Taylor was so different from me. I always wonder if I'm raising him in the way she would."

"Well, you're not," Margot said. It stung. Claire sipped on her wine so she wouldn't respond. Margot clarified right away. "What I mean is, you can't. You're Claire. You aren't Taylor. You can't try to be her, because you're not. And that's okay."

"But it's not." An unexpected well of tears filled her eyes. She turned away. "Taylor was supposed to be here. She was supposed to be the one raising him. Not me. I didn't even want to be a mother yet, and it just happened."

Margot touched her shoulder. "Life can suck, can't it?"

"Yes." Claire blinked and swallowed back the tears before allowing herself to face Margot again. "She was great. You would have loved her."

"I bet I would have," Margot replied. She appeared less tense now that the conversation had shifted away from her and Jeffery. "Would you like to talk more about her?"

"I would," Claire said. She smiled. She stood and motioned for Margot to follow her back and into her office. In there, she had several of Taylor's paintings hung up around the room. Her favorite was the simple drawing Taylor had done of the both of them in college, sitting on the couch, eating mint chocolate chip ice cream. It was framed above her desk. On the wall to the right was the painting Taylor did of Zachary. It had been the only happy painting she'd done over the short time she had lived with her.

"Wow, this is dark." Margot stood in front of Taylor's painting where a fist was breaking glass. Blood dripped from the fist and into the fractures. If you looked close enough, you could see words in the fractures. Dark words such as unworthy, ugly, stupid, and more.

"Yeah, it is," Claire said, her voice quiet.

"Why do you keep it up?"

"It's a good reminder of what a piece of shit Dylan was. That's why I chose it for the foundation's website," Claire said. "But it's also one of her best works. I've sold a lot of her original pieces, but not this one. There are copies of it, which sell the best. People are drawn to it. I've even had insane offers for this particular piece, but I always say no. I just can't give this one away. Zachary can have it when he's older, if he wants it. But no one else."

Margot stared at the piece for several more seconds until her body shook. It was a small shake, but just big enough for Claire to notice. She stepped away and let out a loud sigh.

"Does, um, Zachary talk about his mom a lot?"

"Oh yes. All the time."

"What about his dad?"

Claire made a face. She couldn't help it. It was an automatic bodily response to the mention of Dylan.

"He really doesn't," Claire said. "Though maybe he does in therapy."

"Oh? He goes to therapy?"

"Yes. It's been amazing for him. What happened is such a hard thing to talk about. I hate his dad, but like...it's his dad."

"Does he know that his dad killed his mom?"

"Yes," Claire said with a heavy heart. "He does. It's not something I could protect him from, as much as I would have liked to. The therapist said we needed to tell him so he didn't hear it somewhere else. That was a rough session. I think it's why he doesn't talk about him. His mother's death weighs heavy on his little shoulders. You wouldn't notice, but I do."

Claire did wonder if she should make a bigger effort to talk with Zachary about his father, but she couldn't bring herself to do it. Dylan remained a shadow over her, but she refused to let it be a shadow over her and Zachary. She couldn't protect him from what his father had done, but she could protect their relationship.

Do, do, do, doooooo.

"What was that?" Claire turned up her nose. Was it one of Zachary's toys that made noise? She started to bend down to check under her desk.

"That's my phone. It's the ringtone I made for when Jeffery calls so I know it's him." Margot pulled her phone from her pocket and hit a button, making the sound stop. "I'll call him back when I'm leaving."

"You sure you don't want to call him back?" Claire stared at Margot for a moment, curious about her calmness with her husband trying to call her. Yet, when she looked down she saw that Margot's phone was still in her hands. She could tell how tight she was holding it by the white of her knuckles. Maybe she should ask why she was avoiding his calls and if he knew she was over here.

"I'm sure." Margot made her way over to the picture of Zachary. "I really like this one. I love it."

"Me too."

Margot's phone still remained in her hand.

Ring. Ring.

It was Margot's phone again, but this time with a different ring.

"It's Max," Margot said before answering the phone. She talked for just a few brief seconds and then hung up.

"So? What did he say?" Claire asked.

"That he found some really interesting information. He asked me if I could come by tomorrow morning."

"Oh, that's good. It is good, right?"

"I don't know," Margot answered. "Once I know, there's no going back. Could you come with me tomorrow?"

"Sure. I have Zachary, but I'll make it work."

Chapter 31

Margot

When Margot got back home, Jeffery was standing in the driveway. He moved to the side to let her pull in. Her hands tightened on the steering wheel. She hadn't responded to his phone calls or his texts. After the third text asking where she was, she turned off her phone.

Ignoring his calls didn't come from confidence. It came from fear, because when he answered he would know she wasn't just on a drive. He might find out she was looking into leaving. She told herself she shouldn't be afraid of him. But she was. She'd seen what he could do.

As she stepped out of the car, Jeffery was right next to her. She tried to read his face in the darkness. Even though the outside lights were on, there was a shadow covering his face.

"Where have you been?" His voice was eerily calm.

"Out on a drive," she answered. "Then I stopped by a friend's house."

"I tried calling you."

"Did you?" She lifted her phone. "Oh, it's off. Sorry."

"You keep your phone off when Ari is here?"

"Not usually. It must have turned off. Maybe it's dead." More lies.

"I called Victoria. She said you weren't with her."

"No, I wasn't."

"Are you having a breakdown again?" he asked. She couldn't step back or else her back would hit the car.

"What?"

"Nanny Fay says you've been acting odd, and I agree. You haven't acted like this since your breakdown. Do you need to go back to the hospital?"

"What? No. I'm fine." Her words came out a bit too forced.

"It's okay," he said. His hands came up to rest on her shoulders, while one trailed farther to grab her chin to have her look up at him. Now she could make out his features better. Concern covered them. "It's okay to need help, Margot."

She didn't say anything. He led her inside.

She felt like she was losing it after everything that had happened in the past several weeks. Was she having another breakdown? Had she imagined his outbursts and the violence? She rubbed her temple before shaking those thoughts away. Her mind went to Claire and the conversations they'd had. She wasn't. And she couldn't let him feel like she was.

As she sat on the couch, Jeffery bent down in front of her. His eyes stared at her intensely.

"I'll take you to the doctor myself tomorrow. I can take the morning off."

"No," Margot finally spoke. "I'm fine. Really, I am. I told you, I was with a friend."

"What friend?"

Margot twisted her hands in her lap. "Claire."

"Claire? Who is Claire?"

"You met her before. She came to the house."

His face hardened. "I thought I said I didn't want you to spend time with her. She's bad news."

"You said you didn't want her to come around here. She hasn't been back to the house." Margot got up and walked away so that her back was to him.

"What were you doing at her house this late at night?"

Margot tugged at her hair and then turned back to face Jeffery.

"Just drinking a glass of wine and eating a cupcake. She's a decent baker."

"So you were drinking and then driving?"

"It was just one small glass of wine."

"And that's all?"

"Yes, that's all."

"Okay."

"Okay?"

"Yes, okay. I don't like it, but it seems what I like or don't like doesn't matter anymore. Let's go to bed." There was contention in his voice.

Her shoulders tensed. She knew he was angry at her. What might he do if he knew the truth of what happened that night?

"Yes, I'm tired."

At her response, Jeffery's jaw tightened. She could see his hands at his sides closing and opening before his jaw loosened. He didn't say anything else to her. He just went upstairs to their bedroom. She waited a few moments behind him.

When she reached their bedroom, she avoided Jeffery's gaze. She got ready for bed and then climbed under the sheets, grabbing her book to read. Jeffery slid in next to her. His arms circled her as his chin rested on her shoulder.

"I wish I could read what's in that head of yours, Margot."

"Nothing's going on up here. I'm just tired." She hated this, really. She didn't like being sneaky and suspicious. She wanted to be able to trust her husband and talk to him. However, she knew she couldn't. She wanted to cry, but she couldn't despite the fact that her life was crumbling all around her.

Jeffery took the book from her hands, placing it back onto the bedside table. She fell to her back, making him tower over her. In the past, this would have excited her, but now it frightened her. He'd become so unpredictable.

But nothing happened. He fell back to his side of the bed. They just lay there in silence.

"Don't leave me, Margot." He sounded sad. Margot faced him. She blinked back the tears that threatened to escape. "I love you," he said.

"And I love you." She did. She loved him and their family so much. She cuddled up against him. His arm came around her, holding her close. The tears finally fell, landing on his bare chest. His hand ran up and down her back, causing her to settle.

She thought about tomorrow and about what she would find out about him on that drive. It would change everything. She clung to him, allowing the tears to flow more freely.

Chapter 32

Claire

Claire was glad Margot wanted her to come along today because she was very curious about what was on that USB drive. She was bringing Zachary along with her. Max said it would be fine and that Liliana could watch him in her office. Claire had no idea if Liliana had been made aware of this, but she hoped she had.

"Hi!" Zachary said, skipping into Liliana's office. Claire handed him the bag of goodies she had packed for him which included his iPad, headphones, and a ton of quiet snacks.

"Is it okay that he's in here?" Claire asked.

"Yeah, no problem. Hey, Zachary! How have you been?"

Zachary went right over to her desk. Knowing that Zachary was in good hands, Claire went to wait back on the front porch for Margot. She hadn't heard from her yet that morning and was starting to worry that she had gotten cold feet. She checked her phone again. Still no messages.

Right as Claire lifted the phone to her ear, she spotted Margot's car coming up the road. She slid her phone into her back pocket.

As Margot stepped out of her car, she removed her sunglasses and put them on the top of her head. Her hair was pulled back into a slick ponytail, and she had on a light base of makeup. She placed her purse over her shoulder and came up to where Claire was standing.

"Are you ready?" Claire asked her.

Margot looked the building up and down before nodding. "Yes. I am."

Max's desk was covered in paperwork. His normally tamed hair was a little wild, showing he'd been up most of the night. Claire found she liked it that way. Her fingers itched to reach out and muss it some more, but she held herself back.

"Come on in and take a seat," Max said.

"So what have you found?" Margot asked.

Max swiped all the paperwork up in his hands, hitting them against the desk to make one neat pile before handing it to Margot. He walked around to the other side of his desk so he could rest against the front.

While Margot looked through the paperwork, Claire tried to glance over but she couldn't read anything on it.

"What does this mean?" Margot handed the pile of papers back to Max.

"It means your husband is in big trouble."

"What kind of trouble?" Claire couldn't help but ask. She needed to know.

"Is he in danger?"

"Maybe," Max said. "But he's more in trouble with the law than anything. He's been funneling money illegally from his company."

Claire watched as Margot's face grew pale.

"What?" Her breath was sharp. "No, that has to be wrong. Jeffery would never..."

"I wish it was, but it's not. These files are very clear about what's been going on. And it's not just him. There are other names on the list." Max pointed to one of them at the top of the paper and turned it around for Margot to see.

"That's...that's my friend Victoria's husband. No. I don't believe any of this." She shook her head. "Something is wrong. I know Jeffery isn't perfect, but he's not some criminal!" Margot stood, shoving the seat back as she did.

"Why don't you sit back down and—" Claire started to suggest.

"Don't!" Margot yelled, interrupting Claire. She dashed out of Max's office, leaving Max and Claire alone. Claire looked at the door and then back to Max, who looked just as shocked as she felt.

Claire followed after Margot. She found her sitting on the small swing on the front porch. Her head was in her hands as she swung back and forth. Claire just stood there, not wanting to say anything to upset her any more than she already was.

Finally, about five minutes later, Margot stopped swinging. She sat up, revealing tears that had been sliding down her cheeks.

"I can't un-know this," she murmured. "But there has to be something else. He must have been pulled into this. Maybe he—"

"You're seriously making excuses for him?"

Margot's head snapped up. Her red-rimmed eyes hardened as her lips fell into a tight, steady line.

"This is all your fault," she said, her voice low. She stood, curling her hands into fists at her side.

"My fault? How is it my fault?" Claire was stunned. She had done everything she could to help Margot.

"You...you got in my head." Margot touched her temple. "You convinced me my husband was evil—abusive! We were happy until I met you. He was right about you, messing up relationships. Maybe it's the trauma from what happened with your friend, but not every man is evil."

Despite the fact that Claire knew Margot was likely in panic mode, falling back to denial in her stages of leaving, she spoke up.

"He *has* been abusive with you! You've admitted it!" Claire bit.

"It was...it was only twice. And one of those was an accident. And the other...well, I was half asleep. I probably made it out worse than it was." She grabbed her purse from the swing, bringing it over her shoulder.

Claire stood, stunned. Margot breathed heavily a few times before leaving the porch and going to her car. Claire just stayed there, knowing there was nothing she could do. She hated feeling helpless.

It was a while later when Max joined her on the front porch. She sat in the swing with her knees brought up to her chest. Max just sat down next to her, handing her a tissue.

"Zachary!" she said, remembering he was here with her.

"He's fine. He didn't hear a thing. Had his headphones on, and Liliana is now drawing with him."

"I'll have to buy her dinner or something." She sighed and began picking at the skin on the edge of her thumb. "This is why I don't get involved. It's why I stay back, just donate money. Because you can't save them all. You can't always help them. And then..." A shuddering breath left her lips.

"You can't save them all," Max repeated in agreement. "And sometimes you need someone to look after you, Claire. You're always holding way too much on those shoulders of yours."

"But she's my friend," Claire whispered. "And he'll hurt her again." A hot tear ran down her cheek. Max's arm came around her shoulders and she dropped her head onto his chest. "She blames me, for all of it."

"That's just anger. She'll come around." Max drew a pattern on her upper back with his finger.

"You don't know that. I might never talk to her again."

"Maybe not," Max said. "But I doubt that. You have this force, Claire, that brings people in. She'll realize she was wrong."

"But not until it's too late," Claire hiccupped. "Oh God, Max, I can't go through this again!"

Quickly, Max drew her closer to him, allowing her to cry into his chest. She clung to him, grateful that he was here in this moment. He was the only person in the world she felt comfortable enough to be fully vulnerable with, and it had taken her four years to get to this point.

As her tears subsided, she still held on to his shirt, and breathed him in. He smelled musky, but in a good way. She lifted her head and met his gaze.

"Her husband is going to go to prison, isn't he?" she asked.

"Likely."

"He's into some bad shit."

"Very bad."

"So, like, how bad? Who is he working with?" Claire asked.

Max shook his head. "Can't tell you."

Claire sighed and unhooked her fingers from his shirt and got up. She grabbed her compact from her purse to check her face, not wanting to upset Zachary when he saw her. Her appearance was acceptable enough, so she put the compact back into her purse.

"Do you tell them?"

"Tell who?"

"The FBI?"

"I can't really tell you what I have or haven't done," he said.

"What do you think will happen?" Claire asked. "To Margot? And Ari? Will they be okay?"

"I don't know," he answered.

"And her husband would be put away, unable to hurt her," Claire said.

Max ran his fingers through his hair before shaking his head. "If he is dangerous, like you say, then if he gets any sniff of this being leaked, Margot could be in more danger."

"I know," Claire said. "Oh God." More sobs came. Her fear for Margot just kept growing. "So what do we do now?"

"Right now, *you* do nothing," Max said.

"Nothing?!" Claire screeched. "I am not one to just sit around and do nothing."

Max chuckled. He stood, taking Claire's hands within his own.

"I know, and I love you for it. But for now, you do nothing. I want you to be safe, Claire. And Margot doesn't want your help, not right now. She'll come back around, after the shock wears off."

Claire wasn't sure she agreed. She took a moment to calm down, knowing she didn't want Zachary to see her this way.

"Well, I should grab Zachary," she said, wiping under her eyes. "I promised him he could decide what we're doing this afternoon. Are we still on for pizza?"

"Yes," he said with a smile. "It's all going to be all right," he promised.

She sighed. "You can't promise that."

It was hard to concentrate the rest of the day. Zachary had chosen to go to the arcade and Claire had to pretend to pay attention as he played millions of games. By the time they got to dinner, she was just glad that Max was there to entertain Zachary.

She'd been looking forward to their time together, but now it had been clouded over by everything that had happened.

"What do you think, Aunt Claire?" Zachary asked. He had red pizza sauce smudged on his face and up to his nose. She grabbed a paper towel to wipe it away.

"About what?"

"About going to a movie," Max added.

"A movie? This late?" She checked the time on her phone. It was only seven, but by the time the movie ended, it would be past Zachary's bedtime.

"Not just any movie! A drive-in!" Zachary said.

Claire bit the inside of her cheek. "What movies are playing there? And won't it be too late? Zachary, your bedtime is in an hour. You'll fall asleep in the car."

"That's half the fun," Max broke in.

Claire shot him a look. It didn't seem to deter him; he just grinned some more and batted his eyes at her playfully.

"Come on, it'll be fun. Zachary and you are on fall break. Let's do it," Max said. She knew he was just trying to help distract her from everything going on.

"You're incorrigible," Claire said, throwing the napkin from her lap onto the plate. "But fine, I guess. I'm assuming the movies are on you?"

"Definitely."

"Yay!" Zachary exclaimed. He brought his arms around Claire, hugging her tight. "Thank you, Aunt Claire! Thank you!"

She had been right. About thirty minutes into the film, Zachary was fast asleep in the back of the car. Max sat next to her munching on popcorn and enjoying the film about talking bunnies. This could have been fun, if she didn't have Margot on her mind.

She lifted her phone to text her again. She'd already sent ten texts to her today. No responses had come back.

"You need to give her space," Max said. Claire kept her eyes on Max as she typed.

Just be safe.

"Or you can not listen to me and do whatever you want to do," Max said.

"Thank you."

"Has she responded to any of your texts?"

"No." Three dots popped up. Margot was texting her back. "Wait, she is."

Don't text me again.

Claire dropped her phone into Max's cup holder.

"It's just like Taylor," Claire murmured.

Max didn't say anything. He reached across to take her hand, rubbing his thumb over her palm. At least this time, she had him.

Chapter 33

Margot

Two weeks after she received the information about the USB, Margot had almost forgotten about it. *Almost.* Life was almost back to normal. *Almost.*

This Sunday morning she awoke to breakfast in bed.

"Happy birthday!" Ari exclaimed, jumping into the bed next to her.

"Yes, happy birthday," Jeffery said. He bent down and kissed her on the lips before putting several presents next to her.

"You didn't have to get me anything," Margot said. Though she knew at this point it was all a song and dance. It didn't matter how much she insisted she didn't need anything for her birthday, Jeffery always lavished her with expensive gifts. It seemed this year was not an exception.

"Here! Open this one first!" Ari handed her a small, rectangular box.

Margot carefully unwrapped the paper and set it aside to reveal a velvet box. A beautiful white gold chain with a diamond pendant sat inside.

"Oh, it's beautiful!"

"Don't forget this!" Ari shoved two more boxes toward her. There was a matching bracelet and earrings in them.

"I love them."

"Good, you'll wear them tonight, with the rest of your packages," Jeffery told her.

"Oh?" Margot grabbed the next box. There was a gorgeous green dress.

"I bet the next box has shoes!" Ari gushed.

"I bet you're right," Margot said, tapping her nose. And she was right. Inside the box were silver high heels.

"Tonight, dinner at eight at Dahls, corner booth."

"Like always," Margot said, her voice low. "What if we just stayed in tonight and watched a movie instead?" Her fingers ran over the elegant gown. Her mind went right to what she knew. Had this dress been bought with illegal money? Had all of it? Would their dinner be tonight?

"Don't be silly," Jeffery stated. He stood. "It's your birthday. It will be celebrated with a nice meal."

"Of course." Margot quirked her lips up in an attempt to smile. It faltered, but Jeffery didn't seem to notice. He gave her a quick kiss on her forehead before grabbing his suit jacket to put on over his pressed white button-up. He walked over to the mirror and grabbed a comb to make sure his hair was just right.

"Where are you going? It's Sunday. Family day."

"Can't today. Too much going on with work. I'll have a car pick you up at seven thirty sharp."

Margot panicked. Was he going off to do something illegal? "Can't you just stay home?"

"I can't. I'll be working until dinner, but I'll meet you at the restaurant." He kept looking at his appearance in the mirror. "Oh, also, I have someone coming over to help you with your hair and makeup beforehand. Make sure you shower and blow dry your hair before six."

Margot slumped back against the pillows.

He turned to face her and Ari. "Love you both, and happy birthday again, Margot."

With that, he was gone.

Margot set her new presents carefully back into their boxes so that she could enjoy the breakfast she had been brought. It wasn't her favorite type of breakfast, with mainly fruit and just some egg whites. Usually on her birthday, Jeffery made her one of her favorites like pancakes or French toast, and she wondered if he was trying to tell her something with this meal.

Ari snuggled next to her, reaching out her fingers to pinch a strawberry out of the fruit cup.

Margot was tempted to push her breakfast away and take Ari with her to a local diner for something more delicious, but in the end she decided against it. She was making changes. No more going behind her husband's back. If things were to go back to the way they were, she had to show him that she could be trusted.

"Ari, it's time to get ready for your playdate," Nanny Fay said, standing in the doorway. Around her shoulders was a red shawl that she wore when it started getting colder outside.

"Playdate?" Margot asked. "I didn't set up a playdate."

Even though she'd made changes the past two weeks, things were still awkward between her and Nanny Fay.

"Jeffery did."

"Oh." That was odd. He never set up playdates for Ari. "Where is this playdate?"

"Victoria's house."

"Oh, I could take her." Going to Victoria's today could be a nice distraction. But then her mind went back to the paperwork. Victoria's husband's name was there too. Did Victoria have any idea?

"No, you're to stay home, boss's orders. It is your birthday, after all."

Ari nabbed one more strawberry before bouncing out of the bed and into the hallway. Nanny Fay shot her a quick look and then disappeared with her.

She was thoroughly spoiled on her birthday. After Ari and Nanny Fay left the house, a masseuse showed up to pamper her for two straight hours. Then lunch was brought to her. It was another healthy meal, but a nice one. She munched on it while watching television.

She enjoyed having the house to herself, reading and being lazy for most of it, until Nanny Fay returned with Ari later. But even then, she was mainly left alone. She did as she was told, showering and blow drying her hair before the cosmetologist came to doll her up for the evening.

By the time the car showed up, she was looking elegant, and not much like herself at all. She was helped into the car by the driver and then out by her husband at the restaurant. He had changed into a nicer suit and a matching tie to her dress.

"Happy birthday," he murmured to her the moment she stepped out of the car. His hand fell to her hip so he could pull her close and kiss her. His lips lingered on hers. He tasted like alcohol. She pulled away, surprised by this. He just smiled. "Let's go inside."

As promised, they had the same booth they'd always had at this restaurant. They'd come here every year for her birthday since the year they met. That year, she'd been so excited. They'd only been dating for a little while and she couldn't believe she was eating somewhere as fancy as this.

At their booth, they were immediately asked for their drink orders.

"We'll have your most expensive bottle of white wine. And we're ready to order our food."

Margot tightened her brows. She certainly wasn't. She hadn't even looked at the menu yet. She enjoyed their steak, but she'd only come here once a year and might have preferred something else. She reached for the menu, but Jeffery placed his hand over hers to stop her.

"I'll have the nine ounce filet, medium rare with the steamed vegetables as a side. My wife will have the grilled chicken with the steamed vegetables as well. Thank you."

Margot deflated. Grilled chicken? For her birthday?

"I wanted steak," Margot said.

"No, you should have chicken. It's better for you. You've been eating too much junk food lately. Don't think I don't know about your little treats."

Margot blanched. How could he know? She'd been so diligent about throwing everything away before she got home. Was she being followed?

"Darling, it's only because I care about you," he said. "I want you to be healthy. Don't you want to be healthy?"

Margot nodded, but tears still stung her eyes. She felt so foolish sitting here at this fancy restaurant with her husband calling all of the shots.

Another waiter came by with rolls and butter, but before he could put them down Jeffery stopped him.

"We won't be needing that."

"Why did we even come out to dinner?" Margot asked. "I can't eat anything fun."

Jeffery's hand wrapped around her wrist under the table. He tightened his fingers so that they dug into her skin.

"You just can't be grateful for anything, can you, Margot? I've made sure you were pampered all day, I bought you this beautiful outfit to wear, and I took you out for a nice dinner. And all you care about is that you aren't getting what you want to eat?"

"You're hurting me," Margot squealed. Jeffery only held her tighter.

"It's because of that girl, isn't it? She's turned you against me."

"No, no, she hasn't. I...I love you, Jeffery. Just...please stop."

Jeffery's fingers unlatched from her skin, but his jaw did not unclench. Nor was there any apology from him. The waiter returned with their wine, pouring them both a glass. Jeffery took his, swirled the wine in the glass, and took a long sip.

"You should have some wine," Jeffery said, motioning to the glass with his hand. "It'll help the nerves."

Margot didn't feel thirsty or hungry for that matter, but she took the glass anyway and sipped some of the wine. With her free hand, she rubbed against the spot where Jeffery had grabbed her.

"Don't be so dramatic," he hissed in her ear. "You're fine."

Later that night after Jeffery had fallen asleep, Margot decided to look at apartments around town. Not that she planned on leaving, but she felt like she needed some sort of plan, just in case.

Chapter 34

Claire

Claire yawned after putting Zachary to bed. It was only eight, and she was exhausted. She walked down the stairs to find Max cleaning up all of Zachary's toys.

"Zachary really should be doing that," she said.

"Ah, I don't mind. Come on, sit. You're tired. Or should I leave? Let you go on to bed and rest?"

"Stay," she said. She walked closer to him and rested her head against his chest as his arms came around her. Life had become rather domestic pretty fast, and Claire didn't mind it. It was nice playing family. Max fit with her and Zachary so incredibly well.

"Should we watch something?"

"Sure," Claire said. They both got on the couch, and she cuddled up next to him. Since the other night, he hadn't stayed the night again. And that was how it should be, right now, with Zachary in the picture.

"I've been thinking," Max started.

"That's dangerous," Claire teased.

"What if we went somewhere after Christmas?"

Christmas had always been Claire's favorite holiday, and she loved it even more now with Zachary and his belief of Santa. Every year, she told him the story of when his mom visited her family that one Christmas. It was his favorite part of the holiday.

"Somewhere? What kind of somewhere?" Claire asked, intrigued.

"A trip."

Claire sat up. "Oh, I don't know. I don't think I could be away from Zachary for that long, or how he'd do if I was gone that long. I mean, maybe if we just did something overnight."

"With Zachary," Max clarified. "A vacation with the three of us."

"Oh." Claire pondered this. "I...I don't know. You don't think it's too soon? And where would we go, exactly?"

"Somewhere farther up north, let Zachary experience the snow. He's been talking about wanting to build a snowman. I thought we could rent a cabin and let him play in the snow. Maybe even take him skiing."

"He does want to see the snow," Claire said. "I just...we can think about it."

"Okay," Max said.

"I do want to go on a vacation with you, Max. It just seems so sudden, don't you think so? We've only just started dating."

"We've been together on and off for four years. I thought..." He shook his head. "Never mind. It's fine." He didn't sound angry or frustrated. "I shouldn't have assumed. Let's just watch some television for a bit."

Claire curled up against him. She didn't know the right things to say. It had been a long time since she'd been in any sort of relationship that she recognized as one. She wanted this with Max to work out. She loved him, and she was sure he loved her. She couldn't pinpoint why it frightened her to think of going on a trip together.

"Let's do it," she said. "I'll start looking up cabins tomorrow."

"No, Claire. I don't want you to feel like you have to go on a trip with me. Let's not rush it if you're not comfortable."

"You're saying all the right things," Claire said. "And I love you for it. But I do want to go on a trip with you and Zachary. I want us to have fun together. I guess…I just still have a lot of issues to work through. But I trust you, and I love you."

"I trust and love you too, Claire." His hand brushed against her cheek. "And I don't want to force anything."

"I know that. It's not too much?"

"What?"

"Having to become a father figure to Zachary? He's a great kid, but it's a lot to take on."

"I know. And I want to, Claire. I know that you both are a package deal."

"Good, because we are. Always."

She curled back up against Max. He kissed the top of her head. She settled against him, and before she knew it, she fell right to sleep.

"Aunt Claire?" Zachary said, tapping her shoulder. "Aunt Claire! Wake up."

Claire popped up. She was on the couch with a blanket over her, but Max was nowhere to be seen. She rubbed her eyes. That's when she spotted the note sitting on the coffee table.

You were sleeping so hard that I couldn't wake you back up.

"Sorry," she said. Zachary was still in his pajamas. He had a bag of powdered doughnuts in his hand and handed her one. "Thanks."

He sat next to her, munching on his half-eaten doughnut.

"What would you think about going up to see some snow after Christmas?" Claire asked him. Zachary's eyes glistened.

"Snow? Like real snow?"

"Yes," Claire said with a smile.

"Yes! Yes! Please!"

"And would you be okay if Max came with us?"

"Yep! I like hanging out with Max!"

Claire grinned. She mussed Zachary's hair. "Okay, good. I'll plan it soon. Now, go get dressed and brush your teeth. We have to get going."

As Zachary ran up the stairs, Claire decided to text Max.

Zachary is excited about the cabin.

Good, Max typed back right away.

I think it'll be fun.

Me too.

Chapter 35

Margot

"Y ou are so spoiled!" Victoria gushed as she looked at the new bracelet Jeffery had given Margot that morning before her birthday brunch with her friends. It was a nice thick bracelet that covered the bruising on her skin from his fingertips. He hadn't apologized though. The bracelet was on the pillow next to her head when she woke up, with a note saying it was an extra birthday gift.

"I know," Margot said. Jenna and Abby each took a turn looking at the thick bangle.

"My husband never gets me anything other than flowers for my birthday," Abby said with a sigh. "And the only reason he does that is because he set it up with the floral shop the year we got married. He doesn't even have to remember." She rolled her eyes. "What is it like having the best, most adoring husband?"

"It's...it's great," Margot told them.

"So, how was dinner at Dahls? Did you get the steak and potatoes? What appetizers did you get?" Victoria asked.

"Oh, no appetizer, but yes, the same meal as always," she lied. Even though she was lying, it did feel nice to be at brunch with the girls.

"And Paris after Christmas. Ugh, I'm so jealous," Jenna said. "My husband said we can do a nice hotel overnight for our upcoming anniversary. I suggested a trip and he looked at me like I had three eyeballs."

"Maybe in the future," Margot said. "Or maybe he's waiting to surprise you."

"As if. Randy doesn't have a romantic bone in his body," Jenna said.

Margot remembered why she loved these brunches. She was always reminded how great Jeffery was in comparison to their husbands. Jeffery showered her with gifts and made exciting plans for them. So what if he got angry from time to time? And maybe he'd hurt her a few times, but overall he was a good man who loved her and their daughter and treated them like royalty.

"Thank you for brunch," she told Victoria.

"Of course! Want to go shopping?"

"Sure."

She and Victoria stayed downtown and went to some boutiques. Being alone with Victoria made her think about what she'd found out about her husband, as well as Victoria's.

"Um, does your husband work super late hours?"

"Oh yes, always."

"Has he been, um, more tense lately?" Margot asked carefully.

"Tense? In what way?"

Margot shrugged. She couldn't think of the best way to describe it without raising alarm bells in Victoria.

"I don't know. Just...more stressed?"

Victoria laughed. "John is always stressed. He's been no more stressed than normal. Why, has Jeffery been more stressed?"

"A little bit more. At least, it seems that way. He's always worked late, but I feel like it's been even later."

"Huh. I'm not sure about John. I'm usually asleep right after Jordyn, so I'm hardly ever awake when he gets home."

Margot grabbed a few items and took them to the checkout counter.

"I'm sorry, ma'am, but your card has been rejected," the cashier said. Margot's brows creased.

"Huh, can you try it again?"

"I already did."

"Oh." She opened her wallet and grabbed her other card. "Here." She handed it over to the cashier.

"This one isn't working either."

Margot's cheeks grew warm. She'd never had this happen to her before.

"Oh, there must be some kind of mistake," she said.

"Here, I'll get those for you," Victoria offered.

"You don't have to do that," Margot said, embarrassed. "I don't need these things. I'll just put them back."

"Don't be silly." Victoria gently pushed her aside and placed her own items up onto the counter. She paid for their things and handed Margot's items to her.

"You didn't have to do that. I'm not sure why neither of my cards are working."

"It's not a big deal," Victoria said.

"I'll pay you back."

"Don't worry about it. Consider it more of your birthday present."

After she left Victoria, she called her bank.

"Yes, Mrs. Lewis, your cards have been frozen."

"Were they stolen?"

"No."

"Well, can I unfreeze them? I need to have access to my money."

"Sure, your husband will have to call in to have them unfrozen. It looks like he froze them both this morning."

"Pardon?" She couldn't have heard that correctly. "My husband froze the cards?"

"Yes. And the accounts are in his name, so he has to be the one to unfreeze them. You do not have the access to do it."

She held the phone to her ear, breathing heavily. This couldn't be right, could it?

"Ma'am?"

"Um, thank you." She hung up and then called Jeffery. He didn't answer. What was she going to do? She did have access to her secret account, but she didn't want to touch it until she needed to. And she wanted to talk to Jeffery first about it. Maybe there was some reasoning behind it that he hadn't been able to tell her about yet.

Her phone rang.

"It's nice to get a phone call from you in the middle of the day," Jeffery said, his voice light and happy. "How was your brunch?"

"It was nice."

"Oh, good. I'm glad. Now, what honor do I have for this phone call? Missing me?"

"Yeah, but, um, Victoria and I went shopping after brunch and neither of my cards worked."

"Yes, they've been frozen," Jeffery said, matter-of-factly. "I'm transferring accounts over."

"But what do I do if I need money?" Margot asked. "I need gas in my car."

"I will have that taken care of. But you don't need money right now. If you want anything, let me know and I'll buy it for you. It'll be a couple of weeks until you can have direct access to the money again."

"But why?"

"I told you, I am changing over accounts," he said, now sounding impatient.

"But you have access to some money. Can't I at least—"

"Margot, stop questioning me. You have everything you could possibly need. I'll make sure you have gas in your car, and I'll leave you some cash to use while we wait on your new cards."

"Oh...okay," Margot murmured. "Okay."

"Now, is that all? I need to get back to work."

"Yes, that's all."

Jeffery hung up the phone without saying goodbye. Margot placed it back into her bag. Jeffery's reasoning made sense enough, though she was still confused why she couldn't have any access to their money. Jeffery had never kept her from spending money. He'd always said his money was their money. Her mind went straight to the USB. Did this have something to do with the illegal funds? Or was this more about controlling her? She remembered Claire mentioning that about abusive relationships, and how they like to have control. He had been more controlling lately about every aspect of her life.

She could feel herself starting to spiral so she took a deep breath and closed her eyes. Despite the fact she didn't want to get involved, it seemed nearly impossible. How was she supposed to forget what she knew? The nagging voice inside her head was only getting louder and louder.

Checking her watch, she saw it was time to collect Ari from school. When she arrived at the school, she parked in the parking lot and spotted Nanny Fay already standing up front. Alarm bells went off in her head. She was supposed to get Ari today. She'd even told Nanny Fay before she left that she was going to do it.

Exiting her car, she rushed up to the front. The nanny glanced up at her before making a low sound.

"I said I would pick her up today," Margot said.

"Mr. Lewis asked me to get her. I listen to him."

"Well, I'm here now. I was hoping to do something special with her this afternoon, so you can go on and leave."

"No, I'll be the one taking her home, as per Mr. Lewis's request."

Margot sighed. She grabbed her phone from her pocket and dialed Jeffery's number. There had to be some sort of mistake. His phone went straight to voicemail.

"I'm her mother. You do not get to decide," Margot said as she put her phone back into her pocket. She stared at her straight in the eyes, not showing any ounce of weakness. Nanny Fay did not seem deterred.

"Fine," she muttered. "You'll explain it to him then."

She threw a glance at Margot before heading off to her car. Margot let out a breath of relief as she waited for the end-of-day bell. But that relief was short-lived. Why was Jeffery sending the nanny to pick up Ari when she normally did it? What was he playing at? It felt like he was trying to show her that she had zero control in her own life.

When the bell rang, kids began pouring out of the doors and running out toward the adults picking them up.

"Mommy!" Ari called out. She rushed right to Margot and hugged her. "I thought Nanny Fay was going to be here."

"Nope, it's me." Margot patted her head, trying to quell all the nervousness so Ari didn't see it. "Remember, I told you I was picking you up today."

"I know, but then I got a message from the office saying that Nanny Fay was picking me up."

"Uh-huh, well, that changed." She took Ari's hand, her brows furrowing. She needed to know what this was about. Why she'd lost access to her money and why Ari's pick-up had been changed without letting her know.

"Can I play at Jordyn's again today?"

"No," Margot said. "Not on school night."

"Oh, I just thought then maybe I could see Daddy again."

Margot stopped in her tracks. "What? What do you mean 'see Daddy again'?"

"He was at Victoria's yesterday when I went for the playdate." Ari bit her lower lip, her cheeks turning red. "I just remembered I wasn't supposed to tell you. Daddy said it was for a surprise."

"Oh?" Margot bent down to Ari's level. "It's okay, you haven't done anything wrong. Did you see your dad there very long?"

Ari shook her head. "No, they went inside. We stayed outside and played on the porch. When we went inside, we couldn't find them. I think they were in the bedroom. I guess that's where the surprise was." She shrugged.

A heaviness sat on her chest. Victoria and Jeffery? She wondered how long this had been going on. Panic began to bloom, but she pushed it back.

"We should go home," Margot said as she stood back up. "We can't go to Jordyn's today." *Or ever again*, she thought.

That night, Margot stayed up until Jeffery got home. She sat in the living room with the lights still on. When Jeffery came in through the garage door, she popped up from the plush couch.

Jeffery didn't seem to notice her at first. He flipped the lights off.

"I'm in here," Margot said. Jeffery startled and turned the lights back on.

"Why are you still up?" he asked. "It's nearly midnight."

"I'm aware," Margot said. She tried to bite back a yawn, but it was futile.

"Well, let's get you to bed now."

"No."

"No?" Jeffery asked, surprised. "What do you mean no? It's late. You should get in bed."

"Not until you explain why you froze my cards and why you sent Nanny Fay to pick up Ari when I was going to do it." She didn't mention Victoria. Not because she didn't want to confront him about it, but because she didn't want Ari to be blamed for her knowing.

Jeffery rolled his eyes. "Margot, it's nearly midnight. You stayed up for this? I told you that we're changing over accounts. And I asked Nanny Fay to pick up Ari because you said you were low on gas. Seriously, darling, you're acting paranoid."

"You never told me you changed the pick-up plan for Ari, or that you were freezing my cards. A heads-up would have been nice."

"Margot, seriously, we're having this conversation now? It's late. I'm tired. Also, here." He dug into his pocket and handed her a pile of twenties. "This should hold you over until the new bank is set up."

Margot took the money, counting how many twenties she had been handed. There were five.

"It's just a hundred dollars. How long until you think I'll have a new card?"

"I don't know, Margot. This is a complicated situation. I'll bring you more cash home tomorrow, all right? Now, can we go to bed?"

"Why did you need to change banks? And how do you still have access?"

"Someone has to pay the bills. This way I know exactly how much is left in the account."

"Do you not trust me? Because it doesn't make any sense."

Jeffery made a sound. "I'm doing what's best for our family, just like I have for the past ten years. I feel like *you* don't trust me, Margot."

"I do," she said, but her words were weak.

"Fuck, Margot! You don't trust me!" he screamed, his face up close to hers. She flinched. "I have done *everything* for you! *Everything!* And nothing is ever good enough, not anymore." His voice lowered. He stepped back. She felt a lump in the back of her throat. "And you wonder why I don't trust you. I'm going to bed."

He stormed up the stairs, leaving Margot alone.

Her lower lip quivered. Her heart hammered in her chest. But a calmness came over her. He was cheating on her. He wasn't going to change. He never would change. He had always been like this, controlling and harsh. Only before, it had been easier to forget because he had been better at covering it up in a charming manner. This was it. She needed to leave him. There was no turning back now.

Chapter 36

Max

A knock on his doorframe made Max look up. Margot was standing there with a determined look on her face.

"I was not expecting to see you today," Max said, standing behind his desk. "Come on in."

"I need the copy of the USB. I'm going to turn Jeffery in."

"Oh?" Max asked.

"Yes. I think—no, I know—it's the right thing to do."

Max nodded. He grabbed one of the copies he had, handing it to her as well as the printed copies she'd left the other day.

"It is," he agreed. "But you have to have a plan now. Once he catches wind of this…"

"I do. I'm…well, I've been looking at apartments. The other night I realized it's time to leave him. I just had to make the right next step. Thank you." She gave him a curt nod before leaving the office.

Max sat back in his chair. While he had actually already given the information to the police, he had decided not to tell her. This was an important step she needed to take.

The rabbit hole of the money laundering scheme was long. Max had been hired by the police to find out more. While he'd found a decent amount of information on the USB drive, they wanted more information.

He'd not been able to tell Claire about any of this, as it was confidential information. But he did wish he could tell her something. It didn't feel right keeping secrets from her, especially not when they'd just become a couple.

He got back to his office after following a lead that went nowhere. As he parked his car, he was pleasantly surprised to see Claire's car in the parking lot. He got out and saw her still sitting in her own car. He walked over to her window and knocked. She jumped. Then she rolled her window down. He gave her a kiss.

"This is a surprise," he said.

"I thought we could do an early dinner." She lifted up two bags of fast food. "I was going to surprise you."

"Well, you did. Nice surprise."

He opened her car door for her and took the two bags of food before helping her out. He glanced in the car in search of Zachary.

"Oh, he's at my parents' house. And he's staying the night."

Back in Max's office, they both sat down. His desk was a mess, so he pushed some of the paperwork to the side.

"I don't get it," Claire said.

"Get what?"

"You are so clean at my place, but here is so unorganized."

"What can I say, I work best in this chaos, but I like my living spaces to be clean."

"Huh, interesting." She pulled the chair closer to his desk. "I forgot drinks."

"Oh, that's okay. I have some in the kitchenette. What would you like?"

"Water?"

"Okay."

He headed into the small kitchen. His office used to be a house, so it still had the kitchen attached to it. You couldn't use the stove anymore, because it wasn't hooked up to anything. But he did have a microwave and a refrigerator. It was nice for late nights on the job.

He grabbed two drinks and then went back to his office. That's when he saw Claire looking through some of his paperwork on his desk. He rushed over and pushed it away.

"You are looking into the laundering!" she said. But she didn't look angry, she looked amused.

"You aren't supposed to look into my things."

She just shrugged. "What have you found?"

"I can't talk with you about it." He handed her one of the waters. "You know that."

That didn't stop Claire from trying to peek over to the corner where some of the papers still sat. Max pushed them into his top drawer and closed it before locking it. Claire huffed and rolled her eyes. "Fine, whatever. I don't even care."

"Yeah, right," Max chuckled. "I'm sure you're already plotting how to get to this information when I'm out of the room or when I'm not here. But you won't," he told her. "The drawer is locked. I am the only one with access to the key, and after you leave I'll be locking it up somewhere else. And don't think Liliana will help you. She doesn't have access to any of my stuff."

"Well, that seems irresponsible," Claire said with a shrug. "What if something happened to you? Shouldn't she be able to get to your information to help that person?"

"No. I don't work that way." Max dropped the key for the drawer into his front pocket.

Claire made a sound of disapproval, but her lips curled up slightly in a smile. He knew she'd tried to steal it from him, but he had plans on keeping it safe.

"The food is cold." Claire dropped the food back into the bag.

"Why don't you come to my place? I'll make you something," Max offered.

"Are you finished with your day?"

"Not really."

"How about I come over tomorrow then? I want you to be able to get what needs to be done with the case. Find out all you can about that asshole Jeffery."

"I still won't be able to talk with you about it," he reminded her.

"I know. Oh," she said. "I'll have Zachary tomorrow."

"Sounds great, bring him along."

His apartment was spotless. Of course, it was easy to keep it that way when he was the only person who lived here. He barely ever ate at home either. Most of his days were long and in the car, so he ate takeout more than home-cooked meals.

As he adjusted the tablecloth over the small round table, there came a knock on the door. He stood and scanned the kitchen. Everything was perfectly in its place.

"Hello," Zachary said the moment the door swung open. He shoved a paper into his hand. "Aunt Claire said it's nice to give gifts when someone invites you to dinner."

Behind him, Claire stood with a bottle of wine in her hands.

"Well thank you," Max said. He turned the paper to find a drawing of some cats. "I'll have to hang that up in my office."

"They're James's cats. He has two now! Callie and Milo. I helped pick out both of them."

"Are we allowed to come in?" Claire looked into his apartment.

Suddenly, Max worried about every aspect of his apartment. Was it clean enough? Was it child friendly? What would Zachary entertain himself with after dinner? What if he didn't like what he made?

"Well?" Claire asked again.

"Yes, of course, come on in."

Both Zachary and Claire walked into his apartment. Zachary headed over to his navy couch and sat down.

"Do you have any pets?"

"No."

"Aunt Claire doesn't either, but you know that." He swung his feet. "Any toys?"

"No."

"Cause you don't have any kids?"

"Yes."

"Zachary, why don't you go and wash your hands for dinner," Claire said. Zachary listened to her and got up off the couch. But as he headed toward the hallway, he paused and looked back at Max, confused.

"Where is the bathroom?"

"That first door right there." Max pointed to the door at the front of the hallway. Zachary bounced down that way and into the bathroom, leaving Claire and Max alone.

"Your place is nice," Claire said. "What's for dinner?"

"Chicken parm," he said. "But I did make mac and cheese too, in case Zachary doesn't like it. Oh, and I got some cupcakes from the store."

"Sounds delicious. And good call on the mac and cheese, though Zachary will probably try the chicken parm. He's pretty adventurous."

They stood apart. For a second, it was awkward. Before Max could dwell too much on it, Claire narrowed the space between them. Her lips pressed up against his. He brought his hand to her lower back, pulling her even closer to him.

"*Oooooo*," Zachary said. They stepped back from one another. Zachary was grinning from ear to ear. "You love each other!"

"Yes," Claire replied. "We do."

Max's heart swelled.

Chapter 37

Margot

"**M**a'am," the police officer said, taking the USB, "I'll put it over here and let some of our detectives look at it."

"That's all?" Margot asked.

"Yes, what else do you want from us?"

"I don't know." And she didn't. She guessed it would be bigger and faster. That Jeffery would be arrested right away. Silly thoughts, she realized now. Of course it didn't work like that.

"Just give us your number and we'll contact you if we have any more questions."

"Okay."

Even though nothing had come from it, she felt a sense of relief and pride for taking this step. Now, she had to take the next one.

"And how much is this monthly?" Margot asked the lady as they walked through the apartment building for a tour of the location. It had taken her over a week to narrow down the apartments she might want to live in. There were so many options to choose from. It had been so overwhelming.

"$1,450 for a two bedroom. That is what you're wanting, correct?"

"Yes, I...um, think...yes." Her hands were shaking. She brought them together and held them tightly. The lady looked at her. She gave a nervous smile. "It's nice."

"We have a gym and a pool. There is also the game room on the main floor of the building with a pool table and some board games."

"Fun."

"You said you have a daughter?"

"Yes. She's seven."

They entered the elevator that took them up to the second floor. There they walked into an apartment that was similar to the one she might be renting. It was nice and clean. The building was fairly new, but there wasn't much to it. There was just a small kitchen and living area, two bathrooms, and two bedrooms. She worried that it would be upsetting for Ari moving in here. She still didn't know if she was making the right choice. Did she just take Ari from everything she knew? Did she pull her from their lavish lifestyle? Would the courts even take her side?

"To sign up, we need the first rent and deposit paid."

"Okay," Margot said. She ran her fingers over the island. She inhaled deeply and thought this over. Her hand came up to her aching shoulder where Jeffery had pushed her against the wall the night before. His outbursts were becoming more and more frequent. If she didn't leave soon, she didn't know if she ever would. "Yes, let me fill out the paperwork."

I got an apartment and turned the USB into the police. Margot typed and sent the message to Claire before she could talk herself out of it. She owed Claire an apology for her behavior; she had been awful to her, yet again.

Three dots formed under her message. She held her breath as she waited for Claire's response. The dots disappeared, but no words came. She sighed. She shouldn't have expected a reply after the way she treated Claire.

Her phone dinged. She slid up the screen. There was a new message from Claire.

Good. It was a simple reply.

Margot typed some more, trying not to let her nerves get to her.

I'm not moving in yet. I have to get it ready.

Well, at least you have a safe place to go.

I'm sorry for how I treated you. Margot bit the side of her lip. Her chest tightened. She hit send. Claire's response came back right away.

I know.

Immediately, Margot's phone rang. She jumped. It was Claire.

"Hello?" Margot answered.

"Where is the apartment?"

"About half an hour from my house."

"Does Jeffery have any idea?"

"Absolutely not," Margot said. "I put the apartment in my old name, Margot Bailey. I paid with the money from my account. The only information they have to contact me is my phone number."

"Well, that's good. When will you move in?"

"I don't know. Soon, I hope."

"Has he been violent?" Claire asked.

"Yes, but not too bad." She heard Claire huff on the other end.

"Any violence is bad."

"I know that, but it's just small things, like he's trying to warn me to watch my place." Margot curled a strand of her hair with her finger.

"Just be careful," Claire said.

"I am."

"Don't tell anyone who knows Jeffery your plans, not even your friends in your circle that know him."

"Oh, I won't. I can't trust that it won't get back to Jeffery. They all adore him."

"Eww."

"And I'm pretty sure he's having an affair with Victoria," she added. It was the first time she said those words out loud. She'd been trying to catch him; it was why she had this aching shoulder. He'd found her looking at his phone.

"Oh my God."

"I know. I don't even know for how long. Maybe years. Is that where he's been all these long nights? Where was John? Does *he* know?" These questions hadn't left her mind. She wanted answers—needed them.

"I'm sorry," Claire said.

"And yet, I still love him," Margot confessed. The tears came. Everything was so overwhelming. The past few months her entire life had turned upside down. She wiped below her eyes.

"I know you do." Claire's voice was soft and full of understanding. That just made the tears come on stronger. "But Margot, you're doing the right thing. You are no longer safe and neither is your daughter. You're doing what is best for her."

Margot used her palm to roughly wipe against her cheek. "Could Ari and I come over on Saturday?"

"Absolutely."

She hung up and deleted the messages between her and Claire. Jeffery had never gone through her phone before, but she couldn't take the chance that he might. She remained parked outside the bookstore. There was still an hour before she needed to go pick up Ari from school.

Her house no longer felt like a home. Every moment she was in the house, she felt like she was under a microscope. If it wasn't the nanny watching her, it felt like it was the housekeeper or the cook. When Jeffery was at the house, that magnified. She was always walking on eggshells. The only time she felt free was when she was alone with Ari.

After Margot put Ari to bed, she stepped out into the hallway where Nanny Fay stood. Since picking up Ari, Margot hadn't been allowed one moment to herself. Nanny Fay was always right there. She had even insisted on being part of Ari's bedtime routine. Usually by this time at night, she was already downstairs and in bed.

Margot avoided her gaze and headed down the hallway to her bedroom. She could feel Nanny Fay behind her. She paused her steps and turned.

"Do you need something?" Margot asked, her words full of impatience.

"No. Just heading downstairs." Nanny Fay clucked her tongue. "Mr. Lewis will be out late tonight. I wanted to make sure Ari got to bed all right."

"He's always out late. Most nights I put her to bed."

"Yes, well..." She made a weird motion with her hand. Then she bypassed Margot and went down the stairs. Margot watched her until she turned the corner, making sure she was actually going to leave her alone. Once she was out of sight, Margot was finally able to let out a breath and relax some.

She entered her bedroom and closed the door behind her. She had a lot to do and plan if she was going to leave with Ari soon.

In the bottom drawer of her vanity, she lifted up the small drawer. Beneath it was a stack of paperwork for her apartment. She double-checked that the door behind her was closed. Then she withdrew the papers and put them in her lap to review. She wished she had a locked location she could keep them in. Perhaps Claire would be okay with her keeping all of this at her place.

She heard the sound of the garage door opening and panicked, quickly stuffing the papers back in their spot and placing the small drawer on top of it before closing it back. She stood and went to turn on the water in the shower. Jeffery was home early. Why did Nanny Fay say he was going to be out late? Was this all a tactic to throw her off?

By the time she stepped into the shower, she heard the bedroom door open. She put her head under the water.

"Margot? Darling?" Footsteps headed toward her. "Ah, you're in the shower."

The door to the bathroom closed. Margot didn't respond, though she could hear Jeffery moving around in their large bathroom. She scrubbed shampoo into her hair, keeping her breathing even.

"Hi," Jeffery said, peeking his head into the shower. "Can I join you?" But before she had a chance to answer, he stepped inside. He stood behind her and his arms came around her middle. Right where the bruise had formed on her shoulder, he kissed her. His fingers rubbed her belly. "We should have another baby," he whispered in her ear.

Margot pushed his hands away and turned to face him. She glared at him.

"I'm too old to have another baby," she said with a shake of her head. She used the water to wash out the soap from her hair. "Plus, we decided after Ari was born that it was too much for me. We didn't want that to happen again."

Jeffery grabbed her hips and brought her roughly against him. He pressed his lips to hers. When she tried to pull away, he dug his fingers into her hip.

"Jeffery!" she yelled, shoving him back. He heaved. She held her breath. Her hands shook at her sides as she waited for him to do something. She braced herself for getting hit.

However, he didn't. He stepped out of the shower and grabbed his towel from the hook on the wall. As he wiped his hair, his eyes remained on her. She swallowed hard.

"I'm going into work."

"It's...it's nighttime. You just got home."

"I know. And I won't be back until later tonight. Don't wait up."

"Are you going to see Victoria?" she asked, finally finding the courage. His eyes bore into hers, but he didn't answer. He stepped out of the bathroom and slammed the door, making her jump.

Chapter 38

Claire

"Do you want to go upstairs and play?" Zachary asked Ari the moment Claire opened the door.

"Sure!"

Both kids ran upstairs. Claire laughed and widened the door, motioning for Margot to come on inside her house. Margot already had a jumpiness about her. She came inside with her purse still over her shoulder and her hands tightly closed together in front of her.

"Come on, why don't I get you something to drink? I also made some cake." Claire led Margot into the kitchen.

As Claire cut the chocolate cake onto two plates and got them both a cup of coffee, Margot sat on one of the stools at the island. She dropped her purse on the counter. Claire placed the coffee and cake in front of her.

"Eat up," Claire said. She realized she forgot the forks and grabbed two, putting one next to the plate.

"Oh wow," Margot moaned after taking a bite. "This is amazing."

"So, tell me about this apartment," Claire said.

"There's not much to it. It has two bedrooms. I'll be able to stay there a few months before I have to find a job. I don't want to go through all of my savings." Margot picked at the edge of her thumb-nail. "My mom is planning on moving out here in January, and I'm not sure if I should tell her what's going on or not. That's also when we're supposed to go on our anniversary to Paris. Oh God, how is that going to work out?"

Claire could see the panic growing on Margot's face. She brought her hands over the counter and took Margot's in her own. They met eyes.

"You don't need to worry about any of that right now, Margot. Just focus on getting yourself and Ari out safely. What about my sister? Have you spoken to her again?" Margot nodded. "Good. What did she say?"

"She's writing up paperwork now to try and get me temporary custody once we separate. I've been sending her information about any time he's hurt me, as well as the insane amount of time he's had the nanny following me. I wouldn't be surprised if she's parked outside just watching."

Claire immediately grabbed her phone and checked the cameras around the house.

"Want to check and see?"

Margot took her phone. She scrolled through each of the camera screens.

"I don't see anything. It was hard getting out of the house without the nanny this morning. She kept trying to come along. I finally es-caped with Ari when she went into the basement to find her shoes."

"Wow. Are you sure he's not tracking your phone?" Claire asked.

Margot lifted her phone and glanced at it. She placed it back on the counter and made a quick shake of her head.

"No, he wouldn't do that." Despite saying that, Margot didn't sound so sure.

"Sure he would. I can look at it and see. And then I can ask Max about the hidden ways he could track." Claire reached out for Margot's phone, and Margot didn't stop her. She checked for the different apps she knew of like Find a Friend. Nothing popped up. "I don't see anything. I'll ask Max. Or you could take it by to him tomorrow. I'm sure that would be best."

"Oh, I don't know," Margot said. "That sounds a little extreme."

"It's not extreme," Claire told her. "He's been controlling every aspect of your life. I would be more surprised if he wasn't tracking you."

"I guess."

They fell into a comfortable silence. Margot got a second piece of cake. Claire double-checked her cameras for anyone possibly around the house.

"Tell me more about Max and you," Margot spoke up a moment later.

"Max and me?" Claire asked, shocked by the change of topic. "Not much to say."

"Is he *the* guy? The one you said while we were shopping that you possibly loved and had messed it up with?"

"Yes, he's the one."

"And that's since been fixed?"

"Yes."

"How did you meet?"

"He found my friend's body when she went missing," Claire said. Margot's face grew pale and her cheeks turned pink.

"I'm sorry."

"Don't be. He solved the case. If it weren't for him, I wouldn't have gotten justice for Taylor. I'll always appreciate him for that."

"Is that when you two started dating?"

"No, we just hooked up, on and off. We didn't start dating until very recently. It's been strange, almost too easy."

"Too easy how?" Margot asked. She sipped on some coffee.

"Everything is just easy. Zachary gets along well with him. We fit into one another's lives."

"That sounds nice."

"It is. And scary. I've been miserable for four years. It's hard to allow myself to be happy."

Margot looked longingly at the cake. Claire cut her a third slice. Once again, Claire realized how much she enjoyed spending time with Margot. She needed this type of friendship. It was something she hadn't allowed herself since Taylor died. And now, it frightened her. Of all the women she'd connected with, it was another one in a dangerous relationship.

"This is seriously the best cake I have ever had," Margot said.

"I can give you the recipe."

"Yeah, I don't think that's a good idea. I'm hopeless in the kitchen. But thanks." She finished up the third piece. Her phone dinged.

"Who's messaging?" Claire asked, never afraid of being too nosy. She tried to look over onto the phone screen.

"It's the apartment complex." Margot continued to read the message. "Oh, there's more paperwork I need to sign. Would you mind watching Ari so I can go over? I don't want her to know about the apartment just yet. I'd like to get it done as soon as possible."

"I thought you already had the keys."

"I do. But apparently, this is something they need. I just don't want to mess up having the apartment."

"Sure. Ari can stay here. I'll feed them cake and milk."

"Perfect."

About ten minutes after Margot left, the two children were still play-ing happily upstairs. Claire went up to ask them if they wanted cake, but they were too engrossed in building a large Hot Wheels city in Zachary's room.

Knowing the kids were entertained, Claire went back downstairs. She cleaned up the couple of dishes and put the cover back over the cake. Right as she closed her dishwasher, her phone rang.

"Hello?" she said, happy to see Max's name on the caller ID. "How are you?"

"Hey, um, your friend, Margot...she needs to get away from her husband. He's bad news."

"Yes, we've determined that," Claire said. "She's found an apart-ment. She's just looking for a good time to escape with their daughter. Have you found out more about his laundering?"

"Yes. I can't tell you much, but I can tell you it's bad. It's crashing around him. And Claire..." He paused. "He just bought a gun."

Claire's heart clenched. She knew the statistics of what it meant for a domestic abuser owning a gun and his victim.

"That's not good, but it could be for anything," she said, more trying to convince herself. Yet she knew Max sharing this information with her meant it was bad.

"The police are on his tail right now, Claire. They're closing in. He's trapped. Where is Margot? Is she at their home?"

"No, she went to her apartment building to sign some paperwork."

"Okay, text her and tell her not to go back home after she's done. Where's the kid?"

"My house."

"Does he know where you live?"

"No, I don't think so." Max made a sound on the other end. "I have cameras. I really don't think he has any idea where I live, Max. And I doubt he's going to do anything right now, right?" She bit the inside of her lip. Her fingers tapped against the counter.

"I'm heading over there now. Keep your doors locked."

"Max—"

"It's going to be fine. I'll see you soon."

Claire double-checked the locks on her front door. She'd never been one to be afraid, but something about Max's tone of voice made her think there was more he knew that he wasn't telling her.

Her phone rang as she tried to get in touch with Margot. It rang and rang before going to voicemail.

"Shit," Claire said beneath her breath. It was the fifth time she'd tried to call her.

"*Ooo.* That's another dollar," Zachary's voice said from the top of the stairs. She glanced up to see both Zachary and Ari coming down. Zachary jumped down each stair while Ari took smaller, quieter steps. Her eyes searched around the living room.

"Where's my mommy?" she asked.

"She'll be back," Claire assured her. "She had to run and do something. Would you both like some chocolate cake?" The mention of sweets seemed to make Ari forget her mother wasn't here for at least a moment. Her little eyes widened and her lips curled up into a smile. "You can both eat in here. Zachary, put something on the TV for both of you to watch."

As she headed into the kitchen, she checked the locks on the back door and each of the windows. She cut each of them a piece of cake while trying to call Margot again.

"Come on, Margot," she said into the phone. Again, it went to voicemail. She hung up the phone and slid it into her back pocket. Forcing a smile onto her face, she walked the plates of cake back to the kids. Unsurprisingly, Zachary had chosen *The Parent Trap* to watch.

"Thank you," Ari said when Claire put the cake down in front of her.

"You're welcome. Zachary, did you ask your guest what she wanted to watch?" Claire looked to Zachary. He nodded.

"Yep! She loves *The Parent Trap* too!"

"All right." By now she had the movie memorized.

A knock came at the door. She jumped.

She rushed to the door, hoping Margot was on the other side. She peeked through the peephole and sighed when she saw it was only Max. Unlocking the door, she let him in.

"Any news on Margot?" he asked. She cut her eyes at him and then over to Ari.

"No," she whispered. He gave an apologetic face. "What's going on?"

"Let's go into your office."

Claire made sure to lock the front door behind Max before the two of them went into the office. She didn't shut the office door all the way, leaving it open about an inch.

"What's going on?" Claire asked.

Max ran his hands through his thick blond hair and let out a loud breath.

"Jeffery Lewis is not a safe person. It is assumed he killed one of his co-workers this morning, soon after he purchased the gun. The police are on the search for him. I...I don't like you in on this, Claire. I..." His hand rubbed over his lips as he shook his head.

"Oh my God," Claire said. "What if he knows where Margot is?"

"I know," Max replied.

"Oh my God," she repeated. Her entire body shook with the weight of it all. "Oh my God, oh my God, oh my God..." She paced the length of the office until Max broke in front of her. He took her upper arms lovingly in his hands. She met his gaze. "I can't do this again," she cried. "He's going to kill her, just like Dylan killed Taylor. And that little girl in there—" Her voice caught in her throat.

Max pulled her into his arms, holding her close. She allowed herself to break down, just a little bit.

"You don't know that," he murmured into her ear. "The police are searching for him now."

Claire lifted her head. "What led him to kill his co-worker? What..."

"I don't know," Max whispered, wiping her cheek with his thumb. "Maybe someone confronted him about what he's been up to. I can't say much about what I know. I only said something to you because I was worried about you and Margot."

Claire pressed her forehead against Max's chest. His fingers ran up and down her spine.

"What do we do now? Do we go to the apartment where she is? Do we make sure she's okay? Pick her up?"

"You are staying here with the kids. I'll go to the apartment. Do you know where it is?"

Claire shook her head. "Oh God, I don't know! But we have to do something! Can't you, like, use her phone number to figure out where she is?"

"Um...well, I know someone who could, but it—"

"Then call them! Do something! We have to stop this from happening again!"

Her phone rang. It wasn't a number she recognized, but she answered it anyway, hoping it was Margot calling from a different number.

"Hello?"

"Is this Ms. Donahue?"

"Yes."

"This is Detective Dhar."

Her heart stopped for a moment before she could speak again. The last time she heard that name was when her best friend died.

Chapter 39

Margot

Margot reached her apartment building and got another text. It said the paperwork had been put in her apartment for her to sign and bring to the office as soon as possible. She found it a little odd, but they said it had to do with their new Wi-Fi company and that everyone had to sign. She sighed in annoyance. This wasn't necessary for keeping the apartment, but she might as well do it while she was here.

She went upstairs, inside, and into the kitchen, searching for the paperwork. Nothing was in the kitchen, so she turned to the living room. She flipped on the living room light. Her heart stopped.

"Hey, darling. I see you got my message. Got to make sure you get that new Wi-Fi service." There sat Jeffery on the built-in window seat with a gun in his lap, facing her. Her hands grew clammy. When had he gotten a gun? "You weren't planning on leaving me, were you?"

"You...you're cheating on me," she said. "I..."

He just shrugged. "Yeah, well, Victoria appreciates what I do for her. You never have." His words were eerily calm.

"H-how long have you been cheating on me?"

Jeffery shook his head. "Oh, I don't know. A while. How long have I been staying out late for work?"

"Several years now."

"Oh, then I guess several years."

He shifted in his seat and the gun moved in his lap. Her eyes stared down at it.

This is it. He is going to kill me. The temperature of her body rose. She lifted her foot to step back, but Jeffery lifted the gun in tandem. In this moment, she realized that there had never been anything wrong with her. Jeffery had never been sane; he'd only manipulated her to believe she wasn't.

"Don't move." She dropped her foot back in its spot.

"Jeffery…"

"Where's Ari?" he asked, casually swinging the gun in his hand. His eyes were wild. She'd never seen him this frightening before. Her heart raced in her chest.

"Not here," she answered.

He hit his hand on the wall next to him, making her body jerk.

"She's not home. I checked. That's where I went first. Where. Is. She?"

"I'm…I'm not going to tell you, Jeffery. Not with that gun in your hand."

Jeffery glanced at the gun in his hand and then put it back in his lap, still facing her. He put his two hands together so that the tops of each finger touched.

"Where is Ari, Margot?" he asked in an unnervingly calm manner.

"She's safe," Margot answered. Her voice shook despite trying to stay calm.

"Bullshit!" Jeffery yelled. He stood, the gun in his hand at his side. "If she were safe, she'd be with me." He pointed to his chest with his free hand. "I'm the one who keeps her safe. You're trying to take her away from me!"

"No, I never..."

"Shut up, Margot! Just shut up!" His hand grabbed her upper arm, pulling her closer to him. She whimpered. "I've done all of this for you, for our family. And you gave me away to the police."

"And you cheated on me," she repeated. It was the only thing she could think to say. He tightened his grip on her arm.

"And I still treated you like a queen. You were still my wife. Victoria was just a side piece. Of course, John walked in on us this morning, so...well, it didn't end well." His eyes were crazy.

"What happened?"

"John and I argued. Victoria ran out of the room. He tried to grab her, so I shot him."

Margot paled. She felt sick to her stomach.

"You...you killed John?"

Tears fell down her cheeks.

"I know, it stinks, right? We had a good thing, John and me. But he had to walk in on Victoria and me."

"What good thing did you and John have?" Maybe if she could keep him talking, she could figure out a way to get away from him.

"It was simple scheme. We just skimmed a little off the top from the business and no one was the wiser."

"You stole money from your boss?" Margot asked.

"Money I was *owed*. I worked my ass off for that company for years! Every business we worked with, I took what I was owed. It was easy enough. As long as you don't get too cocky with the amount, it's never noticed. You just have to know what you're doing. John got in on it, too. It kept him busy, so I could sneak over to their house during the week. I'd send him on little errands. Most of them were nothing, but he wasn't the brightest bulb. He never caught on." Jeffery chuckled. "Anyway, he and I started putting the money through our other clients, so it looked legit. It worked really well. I kept all the information secure on a little USB so I could keep track of it. But you'd know that, wouldn't you?"

Margot inhaled sharply.

"I know about the PI. I know about your friend, Claire, and how she's been trying to get you to leave me. I know it all. You see, I put the USB in that bracelet for a little while thinking it would be the best hiding spot. It's ugly, and I never thought you'd actually wear it. Then you started wearing it, so I had to replace it. I didn't realize you'd figured it out though, until recently, when I realized your behavior was becoming more erratic. And you started looking at apartments."

"How did you know that?"

Jeffery laughed. "Nanny Fay. I had her following you more closely. I tried reigning you in to show you I was the boss, but you just pushed against me harder. But now, the feds are after me, thanks to you. And I'm sure they know I killed John too. Victoria probably already called them. So, I have to leave. I don't have time to waste." He swung the gun in his hands. *"So where is my daughter?"*

"I..."

"She and I are headed out of town. We'll be gone before I'm ever found. I already have a plane waiting for us."

"You can't have her, Jeffery. She's just a little girl."

"She's my little girl!" he screamed in her face. "Mine! And I'll do everything to protect her, even if that means taking you away from her. You are the one who destroyed this family, Margot, and don't you forget that. I wanted my life to be with all of us; I wanted us to be a family. But *you* destroyed that! You! I loved you, Margot. I loved our family. But I can no longer trust you."

He let go of her arm, making her stumble on her feet and hit the wall behind her. She prayed he didn't know where Claire lived and that he wouldn't be able to find their daughter, but she had no way of keeping her safe.

Margot attempted to crawl away, not knowing what she was going to do if she made it to the door. Would she be able to reach her car? Would he follow her to Claire's house?

A loud bang hit the door.

"Police! Open the door!"

Relief flooded Margot. Even if he killed her, the police would keep him from getting to Ari. This would be her moment to protect her, like she hadn't been able to before.

A hand grabbed the back of her shirt, bringing her up against Jeffery's chest. He held the gun against her back.

"I will kill her!" he yelled toward the door. "Come inside and I will shoot!"

"Please, Jeffery," Margot pleaded. "What about Ari? Please…"

"Shut. Up." He hit the center of her back with the barrel of the gun. Her body fell forward, and a scream left her lips.

"Don't shoot!" the police yelled through the door.

"You did this," he said to Margot. He lifted his hand, pressing the gun into her back again. "You made the police come after me. I loved you." A tear fell on Margot's shoulder and she realized Jeffery was crying.

"I love you, Jeffery," she said, now crying. "But what about Ari? What about her?"

"Stop it!" He turned her to face him. She watched with horror as he lifted the gun up to her. His eyes widened and then softened. What appeared to be regret flashed over his face. "I'm sorry."

He shot the gun.

Chapter 40

Margot

A female EMT placed a blanket over her shivering shoulders, as a male one stood in front of her checking her body over for any signs of damage. She hadn't spoken since the police came in and walked her outside. Everything that had happened after Jeffery said *I'm sorry* was a blur. She couldn't wrap her mind around it. If she had been asked in that moment, she wouldn't be able to tell anyone how much time had passed since Jeffery shot the gun and her sitting here right now. It felt like a lifetime.

"Ari," she spoke, sitting up. What would she tell her? How would she explain this to her?

"She's fine," another female said, walking up to her. She was a beautiful woman with tawny skin and golden brown eyes. Her dark brown hair was pinned up in a low bun, and she wore a black suit and red heels. "I'm Detective Dhar. Your daughter is safe at your friend Claire's house."

"Thanks for calling her," Margot rasped, her entire body shaking.

Ari was with Claire. Ari was safe. But it didn't make any of this easier, because at some point her daughter would have to know her father had been arrested.

The blue and red lights flashed all around her. Through them, she could see Jeffery sitting in the back seat of the police car. His head was tilted down. She wasn't sure if it was because of shame or defeat. Maybe both. At least, she hoped he was ashamed of what all he had done.

"Ari's okay?" she asked, needing to hear it again. Detective Dhar gave her a sympathetic smile.

"Yes, she's okay. Your friend said she could stay with her as long as you need. We would like to ask you some questions when you're ready." Detective Dhar's voice was kind and gentle. Yet it didn't help the anxiousness that coursed through her body. She wasn't sure she'd be able to calm down again.

A rush of tears flooded her. She leaned forward, covering her face with her hands. How was she supposed to face their daughter now? What was she supposed to tell her? What about Victoria and Jordyn? What did she say to them? The tears wouldn't stop.

"It's all right," Detective Dhar said, not sounding annoyed, but instead understanding. Her hand touched her back. "You take as long as you need. The ambulance is going to take you to the hospital. We will follow behind. There is no pressure to talk until you're ready. All right?"

Margot glanced up and nodded.

Physically, she was fine. The doctors and nurses had looked her over for any bruising or broken bones. There were none. Emotionally, however, she wasn't sure she ever would be. One of the doctors mentioned someone coming in to talk with her about what she'd been through, but she wasn't sure if she was ready for that.

The door to the hospital room they'd put her in opened. She expected the detective, but it was Claire. Claire remained in the doorway, not taking any steps forward, as if she was waiting for Margot's permission to come inside. Her hands were clasped together, and her face was sullen. But she didn't move.

The tears started again.

"Ari is just fine," Claire started, now rushing toward her. "She's with Max and Zachary at my place. She has no idea what has happened, and is just eating all the cake. Probably too much cake," Claire added with a small smile. She carefully sat on the edge of Margot's hospital bed. "She is safe." She would never tire of hearing that. "And you are safe."

Margot hiccupped. Her eyes met Claire's. She didn't know how much she'd been told about what had happened. "He...he chickened out," she said. "He...he pointed the gun toward me and at the last minute, he shot away from me."

"Thank God for that." Claire placed her hand on Margot's knee.

"And then he almost shot himself, but...but the cops came in then and tackled him to the ground."

"I am so glad you're all right."

"But I don't know that I am," Margot admitted. Another hiccup came. She pressed her fingers against her temple. Her head ached.

"Of course you're not." Claire dropped her hand from Margot's knee and glanced around the hospital room. "Have they brought you anything to eat? Drink?"

"Just some water. I haven't felt hungry."

"I could order you something, or go pick something up." Claire's knees bounced in front of her, giving Margot the impression that Claire didn't feel completely comfortable in the hospital room.

"I'd really rather you go back to Ari. I'm fine here, alone."

"I don't think you are," Claire disagreed. "I know I wouldn't be. Ari is fine with Max and Zachary. Someone needs to be taking care of you."

She didn't know why, but those words caused a fresh set of tears. Claire slid closer to her on the bed.

"What do I tell Ari?" A harsh breath left her lips as she met Claire's eyes. "I...I think he didn't do it because when he looked at me...maybe he still loved me. Or maybe it was for Ari..." She'd been thinking of that moment since it happened. She didn't know why in that split second he had changed his mind. She had been so sure he was going to kill her.

"Shh," Claire attempted to soothe. "Maybe. It's a lot. And you have been through so much. You don't have to know what you'll say to her. Not yet."

Margot looked down at her hands as she began picking at the edge of her thumb. While Claire was right, it didn't make it any easier because eventually, she would have to face Ari and tell her some version of the truth. Like Claire had said, she couldn't keep the truth from her. She'd likely have to get Ari in therapy; she'd probably need it too.

"Where will we stay? I can't go back home and I...I can't go to the apartment," she said, continuing with her thoughts.

"You can stay with me, if you'd like. Or I can find you a hotel for the next few nights. Wherever you think you would feel most comfortable."

Margot wasn't sure anywhere would feel comfortable. In this moment, she just wanted her mother. As if she could read Margot's mind, Claire spoke up.

"I could call your mom for you. I bet she'd come right away."

"Yes, actually. Would you? I...I have to talk to someone...um, a detective. Detective..." The name slipped her mind.

"Dhar," Claire told her. "I know her. She's a good one. I don't trust most on the force, but I do trust her. She called me when all this started, when they found him at the apartment with you."

"You know her?" Margot asked in awe.

"She worked on Taylor's case." Claire spun her bracelet on her wrist. "I don't think she was supposed to call me," Claire told her. "But Max had been helping her with the case. And he'd told her about us being friends. I think she just wanted to be the one to let me know that they had found him and they were going to do everything they could to keep you safe." She wiped her cheek. "Now, what's your mom's number? I'll call her right away."

"I gave the USB to the police at the station down on 44," Margot told Detective Dhar. "I don't know if they looked at any of it."

"Oh, I did. And that's when I connected with Max," Detective Dhar said. "He was already working with others on the case and he told me you were connected to Claire." She patted Margot's hand. "Why don't you get some rest now?"

Detective Dhar left, but not before seeing Claire. They gave one another a look of acknowledgement before slipping past the other.

Claire walked back into her hospital room with her phone in her hand, covering up the speaker.

"It's your mom. Would you like to talk to her?"

Tears of relief spilled from her eyes.

"Yes."

She took the phone from Claire, who then respectfully left the room again to give her this private moment alone with her mother.

"Mom?" she cried into the phone.

"Oh Margot," her mom said, her voice pained. "Your friend Claire filled me in on all that happened. I'm packing now. Your friend was kind enough to book my flight. It leaves first thing in the morning." Relief flooded Margot, knowing her mom would be here soon. "I wish I could be there now."

"Me too," Margot said. She wiped below her eye. "I was so scared."

"You had to have been. I just...thank God you're all right. You and Ari. I will be there as soon as I am able."

"I know you will be." Margot tugged at the hospital band around her arm. She couldn't wait to take it off. She just wanted to go to her daughter. "I love you."

Once she hung up, she slid out of the hospital bed. Claire popped her head back in.

"Are you ready to go?" she asked. "We can pick up food on the way to my house. Then there, you can decide if you want to stay at my place or we can find you and Ari a hotel."

"I'd rather just stay at your place tonight. Then tomorrow after my mom arrives, we can go to a hotel."

"Okay."

"And Claire?"

"Yes?"

"Thank you."

Chapter 41

Claire

It was nearly two in the morning. Zachary and Ari had been asleep when they arrived. Margot, with the help of some sleep aids given to her by the hospital, was asleep in Claire's room. Tonight, Claire and Max would sleep downstairs on the pull-out couch. But for now, they lay in the hammock outside. Claire was cocooned in Max's arms as he kept her warm from the coldness outside. Every few moments there would be a gush of wind, causing them to swing.

"Today has been a day," Claire said.

"It has," Max agreed.

"I'm so glad she's all right, that Ari didn't lose her mother."

"Me too."

"I suggested my therapist to her, but maybe it was too early."

Max kissed the crook of her neck. His arms held her closer as another gush of wind passed by.

"Maybe we should go inside."

"Not yet," Claire said. She brought the blanket up to her chin. "Out here, it's just you and me. Once we're inside, we have to face the reality of what happened today. I'm not quite ready for that yet."

"Okay."

He held onto her tighter. Claire never wanted him to let her go.

"I want you to always be here, with me." She tried to turn to face Max, but in the hammock it was impossible. So instead, she turned her head to face him as best she could. It was hard to see him in the dark of the night where only the back porch light was on. "Do you want to be here?"

"Are you asking me to move in?" Max asked.

Claire pondered this a moment. That would be such a big step in their relationship, when they'd really only dated for a short while.

"I don't want you making rash decisions because of what happened today, Claire," Max added. "We don't have to rush anything."

"I'm not," Claire said, sure of herself. "I never make a decision I don't want to make."

Max chuckled. "Well, I know that to be true."

"And I don't want you just to move in with me and Zachary. I want to marry you, Max. If what all I've witnessed has taught me anything, life can change so quickly, and I want whatever time we have to be together. Whether it be just a day or fifty years. You don't have to answer today, and if you need to *be the man* and propose in the future, well then, okay, whatever. We can do—" He cut her off by kissing her.

"Yes," he said when they pulled apart. "I was planning on proposing at the house in the mountains. You beat me to it." Within the shadows, Claire could see the grin on his face.

"Yes, well, get used to me beating you on things like this."

"I wouldn't have it any other way."

Claire hadn't been able to sleep. At some point in the early morning, she had given up and started coffee. She sat at the kitchen island scrolling on her phone as she waited for everyone else to wake up. Max snored loudly on the pull-out couch, making Claire wonder if she'd made a mistake proposing to him the night before, but only briefly. She really did love him and was looking forward to spending the rest of her life with him.

She was so deep in her scrolling that she hadn't heard Margot enter the kitchen until the stool next to her scraped against the flooring.

"Hi," she said, her voice small. Her cheeks were sunken in and pale. Claire knew she hadn't eaten since the incident the day before.

"Good morning. Can I make you something to eat?"

"I'm not hungry."

Claire got up from her stool and went over to the refrigerator, despite what Margot had said.

"I'll make eggs. How do you like them?"

Margot sighed in defeat. "Scrambled is fine."

With ease, Claire cracked and scrambled the eggs. She placed a pan on the stove and turned on the burner.

"Cheese? Onions? Spinach? Tomatoes?" she asked as she looked through her fridge to see what else she had to add to the meal.

"Just some cheese would be fine."

"Okay." Claire grabbed a bag of pre-shredded cheese and added two good handfuls to the mixture before pouring it into the pan.

Once the eggs were done, she plated some for both of them.

"Here, eat up."

"I still haven't spoken to Ari," Margot said as she used her fork to move the eggs around on her plate.

"I know. Have you decided what you'll say to her yet?"

"No."

"You don't have to tell her yet," Claire suggested. "All she has to know is that Grandma is coming into town today."

"I don't know if I can keep it from her. It's Sunday. Jeffery almost always spent Sundays with her. She's going to ask about him." She dropped her fork onto her plate. "I will have to tell her something."

Claire nodded, not knowing what else she should say. This was odd for her. She usually could figure something out. Little steps could be heard coming down the stairs, so she knew the time was here for Margot.

"Mommy!" Ari said the moment she spotted Margot and ran right to her. Margot picked her up and placed her in her lap. Zachary was right behind her, coming in and rubbing his eyes. "Where were you yesterday? Claire said you had some errands to run. They took forever."

Margot looked between Ari and Claire before turning back to Ari and brushing her hair out of her face. "I did. A lot has happened that we need to talk about."

"We'll leave you two alone," Claire said. She took Zachary's hand and led him out of the kitchen.

"I told her that her dad loves her, but that he won't be able to see her for a little while," Margot said as Claire sat next to her outside. They still had about an hour before it would be time to pick up Margot's mother from the airport.

"How did she handle it?"

"Okay, I guess. She just kept asking why and I didn't know what to tell her. I said he hadn't made good choices, and she kept asking what choices." Margot rubbed the back of her neck with her hand.

"Was she happy your mom is coming into town?"

"Yes. I think that will keep her distracted for a day or two at least."

"At least," Claire agreed. "I booked you a hotel—a suite, actually—so you three have some space."

"Suite? No, that's too much."

"It's okay. It's a hotel company that uses my parents for any cases they have, so we get good deals."

"Well, I will be paying you back."

Claire shrugged. "It's fine."

"I guess right now I just take it one day at a time."

"That's all you can do," Claire agreed. "You and Ari are going to be all right."

"I hope so."

Chapter 42

*Margot
(A few months later)*

"Is that everything?" her mother asked as Margot handed her a suitcase.

"Yes," Margot sighed. She glanced back at the house she'd lived in for ten years. The only house Ari had ever known.

Everyone had left, even Nanny Fay. She hadn't spoken to her again. All she knew was that she'd moved in with one of Jeffery's brothers to help with their newborn. It was probably for the best. This house would be seized by the government. With all of Jeffery's illegal money issues, not much would be left for Margot and Ari. Though Ari did have a nice trust fund her grandparents had set up when she was born, so Ari would be set for life once she turned twenty-one. And, thankfully, her savings also hadn't been touched since that had been saved separate from Jeffery's funds.

In charge of making sure everything was where it should be was Claire. She stepped out of the house looking perfectly put together. Her dark curls were pulled up and out of her face. She wore a matching tracksuit and some sneakers, and yet she looked absolutely gorgeous. Margot had found her comfort in her own clothes as well. She got rid of all the fancy clothing, now only wearing T-shirts and jeans and leggings. She'd forgotten how comfortable they could be.

"I'm really going to miss you," Claire said. "But I do think this is best."

"Yes, me too," Margot agreed. "I'm excited about going back to work." Her old pharmacy was thrilled to learn she was returning, though she would have to recertify to be a pharmacist again. For now, she would be working at the cashier desk. She didn't mind. She was just glad she got to be her own self again.

"I'm excited for you," Claire said.

"And we'll be back. I'm bringing Ari back twice a year to visit her father in prison." She made a face. "I never thought I would be saying those words. They think he could get life." She'd spoken to the prosecutors. But she had little faith he would get that long. He came from a wealthy family. He was a white man. At the very least, he should be put away until Ari was an adult.

"How did Ari take it when you told her?"

"Not great," Margot said, groaning. "I don't think she understands the weight of it all. She knows he did something bad, but she keeps asking why he can't move with us. I think it's going to take time. And the move will be good for her too. A fresh start and all of that. I'm so thankful for your sister. She really came through with the custody agreement and me moving out of state. His family tried to fight it, but Mila was not having it."

Claire chuckled. "We Donahue women don't lose fights."

"I can tell."

"We're going to come and visit you too," Claire promised. "Zachary has already been asking for skiing lessons."

"Can't wait. I think Ari might do that too. She says she wants to try everything there is to try. That is the one benefit of all of this for her.

She said with her daddy not there, he won't make learning new lessons stressful."

Claire lifted her arm, showing off the shine of the ring on her finger. "When is the wedding?"

Claire looked at the ring. Max had given it to her at Christmas.

"I don't know. We haven't had a chance to plan."

Margot felt guilty. The past few months had been full of the mess of her life and Claire had been there every step of the way. Claire found them a small house to rent while they figured everything out. She even missed her trip to the mountains she'd planned with Max and Zachary to make sure she had what she needed.

"As soon as we know, you'll be the next to know," she promised. "We're taking Zachary out of school on Friday and going up to Helen, Georgia. Max got us a cabin. So stop feeling guilty, got it?"

"Got it," Margot agreed.

Margot rubbed her hands in front of her. She hadn't spoken to Victoria. She had tried—once. She knew there had been a service for John, but she hadn't been invited. There was too much between them with the affair and Jeffery killing John. Maybe it was for the best that they didn't speak. The other friends had rallied around Victoria. Margot didn't mind. She was ready to leave most of this life behind anyway.

"He wrote me a letter," Margot said, biting the inside of her cheek.

"Jeffery?" Claire asked. Margot nodded. "What about?"

"About why he spared me," she answered.

Claire's face grew apprehensive before she asked, "What did he say?"

"It was long, a mess of ramblings, but in the end, it said the only reason I'm still alive is because of Ari. He couldn't take her mother away from her. Even though he didn't love me, he loves her and she loves me."

"And how do you feel about that?" Claire asked, her words careful.

"I don't know. But I am glad I have some answers."

"Of course you are."

"You better call me every day," Margot said to Claire, wanting to change the topic.

Claire laughed.

"You'll get tired of me, don't worry."

They hugged. It lasted for a good minute or two before they pulled away from one another. When they did, there were tears in their eyes.

"I'm really going to miss you," Margot said. Claire sniffled.

"And I'm going to miss you."

"Margot? Are you ready? Ari is already in the car," her mom called out.

"Go on. You don't want to miss your flight."

Margot hugged Claire once more before heading to her mother's rental car. She waved to Claire and then watched her house grow smaller and smaller as they drove away. Then she looked back at her daughter, giving her a smile. Now, it was time for a new, perfect start for them both. They were both going to be okay.

The End

Also by A.G. Hawkins

Books in the He Did It Universe

He Did It

Perfect Family

Other Books by A. G. Hawkins

Gone

Lucky Ones

Acknowledgements

Thank you to my husband, Braden, and my children, Henry and Lila, for always supporting my dream.

To my family and friends, I am forever thankful for your unwavering support and constant encouragement.

To my editor, Makenna Albert of On the Same Page. My story would be nothing without you. You always encourage me and my stories. I appreciate you reading this story over and over to help me get it the best it can be. I know I can trust you with my work and that you'll help me grow as a writer. I am blessed to have you as part of my team. Thank you.

To my cover artist, K.B. Barrett. You took my vision and made it even better. Thank you.

And finally to my readers, I appreciate every single one of you.

www.ingramcontent.com/pod-product-compliance
Lightning Source LLC
Chambersburg PA
CBHW032019310726

48972CB00002B/462